NOT HORSING AROUND

Jack couldn't miss the pair of hard-eyed hombres loafing around his horse. Both wore bull-hide chaps, vests and six-guns. One looked no older than Luke; the other, maybe near his own age, had a bad scar from a knife cut across his left cheek.

"Can I help you?" Jack asked, wondering what the interest was in the gray horse.

"This is my horse," the older one said as the other blocked his way. "How in the hell did you get him anyway?"

"You got proof he's yours?"

"Mister, I don't need proof he's mine. I raised him from a colt."

"I'm sorry, but a widow woman gave him to me in Austin."

"That's right. Some damn rebel stole him from me."

"The law says possession is nine-tenths of the law. You show me some convincing proof, we'll talk."

"I'll show you—" The man jerked his six-gun out, but Jack's smoked lead first. . . .

Ralph Compton

North to
the Salt Fork

A Ralph Compton Novel
by Dusty Richards

A SIGNET BOOK

SIGNET
Published by New American Library, a division of
Penguin Group (USA) Inc., 375 Hudson Street,
New York, New York 10014, USA
Penguin Group (Canada), 90 Eglinton Avenue East, Suite 700, Toronto,
Ontario M4P 2Y3, Canada (a division of Pearson Penguin Canada Inc.)
Penguin Books Ltd., 80 Strand, London WC2R 0RL, England
Penguin Ireland, 25 St. Stephen's Green, Dublin 2,
Ireland (a division of Penguin Books Ltd.)
Penguin Group (Australia), 250 Camberwell Road, Camberwell, Victoria 3124,
Australia (a division of Pearson Australia Group Pty. Ltd.)
Penguin Books India Pvt. Ltd., 11 Community Centre, Panchsheel Park,
New Delhi - 110 017, India
Penguin Group (NZ), 67 Apollo Drive, Rosedale, North Shore 0632,
New Zealand (a division of Pearson New Zealand Ltd.)
Penguin Books (South Africa) (Pty.) Ltd., 24 Sturdee Avenue,
Rosebank, Johannesburg 2196, South Africa

Penguin Books Ltd., Registered Offices:
80 Strand, London WC2R 0RL, England

First published by Signet, an imprint of New American Library,
a division of Penguin Group (USA) Inc.

First Printing, June 2010
10 9 8 7 6 5 4

THE IMMORTAL COWBOY

This is respectfully dedicated to the "American Cowboy." His was the saga sparked by the turmoil that followed the Civil War, and the passing of more than a century has by no means diminished the flame.

True, the old days and the old ways are but treasured memories, and the old trails have grown dim with the ravages of time, but the spirit of the cowboy lives on.

In my travels—to Texas, Oklahoma, Kansas, Nebraska, Colorado, Wyoming, New Mexico, and Arizona—I always find something that reminds me of the Old West. While I am walking these plains and mountains for the first time, there is this feeling that a part of me is eternal, that I have known these old trails before. I believe it is the undying spirit of the frontier calling, allowing me, through the mind's eye, to step back into time. What is the appeal of the Old West of the American frontier?

It has been epitomized by some as the dark and bloody period in American history. Its heroes—Crockett, Bowie, Hickok, Earp—have been reviled and criticized. Yet the Old West lives on, larger than life.

It has become a symbol of freedom, when there was always another mountain to climb and another river to cross; when a dispute between two men was settled not with expensive lawyers, but with fists, knives, or guns. Barbaric? Maybe. But some things never change. When the cowboy rode into the pages of American history, he left behind a legacy that lives within the hearts of us all.

—*Ralph Compton*

Chapter 1

Lucille Thornton had never before seen the tall man with the black patch over his left eye. She had noticed him right away as he shed his hat like a gentleman when he arrived at the Saturday-night dance and potluck supper at the Lost Dog Schoolhouse.

She nudged her best friend, Sister Farley. "Who's he, Sister?" she asked over the stomping footsteps and the bounce of lively music.

Sister frowned. "I don't know who he is."

"Let's be sure our newcomer has some food anyway." Pulling at Sister's arm, Lucille guided her friend up from the wall bench and crossed the room.

They watched as he spoke civilly to several men and women, then cut through the crowd toward a large tub of lemonade, kept cool by several large chunks of ice floating in the middle.

Lucille spoke up first. "Sir, welcome to Lost Dog Creek and the schoolhouse association's dance."

He turned. He was dressed in a gray officer's uniform, faded from many washings. "Well, ladies," he said in a big, booming voice as he gave a short bow, "allow me to introduce myself. They call me Captain Jack Starr, and I'm very pleased to have found your fine festivities this evening." He pointed toward the couples, young and old, dancing to the toe-tapping music. "Fine-looking neighbors you have."

"Yes, they are, sir—ah, Captain Jack Starr. My name is Lucille Thornton, and this is my friend Sister Farley." She'd have sworn Sister blushed at her introduction. "Let us fix you with a plate of food and some dessert, and introduce you to some of the other folks that are here tonight."

"Why, that would be plumb generous of you-all to do that for a road-dusted stranger."

Lucille smiled. He was certainly not a meek person— no one would ever have any trouble hearing him unless they'd gone stone deaf in the war during a cannon onslaught. But there was something about this man that she found inviting. He had an openness that made her feel as if he was, perhaps, the most honest man she'd met.

"I take it you two live around here?" he asked.

"Yes," Lucille said. "Sister and I both lost our husbands in the war. We each run small ranches of our own. Here's a plate—start filling it."

"I'm sorry to learn that." He took the plate and looked impressed at the spread of food set out. "Lots here to be thankful for. However, I fear many good men died for what looks like nothing now."

Lucille nodded and urged him to fill his dish. "Don't

be bashful. There's plenty here and most folks have already eaten."

He paused and studied the crowd again as if a little awed by the sight of them. "Your people look like you two ladies look: ready to start a new life and rebuild this part of Texas."

"Yes, we're doing that already," Lucille answered.

Sister agreed with a sharp nod.

Lucille, carrying her dress hem, walked beside him as he sampled this and that. Something about the man drew her in and she found that she didn't want to leave his side. She had no notion of doing anything desperate, but Starr was the first man who'd impressed her since she'd learned her husband, Felton Thornton, had been killed in action. Of course, for all she knew, Starr may have been a horse thief, but the big man—with his deep voice, his single sparkling blue eye, his mysterious patch and slightly curled, overgrown brown hair—held her attention.

"Mrs. . . ."

" 'Lucille' and 'Sister' are good enough. We aren't fancy folks, Captain."

He laughed aloud and shook his head. "Well, you two look mighty fancy to me."

Sister had brought him a tin can to use as a glass, with a large shard of ice bobbing in the lemonade. "We can sit over there."

He nodded, spotting an open bench in the corner. But as the three began to move toward the seats, a scuffle broke out on the dance floor. They turned, seeing two young men standing chest to chest and eye to eye. As one of the men lifted his fist to throw a punch, the other swung his arm around the man's neck and threw his own weight down in an attempt to drop his opponent to the floor. Captain Starr sighed and made a face of impatient disapproval.

"Oh no," Sister said. "They're at it again. That's the Bledsoe boy and Alan's grandson, Thad."

"Won't the law stop them?" Jack asked.

Lucille shook her head. "We have no law up here."

Jack handed Lucille his plate and strode over to the boys. In a flash he had both of them by the shirt collars, one in each hand and, their boots hardly touching the floor, he rushed them toward the double doors.

"Open them wide," he said to some bystanders, and when Jack reached the top of the stairs, he hurled both of them out into the night. "Now, stay outside until you learn better manners."

He returned, dusting himself off. Several folks offered their thanks, but he dismissed the act as nothing.

"I must apologize for those rude boys," Lucille said.

"Aw, boys'll be boys," he said with a wink, taking his plate back from her. Lucille steered the threesome to the far corner.

"They're old enough to be past that point," Lucille said; then she turned to the crowd. "Now, everyone please let Captain Starr eat. He can talk later."

Several people repeated his name aloud and most shook their heads—they'd never heard of or met him before. Lucille felt pleased he'd lowered the boom on those two scamps, but she wanted to be protective of the stranger's privacy. He'd tell them his story later.

At last seated between the two women on the bench against the wall, he dug into the food as if he were a starved wolf. No telling when he'd eaten last. But to Lucille's surprise, when the musicians started a polka, he handed Sister his half-eaten supper and took both of Lucille's hands. "I haven't done this in years, so I might mash your toes. Let's polka."

Lucille couldn't manage a single word before he whirled her away as if in a cloud of dust.

She had to admit that he could dance and it was all she could do to keep up. If he hadn't danced the polka in a long time, he sure had not forgotten how. Being whirled around in tight circles by a strong man was an exhilarating experience for her. She'd forgotten all the worrisome things that only a minute before had been weighing her down. Her breath came in gulps, and when the fiddles finally quit he gave her a short bow that made her want to hug him. She straightened her skirt and told herself to mind her manners; at that moment, it seemed that everyone in the county was looking at the two of them.

Later he danced a waltz with Sister, spoke briefly to Eric Wheeler of the Bar 9, then returned to their section of the bench.

"Are you here on business?" Sister asked in one of those rare moments when both women were present. He shook his head wearily. "I'm a man without a place. I came home from the war, found my family had been murdered by Comanches and I've not tried to sink roots ever since."

"Your wife was murdered?" Lucille asked.

He shook his head. "No wife. My parents, sister and little brother."

She nodded. No wife. A man in his mid-thirties who'd never been married was liable to keep right on with his bachelorhood and freedom. Some men were cut out to be husbands; others weren't. Why should she worry about that? She'd only just met him. Knew nothing of his past. Still the notion he'd never been married stung her.

From there on, dancing with him wasn't quite as exciting, but she liked it. Barriers had begun to grow in her thoughts. There was more to lose here. She shouldn't expose any more of herself, only to lose in the end.

"Where will you go from here?" she finally asked as they danced a slow tune.

"Do I need to leave already?"

Her face burned red. "No, no, I mean what will you do next? Obviously you are a man on the move."

"Why, I was hoping you'd invite me to dinner tomorrow."

She avoided his gaze as they slowly stepped to the music. "You're very welcome to come. . . . I have two children." There. If her having big kids bothered him, she'd at least know.

"Good. I'd like to meet them."

"Luke and Tally. They're nearly grown now. Need I say more?" She expected him to look disappointed.

"You must be proud of them." She glanced up and to her relief, his smile was big. The music stopped and he guided her back to their corner.

"I am, but the boy thinks he's twenty-five instead of sixteen. And Tally, well, she's ready to run off."

He laughed. "I'd love to meet them. How do I get there?"

"Oh, ride south along the creek to the crossing. There's a small rock waterfall below it. Turn west and my place is four miles from there. The D-T brand is on the gate."

"Midday?"

"That will be fine. Don't expect too much."

His brow furrowed, and he looked her square in the eye. "Taking a meal with your bunch will be my honor."

She blushed. How was it that this man could make a woman of her age blush as if she were some silly schoolgirl? Why, she hadn't done that in years.

"May I ask why your children aren't here?"

"Luke has a broken leg and Tally offered to take care of him. They told me to go ahead and enjoy myself for a change."

"Nice of them. How did he break it?"

"Oh, riding some bronc he brought home."

He laughed. "I did the same thing when I was sixteen."

With a frown she asked, "Is that a disease among boys?"

"It just might be."

She felt him squeeze her shoulder, but remarkably

she didn't consciously notice it for a long moment. When her mind caught up to the fact that his hand lingered there, she blushed again and looked away.

His presence had become so natural.

Oh, Lucille Thornton, what are you going to do? she thought.

Chapter 2

The next morning, Captain Jack Starr took a bath in Dog Creek. After his skin had dried he heated some water over his small campfire and carefully shaved, using a straight-edge razor, then redressed. It was the best he could do to clean up for the meal he so looked forward to having with Lucille and the kids. Brushing his teeth with a rag dipped in salt water, he admired the hill country's live oak and cedar, a nice land of freestone streams with lots of forage for cattle.

Some doves in the treetops cooed at him and noisy meadowlarks darted in and out of the tall bunchgrass. He liked this hill country of Texas. As he studied the terrain around him, his thoughts turned to Lucille Thornton. Straight-backed and attractive, the woman had spurred something in his brain. No need for him to get too excited—she had her obligations to two children. He looked up at the sound of a horse approaching.

Out of habit he shifted the six-gun holster on his hip. Peering through the brush he could see a single rider approaching. As the man rode in closer, his cow pony dropped his head toward the dust and snorted. Jack's visitor sat in the saddle all dressed for church—Sunday suit and necktie, even a narrow-brimmed derby. His chin whiskers were no doubt trimmed for such an occasion.

The stranger pulled rein within twenty feet of where Starr stood. He didn't seem surprised to find Starr there by the creek.

"I saw you at the dance last night, Mister," the stranger said. "May I inquire about your business in our community?"

Jack frowned at the unfriendly nature of the question. "You the law here?"

"No, but I am considered an elder leader in this community."

Jack wiped his palm on the seat of his pants and stepped forward to offer his hand. "My name's Jack Starr."

The man checked his horse, obviously not ready to shake with him—yet. "Mine is Hiram Sawyer. Now that you've had your dances and free meal, I suggest you just keep on riding."

"I guess you tell that to all the folks traveling through here."

"I beg your pardon?"

"Listen, Hiram. I fought four years for the Confederacy. That's over, but I ain't being run off anywhere by any old goat that's set himself up as the so-called law."

"You'd be wise to heed my words, sir."

"I'd probably be wise to shoot you off that horse and tell God that you died going to church this morning."

"Watch your tongue. I'll allow no slander about the Lord."

"I'm not slandering God nor anyone else but you. And if you think for one minute you can ride down here and order me off, then you've been smoking opium. I'll ride where I want to ride and stay where I want to stay. Now get on to your services before they have to hold your funeral."

"You shall regret this day, sir."

"Hiram, I'll regret lots of things, but one of them won't be because I ran from you."

The fire on Sawyer's face was obvious. He jerked his horse around and in a huff rode off in the same direction he'd come.

Had the old SOB come all the way out here to make him clear out? Or was he simply interested in Mrs. Thornton and didn't want any competition? Snooty old devil—he'd bear to watch. Jack reminded himself that cowards like Hiram always hired professionals to do their dirty work—that would make it harder too, until he came to know the faces and names of his back stabbers.

Still upset by Sawyer's challenge, he went and saddled the stout red roan horse he called Mac and took off his hobbles. He tied his bedroll with his housekeeping gear wrapped up inside behind him. Anger festered by the minute over the man's orders that he leave the country. How powerful could Sawyer be? Major rancher? Banker? Political leader? Or just one of those men that thought God had put him in charge and no one wanted to challenge his authority?

He checked the sun time, figured it was midmorning, and headed for the falls on Lost Dog Creek. The falls spilled over with less than a foot drop off a well-worn limestone outcropping, pure and clean. After Mac took a deep drink, they headed west on the road for Mrs. Thornton's place and the D-T brand she said would be on the gate.

When he arrived Jack dismounted under the arch of the gate and smiled at all the D-T's burned in the lumber. He opened it, led his horse through, closed it and remounted, heading north up a wide, grassy swale. Good cow country. Running water that bisected such great land pleased him.

He topped the ridge and could see the cottonwood trees surrounding the house, corrals, sheds and a creaky windmill, plus some rail-fenced cropland. It was a nice layout and he felt a little jealous that she owned such a homey place. Dogs began to bark and a girl, around fifteen years old, with her mother's brown hair in abundant braids, came and stood in the open, shading her eyes with her hands to better see what made the stock dogs bark.

"Maw! Maw! It must be him," she shouted at the house.

Drying her hands on her apron, Lucille joined her daughter in the yard. Coming off the hill, Jack could see her head bob in agreement. Then she herded her daughter back toward the house. He rounded the corral and noticed a frisky pony galloping around in the pen; Jack figured this must've been the source of the boy's broken leg. Mac did a foot-shuffling gait, obviously excited about their arrival at Lucille's place.

He dropped off Mac at the hitch rail, removed his hat and wiped his forehead on his sleeve. The temperature was rising.

"Good afternoon," Lucille said with a smile from the porch.

He checked the sun time. "Am I late?"

"No, you're right on time. Come in. There's hot water in the basin if you want to wash up."

"Thanks," he said, wrapping the reins on the rack.

He hung his hat and jacket on the porch wall pegs and set about to soaping his hands. When he looked up, Lucille's girl was holding out a tin can for him.

"I'm Tally," she said. "I have some tea. It's pretty cool, but not icy like the lemonade last night. I know how cold that gets."

"Oh yes," he replied, thinking about how refreshing some of that ice-cold lemonade would be now. "Why don't you call me Captain," he said, drying his hands and face on the towel.

"I will, Captain Starr."

"On second thought, that sounds too formal." He took the can and sipped the sweetened tea.

"Maw would want me to call you Mr. Starr."

He reached out and hugged her shoulder. "Darling, we better work this out."

She laughed. "She told us you weren't stuck-up, even though you were an officer in the war and all."

"Tally," Lucille said, sounding shocked after hearing Tally's words from the kitchen.

"She's fine," Jack reassured her. "Is this Luke, the bronc rider?" he asked of the boy who sat with his left leg in a cast across two chairs. He appraised Jack suspiciously, then nodded a quick confirmation. Jack reached out and shook the youth's calloused hand. "Good to meet you."

"Same here," Luke said, firmly gripping the captain's hand.

The room smelled of fresh-cooked food, and the large table was set for four. Jack was about to take a seat when he realized he was still wearing his gun belt. He handed Tally the can of tea and unbuckled it. "Excuse me."

He went to hang the gun set on a coat peg by the door. There was a Winchester rifle over the door and a shotgun standing up beside the door frame. Lucille must be a capable woman, he thought, if she could handle guns like these. Then again, with two children and no man, she had to be.

"How have you been?" he said to Lucille.

"Fine, now that you found us all right." She patted the back of a chair and said, "Come sit. You're at the head of the table."

Jack smiled with pleasure. "May I seat you two ladies first?"

She broke into a smile. "I reckon."

He helped both of them, then took his place. "What about Luke?" he asked, gesturing to the boy, who hadn't moved from his resting place.

"I can eat over here. I'll be fine, sir."

"So long as you don't starve." He shared a wink with the boy. But he was hardly a boy; many men in his outfit during the war had been no older than Luke.

"I'll fix him a plate," Tally said.

"Good. We have to take care of our disabled troopers."

Lucille filled Jack's coffee cup, and made sure that he had the first serving of everything. As she hovered over him with a bowl of mashed potatoes, he gently stopped her. "I eat mess with the troopers. Don't fuss over me."

"We don't get a guest very often," Lucille said.

"I hope I'm not a guest, but a friend you've invited in for dinner."

She smiled, set the mashed potatoes next to his plate and took her place beside him, placing a napkin in her lap. "After you say grace, you're on your own," she said wryly.

The kids laughed.

"Let us pray. . . ." He reached out and placed his left hand over hers. It had been a while since he'd been singled out to do this job.

"Father, we're gathered together here today for our noon meal in fellowship. We're grateful for all the food and the fine weather. Heal Luke's leg quickly so he can go back to enjoying his life. Bring us some rain down the valley for the grass and crops. And, Lord, let us live in peace. Thank you again for our friends and help us forgive our enemies. In Jesus' name, amen. Now pass the gravy, please."

Everyone nodded in approval. He'd passed the first test.

As everyone busily filled their plates, Jack decided to mention his earlier encounter. "I ran into a man this morning. Hiram Sawyer." He checked all their faces for a reaction.

Tally scowled. Luke made a sour look, and Lucille glanced up at him while buttering her bread. "What did he say?"

"I guess I didn't have the right papers to stay in this country. He told me to light a shuck."

"He did?" Lucille blinked her doe brown eyes in disbelief. "Why?"

"Seems my kind ain't welcome up here."

"Kind? What kind did he say you were?"

He shrugged. "I must have failed some test of his."

"Oh no," Lucille said and rose up in righteousness. "He has no right to threaten you."

"What did you do to him?" Luke asked with a snicker, but his mother's frown silenced him.

"What did I consider doing to him, or what did I really do?"

Tally started laughing and the laughter became contagious.

Jack wiped his mouth on the napkin before he spoke. "I told him I sure wasn't leaving on his account."

"Maw, tell him about what you did to Hiram," Luke said.

Lucille stiffened and slowly lowered her knife and fork. "Three years ago, the day I got word that their father had been killed in service to his country, Hiram appeared at my door, ready for me to sign the ranch and everything else over to him. He must have followed the soldier that brought us the news. He said he was calling in the loan Felton, my husband, had made. He assumed since I was a widow that I couldn't pay it, and he was taking over the property."

Jack looked over at her with a hard scowl. "What did you do?"

"I paid him every dime in Confederate money and he had to take it. The money was still good back then. He was the most shocked man in Texas that day."

"How much did you owe him?"

"Two hundred and fifty."

A chuckle came from deep in his throat. "And I bet he still has that money in his safe."

"Ain't any good now, is it?" Luke asked.

"Not worth a dime," Jack confirmed.

"So now you know all about Hiram Sawyer," Lucille said. "You've met one of this family's biggest enemies."

"But that's not all, Maw. Tell him about the other thing. Tell him." Tally elbowed her mother.

"There isn't anything to tell," Lucille said, her face flushing a delicate pink. Jack observed her closely and looked back and forth between the kids.

"Yes, there is," Luke said with a big know-it-all grin.

Lucille sighed. "Sometime back, Hiram came calling, armed with a bouquet of flowers and candy. Said he was there to make amends. I never invited him off his horse. I told him it wasn't necessary because I wasn't excusing him for his bad manners."

"Tell him what you did next," Luke said, egging her on.

Looking peeved, Lucille glared at her son, but decided to go on anyway. "I reached in, grabbed the twelve-gauge and fired it over his head." Jack leaned back in his chair, amazed at the woman's sheer bravado.

"And, Captain, that horse about bucked him off as it ran for the gate," Tally said, clapping her hands together in delight.

Jack leaned forward and gently rubbed Lucille's hand to reassure her. "You did just fine. He had it coming."

"We were sure glad he dropped the candy." Luke was laughing so hard that tears ran down his tanned face.

"What did you do with the bouquet?" Jack asked between choruses.

"Luke's dog, Russel, got it and tore it to shreds," Tally said. "I mean, that collie had a fit about it."

Jack sat back in his chair, letting out a laugh of his own. "Then I don't feel bad about sending him down the road this morning."

Not that he wasn't worried about future run-ins with the jilted man. If there was a fly in the ointment, it would be Hiram Sawyer.

Chapter 3

There was lots to fix around the Thorntons' ranch with Luke laid up, so Lucille didn't turn down Jack's offer to trade work for his keep. There was a spare bedroom in a shed where part-time hired hands stayed, but it had been empty for a while. That afternoon the women swept down the cobwebs, scrubbed the dirt floor and fixed the place up while he spent time with Luke.

"You have any crutches?" he asked the boy.

Luke made a face. "No, I'm confined to a chair most days."

"Well, then, I'm loading you in a wheelbarrow, and we're going down to that workshop I saw near the barn to make you some."

Luke gave a big grin. "That'd sure be alright with me."

The shop, Jack found, was well equipped for blacksmith and carpentry work and just about anything else. He made sticks from some lumber he found and sanded smooth. After taking Luke's measurements, he fashioned saddlelike pieces to go under the boy's armpits. Luke sat in the wheelbarrow, absently petting two stock dogs that came into the shop, looking for company.

"You sure can do lots of things with wood," Luke marveled. "But I'm more interested in horseshoeing. Could you teach me?"

"We can work on it. I'm not an expert, but I could try."

Luke sighed. "Dad always did it, before he was gone. I wished I'd learned more from him."

"I know," Jack said wistfully. "Boys never pay attention enough to what their fathers try to teach them. I was no different. But you can't take it back—you just have to learn from it. Now, let's try this crutch deal."

He helped Luke out of the wheelbarrow and stood him upright, fitting the crutches under his arms. "Take your time. They weren't meant for running. I know you can go faster than they want to. Just be patient."

Soon Luke was easily crossing the length of the shop. His mother leaned against the doorframe and shook her head. "You made it so he can get around, huh?"

"A boy wasn't made that couldn't be helped." Jack admired his charge.

"Well, Luke," Tally said, coming in behind her mother. "Now that you can get around so well, maybe you can go back to milking that dang old cow."

"Not yet," Lucille said sternly. "I'm still going to rely on you for that, young lady."

"Ah, Maw," Tally said with a sour look on her face.

"Your room is ready when you want to move in," Lucille said to Jack, changing the subject.

"I'll have all my stuff in there by dark." Jack smiled at her. "Thanks."

"No, thank you for the crutches," she said, holding Jack's gaze for a moment before turning away. "Let's go find some supper." She led the parade back to the house.

Tally ran into the house with Luke hobbling after her while Lucille lingered at the porch to wait for Jack. "I left some of Felton's clothes on the bed for you. I could wash yours tomorrow."

"That would be nice. They sure could use it."

"Not a problem. By the way, I can tell Luke was very proud of his crutches."

"Well, he's a good kid. They both are," Jack said, brushing aside the compliment.

"Oh, they can be a handful," she responded with a laugh.

"You manage it well." He stopped in the sundown's red light and looked around. How long would he be able to stay? Would Sawyer try to run him off her place after the shotgun welcome she gave him?

"What are you thinking?" she asked.

"I wonder what Sawyer's got on his mind now. What's that small town I rode through on my way to the schoolhouse dance?"

"Shedville?"

"I reckon."

"About eight miles east."

"On the *fur* side of Lost Dog Falls?"

She laughed and went to get him some hot water to

wash up with. "Why do you ask? You plan on paying the town a visit anytime soon?" she called from the other room.

Jack wasn't sure if he wanted to tell Lucille that he planned to ride into town and learn all he could about Sawyer. Jack had made himself an enemy, but he wasn't sure how tough a one he'd be. He'd need to find out.

"No reason," he casually replied. "Just thought I'd get some supplies. So, what're we eating for supper tonight?"

"Chicken again. I warn you: we eat a lot of it in this house."

"No problem. I get to crowing, you'll know I've had enough." They shared a chuckle, but his mind was still on Sawyer.

Chapter 4

Jack awoke suddenly in the middle of the night and shot bolt upright in bed, straining to hear what sounded as if it was a hard-ridden horse coming up to the ranch. What time was it, and who'd come at this ungodly hour? Something must be wrong. He threw back the light blanket and quickly dressed in one of Lucille's husband's shirts and canvas pants, buckled on his six-gun and headed for the house under the stars.

When he rounded the corner of the front porch he heard a man on a hard-breathing cow pony, talking to Lucille. "Jack, listen to Craig Ketchem here. He came over to tell us some real bad news," Lucille said with a worried look on her face.

Jack and Craig exchanged quick nods. "They burned out Jason Holmes tonight on Owl Mountain. They kilt him and his wife. Took all of his good horses."

"Who do you suppose did it?" Jack asked.

"Comanches, we think," Craig said angrily.

"Strange time of year for them, isn't it? They usually come after their buffalo hunts in the fall."

"Them bloodthirsty devils don't care," Craig sneered. "They'll show up anytime they need the loot."

"You're right, but I need to see this for myself. Figure out if there's anything that can be done. You've had Comanche trouble in this area before?"

"Oh yeah, lots of it," Craig confirmed.

"Lucille, I'll be back," Jack called over his shoulder as he headed toward the barn with Craig. "I'm going to ready my horse."

"I'll pack you some food," she called back.

"That'd be much appreciated." He turned to Craig. "How far away is this place?"

"Five miles west."

"Can you take me there?" Jack asked the rancher.

"Sure, but I wanted to tell—"

"Lucille and Tally will tell the others," Jack said reassuringly. When Lucille followed a few minutes later with sandwiches, she wholeheartedly agreed to Jack's plan. "You two see what you can do about those killers. The Holmeses were good people, Jack. Both of them."

After Jack saddled Mac and filled his bags with supplies, he exchanged a few words with Lucille. He learned that Craig Ketchem was a stockman and bachelor who lived close to the Holmeses' ranch. He had seen the flames blazing from their house, and had immediately set out to investigate. He had a few Mexicans watching his place while he was away, so Jack needn't worry that Craig was leaving his ranch open to attack if the Comanches weren't done for the night.

"Keep that rifle and shotgun handy," Jack said close to her ear. "I hate leaving you three alone."

"We'll be double careful. I promise." Lucille squeezed his hand reassuringly.

"I'll be back in a day."

"Just you be careful," she said in a low, concerned whisper.

The two men rode out. Craig didn't have much to say on the ride over, which was fine with Jack. They pushed hard to arrive at the smoldering ranch ruins by daybreak. Many people were gathered, and two graves had already been dug. Wagons were parked all over the ranch, and various women wrapped in blankets cooked breakfast over campfires for the men.

"Isn't that Hiram Sawyer?" Jack asked Craig privately when he caught sight of the man.

"That's him." Craig made a sour face. "I figure he had a note on this place. He loans money to many of the ranchers."

"I know. Lucille told me about him. Guess he came to collect on his loan today," Jack said with a bitter edge to his tone.

"I never thought of it that way, but I bet that's the truth."

Jack led Mac through the crowd. A man with a ranger badge was talking to several armed boys around him.

"Good day," Jack said, dismounting. "I hear you think Comanches did this. I'm curious to know what led you to believe that."

"Why?" the ranger spat out in disbelief, his face reddening. "Hell, they're the only ones that'll kill so brutally. What do you know about Indians anyway?"

"Before the war I served under Captain Steele in the rangers," Jack smoothly replied.

The ranger settled down and nodded as if he were deep in thought. "Clifton, you go and show this ranger the corpses."

"Yes, sir," the young man nodded. "Come with me, sir."

Jack handed the reins to Craig. "I'll only be a minute."

Jack caught up with the young ranger in a few steps, and they went to where the covered bodies lay.

"Don't disturb them," a thickset woman warned as she straightened up from a pan she was tending over the fire, and brandished a large wooden spoon at them.

"I only want to see their wounds," Jack reassured her.

She cut an evil look at him. "You a ranger too?"

"I've been one in the past."

"Well, then, go ahead and help yourself." She puckered her lips. "But it ain't pretty."

Jack knelt and lifted the first shroud. It was the body of an older man, most likely Jason Holmes. A large patch of the man's gray-black hair was gone, but the wound hadn't bled, so he was already dead when they scalped him. The copper smell of death made Jack swallow hard a time or two before he moved to check the next body.

It was a woman, roughly the same age as the man. Her eyes were closed from the beating they'd given her, and she'd also been scalped after she died. Unusual for Comanches not to scalp their victims alive,

Jack thought. They liked to hear them scream. But the rest of the knife work looked Injun enough. When he rose, the ranger captain joined him.

"See anything but blood and a mess?"

"Yes." Jack looked around to be certain he wouldn't be overheard. "Both were killed and *then* scalped."

"Hmm. How do you know that?"

"The scalping never drew any blood. Not that I can see."

"Well, a scalpin's a scalpin', ain't it? Don't make no difference when it was done, er . . ."

"Captain Jack Starr." He stuck out his hand to the captain, who shook it firmly.

"Captain Dully McIntyre."

"In my experience, Captain McIntyre, Comanches like to scalp their victims alive so they can hear them scream."

McIntyre folded his arms over his broad chest and nodded. "If you were with Steele, you saw enough of this to know your business. Who did it, then?"

Jack shrugged. "The ones who herded the horses out of here, I'd say."

McIntyre pondered the information. "I can loan you three privates, well-mounted, to follow them, if'n you'll lead them."

"Let me ask Craig if he wants to go along," Jack said as he turned to head back to his horse. "Oh, and, Captain, don't say a word about the scalping."

"I won't." The big man lowered his voice. "If I even thought a white man had done this, I'd stake him on an anthill."

"Ranger, here, take this food and eat it on the way."
The fat woman handed him a plate laden with food.

"But, ma'am, how will I return the—" Jack stopped
short as he looked over the scrambled eggs, crisply
browned bacon, flaky biscuits and thick gravy, and his
mouth flooded with saliva.

"I ain't worried none about one tin plate," she said,
shooing him off. "Now you go on and get them devils
that done this terrible thing."

Jack thanked her and headed toward Craig, who
was busy eating with a red-cheeked, chubby farm wife.

"What're we doing next?" he asked between bites.

"Captain McIntyre's given us three rangers to track
down the horse thieves. You want to come along?"

Craig's Adam's apple bobbed and he nodded, swal-
lowing hard. "Sure, I want in on the deal. But they've
got a powerful head start on us already."

"I know it. Borrow me a rifle and a box of ammo.
We leave in ten minutes."

"Yes, sir." Craig saluted.

Jack stopped. "I ain't your captain, Craig."

"You'd make for a good one. From here on, you're
Captain Starr."

Jack shook his head. "Eat your food. Tell them troopers that're heading over here to ready themselves for
the ride, Sarge."

Craig smiled broadly. "Yes, sir."

"Now, Craig, you be careful out there." Craig's woman
fussed over him worriedly, like she was already his
missus.

But before he left, Jack wanted to see Hiram one more time.

Hiram stood in the middle of a small crowd, leaning back on his heels, running his thumbs under his yellow suspenders and pontificating aloud as if he were the boss of the country. At the edge of the crowd Jack picked at his plate of food, waiting for Hiram to realize who'd joined his small congregation.

After a few minutes Hiram caught sight of him. "Starr, is that you?"

"Hiram," Jack began. "Five of us going after those horses. I wanted to offer you the option of joining us."

"Ah, er . . . you see—" Hiram colored, fumbling for an excuse.

"Don't worry. I understand you're busy collecting your collateral here. Never mind. We'll handle it." Jack walked away, but not before catching the low guffaws of the gathered men. He knew that everyone within twenty miles would know the story of his challenge before nightfall. It was exactly what he wanted.

On his way to mount Mac, he took the proffered rifle and cartridges from Craig's woman and hugged her. "Thank you. This'll go a long way toward bringing the Holmeses' killers to justice."

"Watch out for him for me." She grabbed Jack's shirt-sleeve, glancing over at Craig.

"He'll be fine—"

"Marsha. Marsha Crown's my name. My first man was killed in Mississippi. I can't afford to lose another."

"Don't worry."

"I sure hope you're right. But it's going to worry me plumb to death until he gets back alive."

Craig's safety, like that of the others, would worry Jack too. He shoved the Winchester in the scabbard, swung his leg over the cantle, and nodded to Marsha before signaling to his men. They rode out on a long trot, with a packhorse following close behind the party. Good of McIntyre for thinking of supplies, Jack thought.

The killers' tracks headed west and Jack kept expecting them to turn north, where the Comanches typically settled. But on the second day, the trail turned south and Jack knew his instincts had been on target.

"Captain, where do you think they're going?" the towheaded Arnold boy asked as the path turned.

"Looks like they're not going out on the Llano Estacada, are they?"

The boy, who looked too young even to shave, shook his head. "No, they're sure not. Perplexing, ain't it?"

"Plumb perplexing," Jack agreed.

"I think they're going to Mexico," short, squat Jangles Townsend chimed in.

"Craig, what notion have you got?" Jack asked.

"I'm not sure, sir. But I'd sure like a cool drink right now."

Jack checked Mac. "I think we'll find them and your drink on the Llano River tonight. You boys ready for a real hot-fire fight?"

Dexter Cotton, the quietest of the three young rangers, drew out his cap-and-ball pistol to check the loads. "I sure got me an itching to get on with it."

Jack nodded. "Any of you boys ever been under fire before?'

"We had one Injun fight," Arnold said. "Up on the San Saba. We all three were there. We kilt one Injun and we got two of our horses shot out from under us."

"Boys, if you can't see a rider clear, shoot his horse," Jack commanded. "It makes him a foot soldier."

Cotton hooted. "I never thought of that. Damn sight bigger target too."

"Well, those Comanche shot your horses and ended the chase, right?"

"They damn sure did," Jangles Townsend agreed.

"Then you got to figure that the same'll work in reverse," Jack reasoned.

"Well, just how in hell's name do we keep them from shooting our horses?" Craig asked.

"Shoot 'em first is what you've got to do," Cotton said, as if the answer were obvious.

Jack found it hard not to smile at the young man's answer. "Well, let's try to do that, then."

They all agreed.

After dark, as they neared the Llano River, Jack sensed they were close to the stolen horse herd. In the distance, they could hear the new horses fighting with the rustlers' animals. They slowed their pace and Jack held a finger to his lips, motioning for his men to stay quiet. Jack and Jangles dismounted and on foot climbed a hill that overlooked the riverbank to size up the camp.

Through the dark, Jack made out six figures on the bank. One of the men was playing a guitar and singing a Spanish folk song near a blazing campfire, three others lounged nearby, and the last two tended the horses as they grazed.

"Six of 'em?" Jangles asked.

"Same as I got," Jack confirmed. Even in the starlight he could see how upset the young ranger was.

"How'd you figure out this bunch of Mexicans done that murdering? You think they figured we'd put the blame on the damn Injuns?"

"Yep, I think you're right about that. But we've got them anyhow."

Jangles nodded in the starlight, still taken aback by their discovery. He swore under his breath.

"We better go back and get the boys ready," Jack said, heading back to the rest of the party.

"If they're like me and learn what we know, I can tell you they'll be ready real quick." They slipped up the draw and made it back to the other rangers, who had set up a quick camp.

Jack explained the situation. At least two of them were boys, even younger than Arnold, but still killers nonetheless.

"Don't shoot each other in the excitement and don't let any of them escape. Count your shots. A six-shooter is worthless when it's empty, so always save the last cartridge. I'd use my rifle first, then the Colt."

He looked them over sternly once more. "Alright, let's go get 'em. Jangles, you and Cotton take the right flank and get those two guarding the herd. Arnold, you and Sergeant Craig take the left side and deal with the ones near the campfire. I'll come straight down. Whatever you do, don't shoot each other. You'll hear my owl signal when it's time to act."

Jangles and Cotton set out to the right while Craig went left, motioning for Arnold to follow on his heels. Jack walked straight toward the camp, dodging from cedar to cedar for cover until he was close enough to hear their Spanish chatter.

Rifle cocked and ready at the hip, he dropped to his knees and gave his best owl hoot.

"*¿Que pasa?*" The men asked in confusion. Before they knew it, gunfire erupted around the camp.

Concentrating hard in the darkness, Jack aimed his rifle wherever the Mexicans' pistols flared. Shots filled the air in the darkness for a minute, echoing through the night. Then there was silence. As Jack approached the camp, he could hear several of the killers groaning as they clutched their wounds and writhed on the ground.

"Jangles, you and Cotton all right?" Jack called into the air.

After a long pause, Jangles shouted back, "Yes sir. We've got them herders."

"Craig, how about you and Arnold?"

"Everything's fine here. Arnold's making us a pitch torch."

Satisfied, Jack set down his rifle and walked toward the campfire with his six-gun cocked. A bright flare from the fire illuminated four of the killers' bloody faces, none of which looked ready to fight anymore. Assessing the blood loss, Jack calculated that only two of them would still be alive in the next few minutes. He kicked their handguns aside as he approached them.

"Well, troopers, we came, we fought and we won."
He reloaded his six-gun, holstered it, and shifted the
holster. "Carry in those other two near the herd," he
directed.

"Yes, sir, Captain," Jangles said with a quick salute.

The dead lay side by side while Jack's men dug a
single, wide grave for them. One of the two who was
still alive was no doubt the leader, judging from his
age. He'd taken a bullet in the chest and was coughing
up blood into his sleeve. He dragged himself upright
and leaned back against a large log, struggling for breath,
while Jack squatted on his haunches before him.

"I can make your last hours better or worse."

The man held Jack's gaze for a long time with a look
of distrust in his eyes. "What's the price?" he finally
spat out, coughing and spitting blood to the side.

"All you have to tell me is who hired you to do this."

The man shook his head. "No one. These dead men
are mine. I run my own operation."

Jack wasn't having it for a second. "How did you
know Jason Holmes had such fine horses to steal?"

The man started coughing violently, his chest heav-
ing up and down. "My men found them."

Jack jerked the cork out of a pint of whiskey he'd
found near the campfire and took a swallow from the
bottle. He wiped his mouth on the back of his hand.
"Good whiskey. I wish I could share this with you, but
I can't if you don't tell me the truth. I need a name."

The man managed a feeble laugh, dropped his chin
to his chest, and slumped over. Jack corked the bottle
and grabbed the man by his long, gray-streaked hair,

then drew his hunting knife. "I'm going to scalp you before you die, you worthless sumbitch. Who sent you up there?"

But it was no use. The man was dead.

The last survivor was a kid and he knew nothing. They hung him at dawn, then tossed his body in the massive grave and buried the six corpses. Jack gave a little prayer for them and ordered his team to mount up. They drove the rustlers' team and the stolen horses back toward home.

As they got closer, word was soon out. The rangers with the recovered horses were returning, and folks lined the road or gathered at crossroads to wave Lone Star flags at them and shout, "Hurrah, rangers!"

The boys waved back and thanked the people. Cookies, pies and fruit bread soon filled their hands, bellies and saddlebags. When they finally drew close to the falls on Lost Dog Creek, McIntyre and his troop met them and took over the horse herd.

"Sawyer will be glad to see them horses. He's got a note on them too," McIntyre announced.

"Well, he damn sure don't have a note on the Mexicans' horses and gear. Those belong to the rangers," Jack said. "You sell 'em and divide the money."

"How much is your part?" McIntyre asked.

"One-fifth," Jack said without batting an eye.

"But you're the captain—" McIntyre started to protest.

"You heard me: one-fifth."

He nodded respectfully. "I'll do it, Captain Starr."

"Good. Now I've got to say my good-byes and thanks

to the boys 'fore I head on back to Lucille's." Jack tipped his hat and readied his horse to leave.

McIntyre grinned broadly and shook his head. "Thanks for the help, Starr. I've learned a helluva lot from you. You ever need a favor, let me know."

Jack spurred weary Mac over to his crew, who were gathered together and hungrily eating the fresh pies they'd collected on their way over. "McIntyre's selling the rustlers' horses and gear for us, and every man will get a twenty-percent cut. I'm proud to have rode with you."

Jangles was all lower lip when Jack shook his hand and clapped his shoulder. "I'm a lot prouder than I was up on the San Saba. You'll damn sure do to ranger with."

"Hell, we got 'em." Jack rode over to Cotton and shook his hand.

"Word'll get out the rangers don't bring in prisoners, Captain. Maybe it'll keep some of the border trash out of Texas, huh?"

"Sure enough, Cotton," Jack affirmed. "You boys are some of the bravest men I ever fought with."

Arnold laughed. "You don't know how scared we all were."

"I didn't say you weren't scared. Only a damn fool ain't scared." Jack walked Mac over to Craig to shake hands. "Craig, when will we all dance at your and Marsha's wedding?" The other men laughed and elbowed each other good-naturedly.

"If—if you'd be my best man, we'd get it all set up real shortly," Craig stammered.

"I'd be honored. Let me know when it is."

"I will, Captain. I will—" But Jack already had Mac headed for the bare-headed woman in the familiar blue dress who had just climbed off a wagon in the rig-choked road.

Just short of her, Jack put Mac on his heels in a sliding stop, dismounted on the fly and caught Lucille around the waist. My God, what a lovely woman, he thought. He swung her in circles, staring into her brown eyes and grinning big as the whole state. When he finally kissed her, the rangers emptied their pistols into the sky. Leave it to them to do somethin' like that, Jack thought with a smile.

Chapter 5

Before Jack and Lucille left, the locals planned a large dance for the following Saturday to celebrate the capture of the killers and the recovery of the Holmeses' horses. While Lucille took part in the arrangements, Jack squatted on his boot heels to watch Hiram Sawyer's men take over the stolen horses and stud. Damn convenient, the rangers returning his collateral for him. Hiram had already taken possession of the ranch. The place wasn't a bad setup either. It was a full section of deeded land, which meant it went west a mile and north a mile from where the burned-out cabin and sheds stood in the southeast corner of the land. And the big talker hadn't offered the rangers a dime in reward; in fact, Jack hadn't even seen him there.

Was Sawyer concerned they might've learned something about his involvement in the deal? If Jack had any proof that old skinflint had any part in those good folks' demise, he'd personally send him to his reward—feetfirst. But he had only his instincts and suspicions to go on.

As Jack surveyed the scene, a bowlegged man in his thirties came toward him, dressed in bull-hide chaps, run-over boots, Mexican spurs, a leather vest and gauntlets. He wore a ratty denim jacket that indicated to Jack that he frequented the brush; it looked like a cat had clawed at his sleeves.

"My name's Red Larson. I'm a maverick man, so if you ain't interested in associatin' with my kind, I'll scoot."

Under the wide brim of the man's Mexican straw hat Jack saw a sly smile and green eyes that didn't give a damn about much except for having a good time. "Sit tight, neighbor. I ain't got a critter to lose so I ain't opposed to maverick work."

"Good to hear. You ever been north of the Red River Crossing?"

"I've been to Abilene," Jack said, wondering what Larson was getting at.

The man bobbed his head. "Well, they've cut a good amount of miles off that trip. Rustlers only have to drive cattle to the Salt Fork on the Arkansas this year."

Jack nodded thoughtfully. "So they've finally got the tracks down to Wichita?" He hadn't heard until now.

Red nodded. "You got any plans for next year?"

Jack shrugged, looking off at the cedar-covered hillsides. "What'cha need?"

"You probably don't know much about it, but folks round here been having real trouble getting their cattle to the railhead. I know all about stampedes and storms. I been there—it ain't no picnic. But our losses have been too high and that means the cost is up per head. Lots of us are looking for a new man to take our stock north next year."

Jack leaned back on his heels and let out a low whistle. "I'd have to sleep on that a long time, Larson."

"Well, you sleep on it for a while. I figure you'll still be here when grass breaks in the spring."

Jack smiled at the man. "Or that I'll be smart enough to say no to the offer."

Red shook his head. "You sleep on it. A man could earn enough to buy himself a real fine place on the proceeds of a well-run cattle drive."

"Or get buried under the prairie sod. I won't lose any sleep over it. But thanks for thinking of me. Good to meet'cha."

Red stood and hitched up his chaps. "I'm sure I'll be seeing you around." He started to head off, then turned back to face Jack. "By the way, we'll be down at Peters this Sunday afternoon. We'll have some broncs to peel. You should come on down. I figure you'd be a real hand at bronc stomping."

"I'll see about it," Jack called back.

Red grinned and strolled off. Jack saw Lucille coming toward him, her brow arched at the sight of Red.

"What did Larson want?" she asked, a slight edge to her voice.

"Just wanted to shoot the breeze, I guess."

She frowned. "What does that mean?"

Jack was taken aback by Lucille's obvious displeasure. "You dislike him?"

She wrinkled her nose. "Oh, I think he's on the wild side."

"Folks think that about me."

"I don't." She reached out and laced her fingers through his.

He glanced down at their hands as they headed for her wagon. "You'll have folks talking."

"I don't care. A man comes busting home with a herd of stolen horses, near runs me over with his horse and kisses me in public. People can't say too much more."

Jack laughed. "I think it was that four-gun salute we got that really set tongues waggin'."

She shook her head, chuckling. "Wait till the kids hear all about it."

"You think they'll be ashamed of us?"

"No." She squeezed his fingers. "And even if they are, it was . . . fun."

Jack hitched Mac to the tailgate and helped Lucille up onto the spring seat, climbed in, took the reins and eased the team in a U-turn for home. Once they were on the road and moving, he settled down on the spring seat beside her, turned, caught her chin and kissed her again.

"Whew," she said, wrapping her arms around him and burying her face in his shoulder. "I've missed you not being here the past four days."

"I did too." He clucked his tongue to keep the team trotting and slapped them lightly with the reins.

Lucille sat quietly in thought for most of the trip home, then suddenly said, "Tell me, Jack, why didn't you ever marry?"

Jack's face flushed a bit, but he decided he owed Lucille an answer. "Cholera took my first bride-to-be on a train out of Arkansas. We were only seventeen. I grew up fast that year."

Lucille rubbed his back in slow, circular motions, a look of genuine sympathy on her face. "I'm sorry, Jack."

"There was another lady in my life a few years later, but she married someone else while I was off ranger- ing. Guess I stayed away too long."

"How long were you gone?"

He shrugged. "Over a year."

"I guess she couldn't wait for you," Lucille said.

He nodded, then flicked the horses with the reins. "She must have thought I was dead."

"She probably did. Anyhow, I'm sorry for asking you such a personal question, but I had to know."

"Aw, Lucy, I'm like every other man; I've got some things I don't like to talk much about, but I will if it means that much to you."

She squeezed his arm. "Well, I'm sure glad you feel that way."

He studied the fading day with the low sun in his eyes. It sure felt natural as anything he could ever re- member, sitting up close next to her. Maybe their new- found love would work out. He sure hoped so.

He'd had casual affairs with other women, but no one had ever fit him like an old pair of craftsmen-made boots—Lucille did.

Chapter 6

On Sunday, Jack took Luke with him in the wagon to Peters' roping and riding. He could tell Luke was excited about the venture, so once they were past the D-T front gate, he let the boy drive.

Luke glanced back over his shoulder as he took the reins. "I wasn't sure if Maw'd let me go with you today."

Jack nodded. "She didn't want your other leg to go too."

"Naw, that ain't it. I guess she never told you, but some of the crowd that attends these events don't have the best reputation, and she'd never let me go 'cause of that. 'Course I've been to them, but she never knew and I never told her."

"You mean they had some fights down there?"

Luke chuckled. "Sure. Women don't understand that fighting's kind of a regular thing in this world, do they?"

Jack nodded in agreement. "There were two boys that got into it at the schoolhouse dance the other night."

Luke grinned big. "I heard you threw them outside."

"Aw, they shouldn't have been fighting inside. It was a dance and all."

"Jody Bledsoe thinks he's real tough and Thad Simmons does the same. But I bet they won't do it again if you're around."

Jack dismissed the compliment. "You ever been cross with them?"

"Yeah, Bledsoe once at a pie supper."

"Were you tryin' to buy pie from the same gal?" Jack thought about some of his past fights—usually over his pride or some girl—in amusement.

Luke shot him a glance. "You guessed it. I was sweet on Lorna May and had my money saved to buy her pie. Bledsoe ran her pie up past what I had, and then he wouldn't pay for it. Well, he kinda ran over the people holding the auction and said he'd pay them later, but he never did. It made me mad as hell. He cheated and got to eat with my girl. I knew he'd never pay them, so when it was over I challenged him to a fight—called him a *damn* liar.

"We fought for a while. He gave me a black eye and I busted his pretty nose, so he claimed. But it came out a draw. Some older folks finally made us quit. When I got home with my knuckles all skinned up, a black eye and a big bruise on my left cheek, Maw was mad as a wet hen."

Jack nodded sympathetically. "My mother would always react the same way."

"Women just don't understand you've got to settle things once and for all."

"That's why they call them the gentler sex." Jack clapped the boy on the shoulder. "That the place we're going to?"

Luke looked over at the horses, tarps strung up for shade, and parked wagons and nodded in affirmation. There were little kids chasing after each other, women cooking in pots and men talking horses and trying to make trades.

They parked and Jack hitched the team. He helped Luke down and got him on his crutches, and Luke hobbled away to find his friends. After Luke left, Jack saw two men—one tall and gangly, the other short and squat—in suits coming over to greet him.

Joe Kimes, the taller man, stuck his hand out to Jack and introduced himself and the shorter man, Israel Kimes, his brother. Jack shook hands warmly and they squatted down to visit. He knew they had something on their minds and they weren't long getting to the matter.

"You ever been to Kansas?" Joe asked.

"Yes, twice," Jack answered. "I was in Abilene with cattle herds."

"You ever ramrodded a herd up there?" Israel asked.

"Sure did; delivered ninety-five percent of them too out of the Rio Grande valley country."

"That's big numbers," Joe said, impressed.

Jack shook his head to dismiss the man's words. "Got lucky."

Israel appreciated the humility. "Well, I guess Red Larson told you we need a ramrod for next year. Said he'd spoke to you about it."

Jack nodded. "He tell you what I told him?"

"Yeah," Joe said, "but we figured if you heard our story, we might reverse your thoughts on the matter."

Although he had set his mind against it, Jack decided it wouldn't hurt to hear them out. "Okay, I'm listening."

"We never sent no cattle north this year," Israel said, shaking his head as if he regretted it. "Figured if we saved them up to build a big enough herd, we could find us a real ramrod. Truth is, we haven't found one yet, and we're losin' out."

"You'll probably be able to find a dozen good ones at Fort Worth this winter," Jack said, unswayed.

"Some of us are thinking you'd make a good one," Joe chimed in.

"Why? Cause I threw two boys out of a schoolhouse dance for fighting? Wranglin' boys ain't the same as herdin' cattle."

"That and you brought back them horses with three boys who were more than a little wet behind the ears," Israel said, clearly impressed with Jack's work.

Jack shifted his weight to his other leg. "Craig was in on it too."

"He's a good man," Israel said. "But he couldn't've took a posse and got them ponies back." Joe quickly agreed with his brother.

Jack shook his head. "I'm sorry, boys, but I don't know where I'll be next year."

"We're sorry to hear that, but you think on it and let us know if you can't find a way to make it work," Joe said. "We'd be mighty pleased to have you."

"You boys get a chance to hire a good one, you better sign him on." Jack stood, ready to excuse himself.

"Captain, Captain," Luke called, hobbling toward Jack on his sticks and nearly falling over in excitement. "They've got a broom-tail mare here they say no one can ride. Offering thirty bucks to the man who can."

"What's the fee to try?"

"Ten bucks. You want to try her?" Luke was out of breath, leaning on his sticks, his face flushed with excitement.

"Excuse me, gents," Jack said to Joe and Israel, who tipped their hats to him as he headed off with Luke. "You ever tried to ride her?"

"Once." Luke said. "I couldn't hold on. But I got a feeling you could do it." Luke looked at him eagerly.

Jack shrugged. "Aw, why not? Let's try her."

Luke whooped and pulled Jack toward the waiting bronc.

They walked slowly toward the gathered crowd to allow Luke to catch his breath on the crutches. The day's temperature was climbing and a good rain wouldn't hurt anything, for his money. Jack wanted to put the cattle-drive business out of his mind, and a real challenging bronc ride might do just that.

"What do they call her?" he asked Luke as the boy worked to keep pace.

"Black Widow."

Jack let out a low whistle. "I bet she's a real one too."

"She's the worst bucking horse I've ever seen or been on," Luke confirmed.

When they found her, they noticed the onlookers were standing a safe distance back from her heels and teeth. The mare had a black broom tail, coated in dust, which she gently swished from side to side. Her head down as far as her binds would allow, she stood hip shot between two posts, practically unmoving. Her face and eyes were hidden behind a long double mane that hung way down on both sides of her neck. Unfortunately, the mane couldn't hide her ragged right ear, which looked like it had been bitten off. Hardly taller than twelve hands, she looked more like a kid's buggy horse, but neither her small size nor her seemingly calm disposition fooled Jack. He knew that blasting powder came in small, tight packages.

A tall Indian came toward him. The hot afternoon wind rattled the eagle feather tied on his unblocked hat. "You want to ride her?" he asked.

Everyone stopped talking to hear Jack's answer.

"She looks pretty tough," Jack said.

"Naw, just a pony," the Indian said, concealing his real thoughts behind a smug smile.

"I suppose your squaw rides her to church every Sunday."

The Indian laughed, as did the onlookers.

"How many men has she stomped?"

"A few," the Indian said cryptically.

"I'll take ten dollars of her, but first I need a shorter girth. Mine's too long to screw down a saddle on her."

"I'll get you one," a cowboy offered.

Jack thanked him, then beckoned to a boy of about ten who was standing nearby.

"Yes, sir," the boy said, sweeping the red hair back from his freckled face.

"There's a D-T wagon down there." He pointed to the branded one. "There's a saddle in the back. Bring my rigging up here and there's a dime in the deal for you."

"Yes, sir!" The barefoot boy tore off to get Jack's gear while everyone laughed at his eagerness.

"How did you figure out the girth deal?" Luke asked under his breath.

"Part of the game. They get you-all ready. Toss the usual saddle on, draw up both sides—but it just won't come all the way. 'Oh, the saddle is on tight, but not tight enough,' they'll say, and you'll say, 'Aw hell, let's go.'"

Luke laughed and shook his head at this newfound knowledge. "Damn. I won't forget that for next time. That's what happened with that miserable horse at home that broke my leg. I thought it was tight enough. Only lacked a little notch, but the girth was all the way up."

Jack smiled. "I've been suckered in like that before too."

The redheaded boy delivered the saddle and they stripped off the longer girth and replaced it with one Jack borrowed from Hoy, a local cowboy. Hoy was a tough man with steel blue eyes, which pierced the Indian as he straightened the double girth, making certain that the Indian wasn't trying to pull one over on Jack.

"She's a stem-winding sumbitch," Hoy said under his breath.

"I figured she must be. How does she break?" Jack asked quietly.

"She'll tear out furious in crow hops, then she'll plant all four. And if she ain't thrown you, she'll turn her old belly up to the sun. A sun-fishing son of a gun. And the longer you ride her, the madder she gets."

Jack straightened. "Guess you tried her, huh?"

"Twice. I never lasted very long."

"Well, let's see what she can do today."

A crowd was beginning to circle around them. Kids climbed on wagons for a better view. Money started to change hands. As he sat on the ground, Jack used some leather thongs to better tie down his spurs. He caught parts of conversations around him as he busied himself with the straps.

"The new guy. . . the one that brought the stolen horses back . . . Lucille Thornton's new man . . . a captain in the war, they say . . . Cap'n Jack they call him . . . How should I know if he can ride?"

Amused, he rose and brushed off the seat of his pants. Luke rested on his crutches, watching the mare stomp impatiently at the flies buzzing around her.

"See her temper, Captain?" Luke asked worriedly.

"Yes, I do. How far did you ride her?" Jack asked.

"Not far at all. Maybe ten yards. She shook me off like a tick both times."

"Your mother know about it?"

Luke shook his head. "No way. She'd have given me a real licking."

"Heck, she might give me one."

They both chuckled at the thought.

The Indian and his helper put the blinders on Widow. Jack noted how careful they were of her front hooves.

After you were bucked off, she might come back to pay you for trying her.

Widow began making deep-throated threats and Jack could see the knowing nods in the crowd of onlookers; the devil in her was waking up. They sure weren't horse sounds.

The last-minute bets were going down as the Indian led the mare to the center of the open field, with Jack following close behind. As he placed his foot in the stirrup and swung himself onto the saddle, he could feel Widow trembling beneath him. Her trembling felt more like an earthquake as the Indian handed him the leads, jerked down the blinds and ran away.

Her hooves left the dirt and flew skyward, her head between her knees as she made a high-kicking, fierce run-buck like Hoy predicted. She landed in a four-footed stop that would have loosened most punchers and sent them flying over her head, but Jack was braced for landing and managed to hold on, every muscle in his body strained.

In a flash she whirled to the right, rising on her hind legs and showing her old belly to the midday sun. It felt like she was trying to turn herself inside out. Jack kept his seat, punishing her with a quick jab of his spurs to the flank.

She bucked left, then right in a furious fashion to shake him loose. With the arches of his boots pressed down firmly in the stirrups he spurred her even harder. Her fury grew more powerful and Jack had to struggle to hold tight. Instead of getting tired the little Widow was bucking harder than ever.

Her fierce bucking began to shake him and he knew how sore he'd be after this was over. Sharp pains in his neck and shoulders jolted him like lightning. He was satisfied with his performance and knew that prolonging the ride would only break her spirit.

He kicked his right boot out of the stirrup and propelled himself off Widow. Landing on his feet, he swept off his hat and bowed to her as she reared up on her hind legs.

The crowd, puzzled at first that Jack had chosen to dismount, soon realized that he did so out of respect to Widow. A sense of awe pervaded the crowd as they began to clap, the applause building and building.

The Indian led the horse away, and Luke hobbled quickly toward Jack, a look of wonder on his face. "You rode her. You rode her good!"

"That I did. But I didn't wanna break her. She's too great a spirit." He stretched his arms high over his head as he scanned the smiling crowd. "All the riding's got me starved. Let's go find us some lunch."

"Wait, wait!" the Indian called, running to catch up with them. "You rode her longer than any man ever rode her, but you didn't try to break her." A look of respect briefly crossed his otherwise immobile face. "She'll live to buck some more." He handed Jack thirty dollars, then went after his horse.

"That mean the bet's off?" someone asked. Everyone laughed as the crowd disbanded.

Jack bought two bowls of beef stew at a dime a bowl from a woman that Luke knew. They squatted under the shade of a tree to eat their lunch. The food was hot and the chunks of beef were tender as well as flavorful. The sweet, buttery cornbread crumbled in Jack's mouth, drawing saliva in a flood.

The woman came by and collected their bowls when they were finished with the stew and filled them with cherry cobbler.

"Sure is good eating," Jack told Luke. The youth grinned in return, his mouth full of flaky pastry and warm cherry compote.

"I'm just glad you brought me along."

Several townsfolk came by and introduced themselves to Jack. Friendly folks, he decided, despite the fact that he had heard them quietly arguing about his decision to bail off Widow short of a so-called conclusion. He paid it no mind.

After exchanging pleasantries, he excused himself as he saw Jangles, Cotton and Arnold—his three ranger friends from the rescue missions—approach.

"Damn, heard we missed a wild ride," Jangles said, shaking his head. "I'd like to have seen that."

"Aw, I'd bet on the captain," Cotton said as he looked hungrily at Luke's bowl of cobbler.

Jack caught the look. "I'll buy you jaybirds some pipin'-hot stew and cornbread if you're willing to sit and visit a spell," he offered. He knew that the state didn't pay them for their services, so a free lunch would be much appreciated.

"That would be nice," Cotton said while the other two bobbed their heads eagerly. "But what we really came by for was to tell you we found a few signs that Indians've been snooping around the country. We'd like your opinion on the matter."

Jack considered the boy's words thoughtfully. "What does McIntyre say?"

"Well, he's gone to Fort Worth for the week and we don't trust just anyone else with this information," Cotton whispered conspiratorially.

Arnold, who had remained silent until then, looked around to be certain they were alone. "We don't want folks panicking over nothing, but if them red devils're scouting things we need to stop them."

Jack paid up and passed bowls of stew to the boys, contemplating Arnold's words. But before he could answer, he was distracted by the sight of two men in conspicuous dress pulling up to the gathering.

"Who are those two men wearing coats in this heat?" Jangles nodded toward the riders.

"Looks like the law to me," Jack replied.

"You mean the carpetbagger's law?" Luke asked, with a sneer of disgust.

"Could be." Jack frowned when he noticed the pair talking to someone in the crowd who pointed in his direction. The riders appraised him with cold eyes as they turned their horses toward him.

The older one, with a white mustache and cold blue eyes, rode in the lead.

"You Jack Starr?"

Jack nodded, but refused to say a word.

The younger one drew his six-shooter, keeping it

low at his side. "You're under arrest for the murder of Judge William Streeter."

"Who?" Jack said in confusion. This had to be a mistake. He certainly didn't know any Streeter.

"I'm afraid we're gonna have to take you in, Mr. Starr," the older man said, a cruel smile on his face.

"You can't do that—" Luke defiantly protested, nearly losing his balance on his crutches.

"What in the hell is going on?" Jangles asked, returning with his second bowl of food.

"These men are arresting me for murder," Jack said in a soft voice. "But don't no one interfere. Cotton, you three boys see that Luke gets home alright with the wagon."

"Mister," Cotton said to the older man, "we're rangers. This man is one of us."

The older man sneered beneath his thick white mustache. "I don't give a gawdamn who he is. He's wanted for murdering a government official."

Cotton readied himself to fight back, but Jack clapped a hand on his shoulder. His greatest fear was a gunfight breaking loose between the boys and the police.

"Cotton," Jack quickly interrupted, "I'll be fine. They've made a mistake. I'm sure I can clear everything up a lot easier if I just go with them peacefully."

The four boys swallowed hard as they sized up the younger man's gun and watched the older man dismount and clamp cuffs on Jack's wrists, which he held calmly before him.

"Under the power of the emergency act for civil

disobedience, we're taking that horse." He gestured to Jangles' horse nearby. "You may recover him in town. Mount up, Starr."

"Easy, boys." Jack said under his breath. "I can work this out."

"Yeah, you can work your neck right into a noose." The younger man jabbed him in the ribs with the gun to force him toward Jangles' waiting horse, not realizing how easily Jack could've reversed the situation if he wanted to.

"Hurry up, Yonkers," the older man said. "We're going to draw a crowd."

"I don't give a gawdamn. Just be another dead reb to me."

"Shut up." With that the older man jerked the reins on Jangles' horse and they started to leave.

Jack could see people running over to find out what was going on. He closed his eyes. He'd done all he could to contain this thing. Mobs only made trouble. They needed to get out of there fast before things got worse.

"Captain! We'll get you out—I promise!" Jangles shouted after him.

Chapter 7

The jail in Shedville was an adobe jacal with bars on one high window and an iron bar door. Seldom used for more than drunks, it stank of piss and was buzzing with flies. The two state policemen never removed Jack's handcuffs, and simply shoved him inside and put a padlock and chain on the door before heading off to find some food and whiskey.

On the trip into Shedville, Jack learned the two lawmen were a special team from Austin brought in to arrest criminals wanted for high crimes, like the murder of a public official. This Judge Streeter, he learned, was murdered two years before in July on the streets of San Antonio. He'd been some kind of federal judge appointed by the then-current regime to hear cases prior to federal occupation.

"When did you say this happened?" Jack had asked his accusers.

"July 1866."

Two years earlier. Hell, he'd been in Abilene. There was no way he could have been in San Antonio.

But that still didn't get him out of the stinking jacal as he sat on the iron bunk and wondered how the devil he'd ever prove his innocence. A wagon pulled up outside and he wondered in dread who that could be.

"Jack? Jack?" He could hear Lucy's voice at the door as she made her way toward his cell. He wondered how she had gotten past the guards, but quickly realized that no one was there. She clung to the bars as he rushed toward her and squeezed her hand. "What is this all about?" she asked.

"They say I shot some judge in San Antonio back in '66 when I was in Kansas, or at least on my way up there with cattle."

"What can we do?" She looked close to crying. Jack noticed Tally behind her, hugging her mother's shoulder and trying to comfort her.

"I'll hire a lawyer."

"They say this is a military trial, not a regular one."

Jack was taken aback. "Wow, I had no idea—"

"I should have been there," Lucille said bitterly.

He shook his head. "Now, don't go blaming yourself. It would've happened whether you were there or not. But don't worry. I'll get it worked out. You have a family and a ranch to run. Go home and take care of them."

"What if they won't listen? Oh, Jack, these kinds of men shoot people in the back while they're sitting in their cells. . . ." The tears began to flow.

"Lucy, I'll be fine. I have friends in Austin. I rode for the rangers."

"I'm so afraid . . . so afraid for you."

"You go home. This will all be over in a few days.

I'll be back and we'll fix those fences that worry you so much."

She pressed her forehead to the bars. "Oh, I hope you're right. Have they even fed you?"

"Sure," he lied to dismiss her concern.

"I should go down to Austin with you. Maybe they wouldn't shoot you if a witness were standing by."

Jack sighed. "Lucy, no one's gonna shoot me. They're lawmen."

"No, they're not. They're scum of the earth that've been hired as lawmen. Why, Luke told us what one of them said about you: you'd be 'just another dead reb.' He heard him!"

"Lucy, you and Tally go home now and take care of things. This old cowboy will be fine."

"We should bust down this damn door and take you back with us."

"Nothing foolish. Please. That won't solve a thing."

Lucy wiped her tears, taking a minute to catch her breath. "Oh, Jack . . ."

She finally agreed to leave, and he was once again alone with the crickets. Later a small Mexican boy brought him two cold bean burritos and a canvas bag of water to wash them down. The food was gummy in his mouth and water ran down his chest when he drank from the bag. After the youth took the dishes away he was alone again. No one else checked on him.

In the middle of the night he woke to the sounds of a large team of mules in harness stomping around at the jail's front door.

He heard the front door open. "Easy, easy," a voice that sounded suspiciously like Arnold's said through the darkness. Jack heard the clopping of hooves and the clinking of chains as they were wrapped around the bars of his door.

"Boys!" Jack shouted. "Boys, don't break me out of here! That's not the answer!" He rushed toward the bars as he heard the mules straining. Before he knew it, dust was flying everywhere as the entire door casing fell to the ground in a cloud of dust.

"You alright?" Jangles asked, out of breath.

"Yes, but—"

"We ain't got time to explain much," Cotton said. "A war party kidnapped Mrs. Lerner, her baby and her twelve-year-old daughter, Mandy, this afternoon. We need you, Captain. McIntyre is clear up in Fort Worth. Sergeant Craig is bringing packhorses and supplies to meet us tonight."

"Damn. How do we get these off you?" Jangles asked as he fiddled with the cuffs.

"We can do it later," Jack said.

"We told folks we were getting you out to help us, and they'll all testify we needed you for this job," Jangles said.

Arnold added, "We brought your good horse too, sir."

Jack shook his head in amazement. They quickly headed out the door, and holding his cuffed hands in front of him, he took the reins and mounted. *Sorry to mess up your plans, state policemen,* he thought. *They need me.*

"Wouldn't you rather ride off with us than sit in that

piss-stinking jail?" Jangles asked, swinging by him as they rode off.

"Yes, I'd a whole lot rather ride with you boys."

They all laughed.

Craig met them in Flagstone Gap with five pack-horses and they rode west through the hill country until a few hours before dawn. Once they made camp they curled up and slept a few hours, satisfied that the tracks they were following would still be warm enough to follow in a few hours.

When they arose they dressed and quickly ate. Their breakfast consisted of boiled oatmeal with bugs (raisins) and some lick (molasses syrup) for sweetener. They washed it down with strong black coffee and hit the trail. Jack had picked one wrist lock open the night before and worked on the other one while he rode. It was hard for him to do at a trot, but at least his hands were separate now.

A few clouds were gathering by midmorning. Jack noticed them as he looked back over his shoulder for any signs of pursuit. Those two state policemen would be sure to follow them once they discovered he was missing. The question was, How much time did they have? No doubt they were hungover from celebrating their success. They might get a late start that day before discovering the door was gone . . . as well as their prisoner, thanks to Cotton's father's draft mules, who had already been dropped off at home. The doorless adobe jail would be a sobering sight for the pair when they discovered it.

* * *

Midday, Jack and his crew ate some crackers and dry cheese and washed them down with gyp water. After they filled their canteens from the milky-looking water hole and watered their animals, they rode on.

There was no doubt the Indians were headed for Llano Estacada. Later that afternoon the rangers' attention was drawn to some buzzards poking around along the side of the trail in the stirrup-tall greasewood. The rangers, fearing the worst, dismounted to see what was attracting the carrion. When they found the abandoned baby's dead body, its eyes already picked out by the buzzards, tossed into the grass, they were nearly sick. They scattered the large black birds away from the small corpse and got to work on digging a small, shallow grave. Jack said a few words from the Psalms, and Baby Lerner was quietly buried. They hoped her body was burrowed deep enough to avoid attracting wolves.

The crew mounted up again and continued on the path. To the west a hammerhead cloud formed, rising high in the azure sky. The brewing storm spread wider, threatening to descend on the small band of horses and huddled riders as howling winds swept in a red wall of blinding dirt. Sharp grains of sand stung Jack's face. He pulled up his bandana. Soon after, the thumbnail-sized hail began to beat on his shoulders and hat brim. They sought relief in an arroyo, but without a roof it was impossible to escape from nature's fierce beating.

They dismounted and stood with their horses, battered by the hail and jumpy from the blinding lightning and ear-shattering thunder. The storm was so bad that Jack began to question if they'd survive to see the sun again. Soaked through and through, his ears ringing, he kept a sharp eye on the ground around them; all they'd need was a flash of water to come down on them. But the arroyo was high enough that he felt certain they could avoid a flood.

Before they knew it the downpour let up and he nodded at the others to get going. Numb, they mounted and topped the hillside. All evening they rode northwest in the rain, but Jack well knew that the precious tracks of the Comanche had been erased by the storm's assaults. In that vast, unchanging land, they were on their own.

The watery sun threatened to dip away in a bloody smear when they finally stopped for the night. There would be no fire, no hot food. The best they could do was pray that their bedrolls were still dry. With water-wrinkled fingers, Jack dug the latigo leather out to loosen the girth and remove his saddle.

"Some damn rain," Craig said with a wary head shake. "I could have used it at home."

"Maybe it went that way." Jack smiled at him.

"I doubt it. What're we doing for tracks now?"

"Good question. I guess we start by asking trading folks and Comancheros where we can find any. Someone will know or will have seen the two white women in a Comanche camp."

"That could take forever," Craig said, disheartened.

Jack looked him in the eye. "These deals usually do take forever. But this is our mission. You need to get back?"

Craig shook his head, a little ashamed. "Not yet."

"Good. I need you as long as you can stay."

"Oh, I ain't running out on you, Captain."

There was no need for more words between them. Jack understood the man's concern and disappointment. But a big rain was just one inconvenience in this search. There'd be others. Maybe worse ones.

After a restless night the crew made ready to continue on their journey the next morning. With Jangles singing "Ole Dan Tucker," they rode out. The rising sun promised to steam out their wet clothing, but the water holes were full and the rainwater had not turned to alkaline. It was easier to swallow and better for their ponies.

A feeling came over Jack as he rode across the great cap rock: They must be the only people out there. Sure, there may be a coyote, some jackrabbits, prairie dogs, burrowing owls and a few ravens circling above. But there wasn't another soul to be found.

Riding in the lead, Cotton pointed at a small, dirty piece of cloth in the mud. He launched off his horse and waved it in the air. "It could be part of a dress."

They all dismounted, careful not to disturb a thing, and began to search. They detected some barefoot pony tracks near the scrap.

"Could these be their tracks?" Craig asked.

Jack nodded.

"You think we have their trail again?" Arnold asked Jack.

"It looks that way. Craig, you ride ahead and stay

off this trail to the side if you can and look for more signs. We may have stumbled on to something good." His hopes up, he swung back in the saddle, waving the boys out of the creosote brush.

Staring hard at the trail, the rancher nodded. "I think we've found 'em."

If an echo could be produced in that vast country, it would have been from Jack's shouts of "Hallelujah, yah!"

Chapter 8

Jack thought he could see a square gray object far to the west, but his vision came and went, blurred by the rising afternoon heat waves. It looked to be about ten miles away. They rode on. He hoped to be able to distinguish it, but the distance seemed to stretch on. The closer he came the more his curiosity was aroused. Soon the boys noticed the object as well.

"What is that thing out there?" Cotton asked, riding in close to point it out to Jack.

"I'm not sure. I've been watching it for an hour," Jack said.

"It ain't ordinary desert stuff."

Jack agreed.

"It's a canvas shade," Jangles said.

"What's it doing out here?" Cotton asked.

"Be gawdamned if I know." Jangles shrugged. "But that's what it is, boys."

When they drew closer, they could hear someone wailing. Jack told them to stay back in case it was a trick.

He'd go up there and check out what it could be. He gave a spur to Mac's side and short-loped him up the grade to where the ends of a crude tent made of canvas, suspended between short mesquites, flapped in the strong wind. When he swung off the saddle and onto the hillside he held the .45 in his fist.

Climbing the steep grade, he caught the flap and lowered his head to enter. The sunshine's yellow light shone through the material on a half-naked white woman seated on a rag of a blanket and pleading with the gods, "Bring my baby back. Oh, please bring her to me."

Shocked by his find, Jack holstered his gun and backed out. "Craig," he shouted. "Cut a hole in a blanket so we can use it for a dress. I think it's the Lerner woman we've found. But she's mostly naked."

"I know what Mrs. Lerner looks like," Cotton said.

"Wait till I get her dressed. I'm afraid she's lost her mind as well as her clothing." He shook his head, feeling more nauseated by the moment. If only they could have come on faster. But the Comanche probably would've killed her if they'd closed in. Craig delivered the blanket, a hole cut for Mrs. Lerner's head in poncho style. After taking a deep breath Jack went back into the flopping shelter and crawled on the ground toward her. When he rose to put the blanket over her head he heard a dry rattle. Throwing his body aside, he whipped out his .45 and pointed the gun at the viper ready to strike.

He managed to get a shot off, then kicked away another rattler, stomping it with his boot heel. The place was alive with them; she was the bait. Get out! Get out! he silently screamed as he dove out of the shelter, hit the ground and rolled almost to Mac's front hooves.

Their guns drawn, his rangers scrambled uphill to join him.

"What the hell—gawdamn rattlesnakes!" Jangles swore at the sight of one slithering out of the tent. The rangers stood on their toes and quickly scanned the ground for more.

The canvas flopped. The snakes rattled and the wind blew stronger. Mrs. Lerner cried for her baby. The child that Jack knew his men had buried the day before.

Soon a thick sidewinder came slithering out from under the tent's hem, intent on escaping to some lesser place that was shady and cooler than the tent. Arnold blew its triangular head off when it stopped to use its forked tongue to sense the direction of the heat.

While the headless back section roiled on the ground in death's arms, Jangles pointed out the long leather thong tied on his beaded tail. "They had them staked out for you, didn't they?"

Jack nodded in silent agreement, still recovering from the shock of his discovery.

Using his rifle butt to stomp them, Cotton held the tent back and Jangles smashed two of their heads in. Another rushed off to the back and was gone before the cautious boys could raise the roof high enough. Arnold used a big rock raised high over his head to dispatch another.

Jack dressed the numb woman in the blanket. It made no difference if the boys saw her full breasts weeping milk and smudged in dirt. There were dried muddy hand-prints on her bare shoulders and body. But soon she was clothed in the blanket and Jack swept her up in his arms to carry her out.

"No! No!" She began pounding him with her hands. "Give me back my baby!"

Dodging her fists and flailing arms as best he could, he sat her down by the horses and told her to stay there, but she jumped up and tried to flee. Jack ran her down, caught her arm and brought her back. He knew she was out of her mind, lost in such terrific grief and stunned by the torture. But if she didn't settle down he might be forced to handcuff her with the pair that he'd finally taken off his other wrist the night before. If only she'd listen—but it looked doubtful that he could even reach her.

"Do you think that one of those rattlers bit her?" Cotton asked, joining him.

"I don't think so. She'd be showing signs by now." He sure didn't intend to inspect her inch by inch. Even if he did, how would he be able to see two tooth punctures on her scratched, bruised skin anyway? She looked like she'd been dragged through a thicket of rosebushes or briar brambles.

"They certainly could've," Cotton said, eyeing the battered woman apprehensively.

"I guess you're wondering what we do next, huh?"

Cotton nodded as the others joined him.

"Guys, I'd give a good month's wages to find the redskin feller who set that trap. He ain't your ordinary red buck, but I'm afraid we need to send Mrs. Lerner home. That might be why he set the trap—to steer us away from him." He dropped his gaze to the dirt, then began giving commands. "I'll take two rangers with me. Craig, you and whoever stays behind can surely get her back to her people. The three of us'll ride two days farther after the Comanches and see if we can find her other daughter, Mandy. If we don't hook up with them by then we'll turn around and return home."

"We knew you was concerned about them state police," Craig said. "But we're all going to help you whip that deal when you get back."

"That's fine . . . I'm lost as to who even thought I was in San Antonio that summer."

"There's plenty of sons of Texas will stand with you on that one."

The others nodded.

"I want no trouble with them. Right or wrong, they're the law now." Somehow he had to reinforce in these boys' minds how those worthless jerks were law in their state, even over the rangers.

"Wait! Wait," Jangles said, as Mrs. Lerner struggled up to her feet and started to try to run away. Jangles caught her by the waist and dragged her back.

"You may have to tie her on a horse." Jack shook his head in defeat. "Let's cook a good and hearty meal. Then we can sleep and split up in the morning."

They tied her hands behind her back and left her crying and wailing on a blanket while they scrounged up some fuel to cook with. She looked pitiful, her red-eyed, tear-stained and dirty face badly sunburned and her hair plastered to her head.

The image of her battered body wouldn't soon leave Jack's thoughts. Another reason he wanted those damn Comanches in his gun's sights.

She refused to eat, so they left her tied up and moaning and went down the draw to spoon up their bacon and beans in glum silence. After dinner they decided that Arnold would go back with Craig in the morning. Cotton and Jangles were the best shots and the most experienced—the choice wasn't hard.

They parted before sunup. Craig cleared one of the packhorses of its burden for Arnold. They led Mrs. Lerner, mounted and with her hands tied to the horn of his horse's saddle. In the weak, predawn light everyone shook hands and the two groups separated.

Jack's crew made little progress and he started to get the feeling they would never find the Comanches. But late the next day they found warm ashes where the Comanches had eaten part of a horse they'd killed or lost. Running off the buzzards, Jack used his knife to take out a portion of the flank for them to cook. The meat wasn't hurt and only hours before the war party had feasted on it, so it wasn't decayed.

"If I wasn't so damn hungry for some meat, I'd never eat it," Cotton said, looking glumly at the strip of bloody meat.

"Forget it. Meat's meat in this case," Jack said.

Roasted over a fire of dry mesquite wood, the horse meat tasted like corn-fed filet of beef. Maybe a little tougher, but they ate lots of it. Everyone went to bed full and content.

* * *

They ate more of the cooked meat in the morning before they set out. Jack hurried them onward, knowing this would be the decisive day. If they found nothing, they'd turn back for home. All day they pushed their horses hard, and in the late afternoon Jack saw some color moving ahead. Spotted horses could be seen from miles away. As the rangers pushed their own tired horses closer in a hard trot, the animals became clearer through the distorted heat waves.

"That's them, ain't it?" Cotton asked.

Jack nodded.

"Come back here, you red bastards," Jangles shouted, riding in beside him.

"Will they fight us?" Cotton asked.

"They say they'll fight a buzz saw."

"We ain't *exactly* a buzz saw," Jangles said.

"But we can fight like one, can't we?" Jack asked.

"I reckon we can. If they'll hole up we'll damn sure show them," Jangles said with a whoop.

"I doubt they'll stop and fight," Cotton said.

"Why not?" Jack asked.

"Why should they? They've got the girl, the horses they stole and the other things they took."

"I'm counting on one thing," Jack said. "That bastard leader's pride. He thinks he's so damn smart, setting snake traps for us and all. He's thinking that if he don't show them young bucks how he can ass-whip three rangers, then he might not get as big a following on the next hunt."

"You've been thinking on this a lot, haven't you?" Cotton asked, reining in his bay beside him.

"A whole lot." Jack set Mac off on a long lope. They rode three abreast through the greasewood brush, polishing their boot toes and the bottoms of their bull-hide chaps on the brush tops. Their spur rowels rang like distant church bells. Jaws set, eyes firmly locked in hard stares, they breathed hard and let the pungent desert smells fill their nostrils. The dark skin on their faces was drawn taut by the eternal wind and baking sun. Their hat brims were pulled down enough to cut off the sun's lower glare.

Jack thought, Three Texas rangers are coming after you, Injuns. And we're going to nail your red hides to the shithouse wall. . . .

Chapter 9

"They're coming back for us!" Jangles shouted, and cocked his Spencer rifle. The three of them lay on their bellies, surrounded by loaded tubes and cartridge boxes. Each was faced in a different direction to prepare for a Comanche attack from all sides.

Jack could hear the shouting and coyotelike yipping of the war party out of sight in the brush as they tried to gather their courage for a second attempt. They had attacked first, but the rangers had left two dead warriors, while they remained unharmed. Jack knew the leader himself would be back this time, so they chose to hunker down in a dried-up lake to defend themselves. The horses were ground tied in the center and, he hoped, low enough to avoid getting shot. Even if they whipped the Comanches, he and the boys had to get out of there— and that, of course, would require horses.

"You reckon they've killed that Lerner girl?" Jangles asked, lying on his side and holding his rifle in both hands.

"How would I know?" Cotton said.

"Easy, guys. We've got Injuns to fight," Jack said to ward off any cross words.

"How many of them are left?" Cotton asked, rising but seeing little more than the tops of greasewood trees flagging in the wind.

"Several," Jangles said.

"Less than there were before," Jack said. "Unless their leader is a strategist, he can't whip us."

"What in the hell is a strategist?" Jangles asked.

"A military man who knows the rules of warfare."

"Oh hell, here they come—" Jangles exclaimed.

The sound of the Comanche screams pierced Jack's ears. He rose and took aim with his new Henry rifle. The leader, a full war-bonnet rider dressed in black on a piebald horse, charged forward, a Winchester cradled in his bare brown right arm. His war whoops urged the others on.

Jack struck him in the chest with his first shot and he jerked, but not quick enough before another hot slug of lead tore through his chest. He cartwheeled off his horse and fell to the ground in a heap. Close by, Jangles shot a horse out from under another young Comanche.

Cotton shot down another Indian whose horse stampeded toward them while Jack took quick shots at the mob of Indians encircling them. One by one the Indians fell to the ground, just as their leader had. They were making their bullets count.

The Comanches, growing fearful of the rangers' dead-on accuracy, soon had enough and drew back. When their yipping at last ceased, Jack felt relieved. The battle wasn't over, but his rangers' fierce defense had turned them back for the moment. All told, they had cut the war party in half. Taking down the leader right away had slowed the bucks' appetite.

"Look, Captain. They've got a truce flag." Jangles motioned toward a bare-chested buck who was walking cautiously toward them with a white flag tied to his gun barrel.

"Want me to meet him?" Cotton asked.

Jack scowled. "It could be a trap to pull one of us away. Jangles and I will train our rifles on him until you get back. First sign of anything wrong and you ride like hell back up here."

Cotton nodded, quickly mounted his horse and spurred him hard. Jack, nervous for Cotton, dried his sweaty palms on his pants. Rifle at the ready, he watched the two as they came together. After a moment, Cotton nodded to the Comanche messenger and raced back, sliding his horse to a halt in front of Jack and Jangles.

"They'll give us the Lerner girl for their leader's body."

Jack squinted against the glaring sun. "I wonder why."

"What do you mean?" Jangles asked.

"Don't make sense. We ain't gonna eat him. We'll pick up and leave here, then they can have him. I figure he's dead or dying."

"Don't we need to trade?" Cotton asked. "I mean, for her sake."

"Of course we will. I'm saying, though, it seems like too easy of a trade. I don't trust 'em."

"There ain't much for us to do but trust 'em." Jangles made a grim face.

"What're we going to do?" Cotton looked back toward where the handful of bucks sat on their battle-weary horses.

"Cotton, give the go-ahead to the messenger. But we'll have to watch every move they make."

Cotton nodded and headed off toward the waiting messenger.

If they cut the boy down it would be him and Jangles against the five or six Indians left. He liked three better than two and wanted ten more.

Cotton and the messenger quickly exchanged words while Jack and Jangles cleaned their rifle bores with rags, preparing for the worst.

Cotton stepped off his horse. "They say they're sending her. Damn, I hate to see the poor thing."

"There's three of them with an extra horse for the fallen leader," Jangles pointed out.

"I see her coming," Cotton said. "Aw hell, she's naked too, or near it. We won't have a damn blanket left without a hole cut in it."

"Better cut one. She'll need it." Jack could see that all she was wearing was part of a skirt. He drew his six gun and took the blanket Cotton had prepared for her to wear.

He tossed it over his shoulder and started toward her through the greasewood. "You boys be on your toes. This could be the tricky part."

"I'll feel a damn sight better when we're all back

here together," Jangles said as he watched the Indians loading their leader.

"So will I," Jack spoke over his shoulder.

The dirty-faced girl, with her hair full of sticks and straw, came hurrying down the slope toward him. He wondered how she could walk barefoot across the ground, which was covered in stickers. Her state of undress appeared to be of no concern to her.

"Is my mother still alive?" she asked as he covered her nakedness with the blanket poncho.

"Yes. I sent her home two days ago." He made a check to see that they were alone.

Tears of relief welled in her eyes. "That's good."

"Come. I want to get you back to my men." He was still worried about being out in the open. He could only hope that her captors were too busy gathering the body of their dead chief, which the rangers had laid out in front of their "bunker" on the shore of the dried-up lake.

"Do you have many men?" she asked, stepping around a cactus bed.

"Two. You may even know them. It'll be nice for you to be around familiar faces."

She nodded, tight-lipped.

He looked back over his shoulder, his muscles itching. Any moment he expected a bullet in his back.

"They must have gotten their chief," he said under his breath more to himself than to her.

"He's Ten Bears' son—the real chief. They're worried he'll blame them for his death, that they didn't do enough to save him and kill you."

Jack nodded, impressed at her words. "For someone

in such a sticky situation, it's amazing how much you managed to figure out."

She lowered her blue eyes and nodded. "Some of the things I learned wasn't that good."

Jack tipped her chin up. "I'm sorry. We came as soon as we could."

"Thank you . . ."

"Captain Jack Starr."

She swallowed. "Captain Starr."

"It's no matter, Mandy," he said, giving her shoulder a little reassuring squeeze.

"Men," he announced as the two boys swept off their hats for her. "Say hello to Mandy Lerner. Mandy, you might know Jangles and Cotton."

She nodded. "Thank you for coming for me."

"You're sure welcome, ma'am," Jangles said.

"Yeah, you really are welcome," Cotton echoed.

Both young men looked at a loss for words. Jack could tell they were shocked she wasn't a raving idiot. Despite her disheveled appearance, she was perfectly poised.

"What now?" Cotton asked.

"She can ride double behind you," Jack said. "Load up—we're going back. We've done all we could here."

They rode all night, posting one man guard when they finally stopped, just in case the Comanches changed their minds. Jack took watch for the last two hours. Sitting cross-legged on his bedroll he listened to the gentle night winds and insects. There was a lot on his plate. They were several days from the girl's home—no doubt burned down. On top of that the matters of the state police and murder charges against him needed to be settled. Thank God he'd met Lucille Thornton. She was the only thing holding him together.

Other women had swept in and out of his life before her, and he hadn't batted an eye. But Lucille was different. He didn't want to lose this one, but he had so little to offer her. Had he spent the past years since his discharge establishing a ranch or business, he'd have nothing to worry about.

A nearby coyote let out a mournful howl and Mandy came over, huddled in her poncho against the predawn chill. "May I sit here, Captain?"

"Sure. That old sundog won't hurt you. He's just looking for the rest of his pack. They'll find each other and sleep the hot day away."

She lowered her head. "I thought it might be the Comanches coming back."

He shifted the rifle in his arms. "I think they've moved on."

She nodded and they sat together in silence until they heard Jangles and Cotton stir.

For breakfast they drank fresh coffee and ate boiled cornmeal and gruel with brown sugar. Still sleepy-eyed, they climbed in the saddle before dawn and prepared for another tough day of riding. Jack rationed the corn the horses received so it would last. But between the barely potable gyp water and lack of forage, their mounts grew weaker with each long day.

Dead tired in late afternoon, they reined up on a ridge. Below them was a large construction crew building a sprawling ranch headquarters near a thicket of cotton-woods. Several dozen men scurried around doing this and that. There were stacks of bright, fresh-cut lumber, to which the workers added plank after plank, while row after row of adobe bricks were drying in the sun. Hammers clapping and saws whining, the operation looked impressive.

Jack rode in the lead toward them and met a red-complexioned man mopping his sweaty face with a large handkerchief.

"Good day, sir," Jack said, tipping his hat. "I'm Captain Jack Starr."

"Windy Hardy's my name. What are you and these children doing out here?"

"We're rangers. We've been chasing down Comanches and returning captives."

Hardy nodded slow-like. "Well, I wouldn't turn away heroes. Welcome to the Wagon Bar Ranch. I'm the general superintendent here. You-all get off your horses; you look plumb tired to me. Ramon"—he waved to a Mexican boy to come over—"fix these boys' horses up and then I'll take 'em to the chow hall."

He turned back to Jack. "You three and the young lady come with me."

At the chow hall, one of Hardy's helpers presented Mandy with a hairbrush, and thanking him she combed through the tangles and tried to make herself look as presentable as possible. Despite all her trials, she remained self-possessed.

"Whose ranch is this?" Jack asked Hardy.

"Feabius T. Newcastle's."

"I don't guess he ever comes around?"

Hardy smiled. "It's real long ways out here. He's a rich tycoon who lives in New York."

"How many men are working here, Mr. Hardy?"

"Seventy-eight, but ten more are due here in a month."

"Sleep with your guns. The Comanches are still out there."

Hardy scoffed at him. "They wouldn't dare raid this place."

"Comanches will do a lot of things you don't expect."

"I'll try to be ready for them."

Jack knew the superintendent felt too secure with all those mechanics and craftsmen on the premises. But a raid could, and in Jack's book would, happen before summer was over. Way out here, Hardy would sure learn the tough way.

The coffee that the crew cook served tasted wonderful. Mandy ordered pancakes, as did Jack.

They recounted the details of Mandy's recovery to Hardy. Hardy shook his head in disbelief at several points during the story. "You boys sure did good work. Thankfully, I haven't seen an Indian on this ranch since we arrived here."

"I'd bet a hundred dollars they've seen you. They can stay hidden better than anyone," Jack said, pressing the issue.

"If you and two boys could take them on they must be dandy fighters," Hardy said with a chuckle.

"That doesn't say as much about the Comanches as it does about my boys. We took on a band of Mexican horse thieves and laid them to rest just as well."

"So that's you boys, huh? I've heard about you," Hardy said, the realization dawning on his face.

Jack was pleased to hear that Hardy had heard of their travails, but could see that no amount of talking would persuade the superintendent that he was susceptible to attack.

They ate their meal quickly and rested. Hardy assigned Mandy a room of her own in some temporary quarters, had bathwater drawn for her and apologized for the fact he had no females to help her. Jack and the boys were assigned hammocks to sleep in.

After sundown, Jack and his crew ate supper with the men. A young man played the fiddle for their entertainment, and the barbecued beef, sourdough bread and beans filled Jack's belly for the first time in more than a week.

"I suppose you'll have to go on in the morning?" Hardy asked.

"I might stay here a year or two and eat your grub," Jangles said, rubbing his belly. They all laughed.

"We appreciate your hospitality, but we do need to move on," Jack said. "I'm surprised my two men who rode back this way earlier didn't find you."

"I've not seen hide nor hair of anyone else," Hardy admitted. Jack hoped they had made it back alright.

He thanked Hardy again and the fiddler played more

music. While the strains of fiddle music floated around them, Jack thought about the construction work going on around them. Hardy's team was erecting a great house, large horse barns and hay sheds, the kind that were popular in the East but would be of little use in West Texas. But it wasn't Jack's place or money to worry about.

The next morning, loaded up with food and fresh supplies, they mounted and rode their rested horses out at dawn. Their spirits lifted, they made many miles and were fast approaching home. After two days in the saddle they reached the fort at San Angelo. A colonel at the fort, who could hardly believe their story of Mandy's recovery, invited them to rest and fed them a large meal. The officers' wives found Mandy a new dress to replace her poncho and held a small dance that night to celebrate.

In all this no one reported seeing Craig, Arnold or Mrs. Lerner. How had Craig missed both the Wagon Bar and the army outpost? Jack was worried but gladly accepted when a lady named Mrs. Chapman asked him to dance a waltz with her.

"You look like a very industrious man, Captain," Mrs. Chapman said good-naturedly. The story of Mandy's recovery had circulated throughout the entire fort.

"Well, I didn't really have a choice. The boys forced me into it."

She laughed, then covered her mouth to suppress her amusement. "You're either modest or a liar. I don't know which one I like more."

Jack detected a flirty tone in her voice. He knew she was married, but that didn't seem to keep her from pulling him closer.

She lowered her voice to a husky whisper and leaned forward. "My husband's a major. He's currently on patrol in that disgusting dust and scrub brush. If you were discreet we could find some mutual company in my quarters later this evening."

Jack's back stiffened. His thoughts immediately flew to Lucille. "Thank you, Mrs. Chapman, but I'm gonna have to decline."

"Be sure before you decide, Captain Jack. You don't know what you're missing."

He looked down into her baby blue eyes, which were sparkling with mirth. "I'll be moving out real early in the morning," he said slowly. "I have to get back. People are counting on me." The waltz ended just then and he pulled away and tipped his hat graciously. Mrs. Chapman, looking embarrassed, nodded and hastily departed. Jack smiled to himself. He was definitely a one-woman man.

The next morning they were on the road again. Word soon spread that they were returning with the girl. A large group of settlers met them the next evening at the San Saba River crossing. They were cooking beefsteaks to celebrate. Word came to Jack that Mandy's uncle had ridden out to see about her.

Anxious for news, Jack asked the uncle about Mandy's mother.

"Ah, they brought her back a week ago. But"—the

man lowered his voice—"she's raving mad. They had a mighty rough time getting her back."

Jack nodded. They must've been avoiding the ranch and camp. "What about my rangers?"

"I think the trip really upset the older one. He wouldn't talk hardly at all—just rode on home."

"Was Arnold alright?"

"I guess so."

Jack was frustrated that the man didn't have more to tell him.

"Mandy's pretty spunky, ain't she?" the uncle said, leaning on his Kentucky rifle and fondly watching his niece as she played with some of the other children gathered there.

"She's a strong young woman," Jack said.

"Damn shame she ain't pure anymore."

Struck by the man's words, Jack frowned at him. "Don't even say what you're thinking."

The uncle reddened. "Well, you don't have to get all huffy about it. We know she's been out there with them bucks—"

Jack balled his hands into fists. "Get away from me before I blow you to kingdom come."

"Well, I never—" the uncle tried to retort, but he saw the look on Jack's face and scampered away.

Jangles got up and came over. "What made you so mad at him, Captain?"

"Some people make it sound like that girl went with those Indians of her own free will."

Jangles shook his head. "I hear that. There's all kinds of gossip about her out here."

"It's a damn shame. A real damn shame. Maybe you have to come back without your mind to gain any sympathy."

"So, what did he say about Sergeant Craig?" Jangles said, wanting to change the subject.

"Said he thought Sergeant Craig was real upset about having to bring Mrs. Lerner back."

"It would have been a tough job."

"I'll go see him when we get to Shedville."

"We'll all go."

Jack frowned at him. "You boys—"

"Captain, till we get your name cleared, us rangers are going everywhere with you."

Jack didn't want to think about it. Less than two days' ride away and they'd have her home, but his own life would be back in the quagmire. Damn.

Chapter 10

The entire Lost Dog Creek community turned out for them. Mandy's father was on crutches, no doubt from wounds received during the raid. He hobbled out and hugged his girl. They both cried. On the road Jack had broken the news to Mandy that her mother suffered serious mental problems, a fact she took with a nod as she chewed on her lower lip. Jack wasn't sure if she had spoken with her uncle back at the San Saba River. He suspected the man was there only for his own glory anyway.

He dismounted and Cotton collected his reins. Somewhere in the crowd was Lucy Thornton. He looked expectantly for her face among the others, but instead he spotted Luke on his crutches. Smiling ear to ear, Jack covered the distance between them with great strides.

"Maw's working on putting out the food back there," Luke said, motioning to where the women were laying out a delicious feast. "Said you might want to see her."

"Might? I think it's more than 'might.'"

"She said that, not me."

"Lead the way. How's everyone?"

"Doing fine. We've sure been worried about you ever since Craig came back."

"He tell you I was fine?"

Luke stopped to catch his breath and shook his head. "He ain't talking much. I guess bringing that Lerner woman back shook him."

"Seen him today around here?" Jack looked but saw no sign of him.

"No, sir."

"I'll find him."

He looked up at the tables piled high with food, but all he could see was Lucille, who had her dress gathered up in her hand as she came running toward him. He caught her in his arms, swung her around like she was a feather and kissed her with no regrets.

She swept the hair back from her face when he set her down. "I'm so glad you made it back safely. How are you feeling?" She studied him carefully. She must've heard about Craig, he figured.

He held her tight. "I'm doing just fine. Glad to be back. How about you?"

"Oh, I was so worried," she said as she fussed with his vest.

"Jack Starr?" a deep voice behind him asked.

Lucille sucked in her breath.

He let go of her and turned to face a short man with snow-white hair. "May I help you?"

"Everett Hale, sir." They shook hands.

"What can I do for you?"

Hale shook his head. "No, the question is, What can

I do for you? I'm an attorney. I've been hired to defend you."

Jack was taken aback. "Sorry, sir, but I can't afford you."

"You aren't paying me. There's a private organization in the state set up to prepare the defense of leading sons of Texas who are being harassed and wrongfully charged by this carpetbagger government saddled upon us."

Jack shook his head. "I don't hardly consider myself a leading son."

"Yes, you are, sir." Hale said it in a firm voice no one could argue with.

Jack nodded slowly. "Well, thank you very much, sir. What do you have in mind?"

"I suspect we should remove you from these grounds."

"But this celebration is for him and his rangers," Lucy interjected, her voice filled with disappointment.

"I suspect they'll bring a posse in here to make a big show of arresting him," Hale said.

"That could mean big trouble." Jack knew what the consequences would be: a riot. It would just give them more ammunition to close their iron glove tighter on the state's population.

"We need to transport you to Austin so you may surrender to the authorities there and prepare for a proper trial. But I have to tell you, your chances of making it alive there from here are less than fifty-fifty."

Lucy was tight-lipped, but she nodded her head firmly. "We can't afford to let them get near you, Jack.

Mr. Hale, please arrange the trip for us," she said, unty-
ing her apron. "Where will we meet you in the morning?"

Hale blinked at her words and then recovered. "Sunup
at the north edge of town. I'll have a buckboard and six
armed guards duly sworn in to take him to Austin."

"We'll meet you there. Where's your horse?' she asked
Jack.

"He's—"

She guided him by the arm in the direction he pointed.
"Luke can find his way home in the wagon. Mac'll carry
double, won't he?"

"I'm sure he will. But are you sure—"

"I'm sure as anything. We'll have one night together
before they take you away."

When he found Mac he tightened the cinch. Seated
in the saddle, he reached down and swung her up behind him. She must have caught a heel near his flank
getting in place behind the cantle, for Mac humped his
back.

"Get your feet forward." He laughed, holding the
horse in check as he danced underneath them. Her arms
closed tight around his waist. They left out the back
way and headed north. Her arms locked around him,
her firm form pressed hard to his back, she whispered,
"Take me away."

Dawn's pink rose touched the sky as Jack and Lucy sat
on the wagon seat, wrapped in a blanket against the
chill. Trying to get as close as they could to each other,
they inhaled each other's short breaths.

"How long will you be gone?" she whispered.

"I have no idea. It may be a year before I go to trial."

"I can wait. I can wait. It won't be like the last time for you." They kissed, lips pressed together, hard and desperate.

"There's a rig coming. Must be them."

"What if it isn't?"

"I'm not wearing a gun."

"I know, and that worries me."

"Lucy, stop worrying. This is going to turn out fine."

She sniffed, but too late; tears streamed down her face. She blotted them with a kerchief. "I'll be coming down to see you in jail."

"I'll be out in no time."

"Oh, Jack, I don't know what I'll do without you."

"Smell the roses. I'll be back."

She laughed through her tears. "I'll try."

Hale stepped off the buckboard and introduced U.S. Marshal Tim Harris.

Jack shook the marshal's hand.

"These men are duly sworn-in deputy U.S. marshals," Harris said with a sweep of his arm toward the rest of the men. "We have more authority than the Texas State Police. We will go as directly to Austin as we can, sir."

Jack nodded. "I'll be in your debt, sir."

"No, we are in your debt for recovering those horses and successfully saving those two women."

Jack kissed Lucy good-bye. "I'll be fine with them."

"I'll still worry."

He was half sick to part with her and cause her the pain of separation, but he turned to go. It was the hardest thing—to turn his back on the woman in his life. A knife stabbed him in the heart. If they didn't clear him he might never see her again except through bars or from the gallows scaffolding. There had to be justice somewhere.

If it had not been for her he might have rode on west after recovering the girl. Gotten lost in the madding crowd swarming into this part of the country. He'd come back to his own possible demise, but as he climbed on the buckboard beside Everett he had no regrets. Fate sealed or not, he had friends and the love of a woman. He couldn't turn his back on them and he knew they felt the same. Maybe they could deliver him from this mess.

With a cluck to the horses they set off for Austin.

He was surrounded by seven men with rifles. But how safe was he really?

Chapter 11

The jail in Austin looked as bleak as most places like it. Jack felt the police desk sergeant look him over like a man ready to exterminate a stray dog with his handgun.

"This man is wanted for murder?" the desk officer asked as he shuffled the arrest papers.

"Yes, sir," Marshal Harris replied.

"Is he crazy?"

"No, sir."

"Do I need to restrain him?"

"No, his lawyer plans to ask for a bond hearing in the morning."

The jail official scoffed at his words and said, "He can get on the list, but it'll be days before he gets his turn. Judge Hefner does all them hearings, and his list is longer than my arm. And I can tell you right now, he ain't letting no gawdamn reb loose that done killed a federal judge."

"That's not my concern," Harris said. "The man is in your custody now."

"Tell me one thing. You brought him in here with a large armed guard. Any reason for that?"

"His safety."

The official laughed and shook his head in dismay. "I swear this gawdamn world is screwed up when the safety of a killer headed straight for the gallows has to be accommodated."

"No, Sergeant, it's not. When an official in charge of preserving our law and order assumes a man is guilty until proven innocent, that's when I worry," Harris said curtly.

The desk sergeant's large ears and face turned red. He scowled over the high desk at Marshal Harris. "Well, personally, I hope they hang the rebel son of a bitch. Good day, Marshal, uh"—he looked down at the sheet for his name— "Harris."

To Jack the Austin City Prison stank so badly of unwashed bodies, piss and fecal odors that it made most outhouses seem by comparison as if they were refined places to hold celebrity dinners. In a cell by himself with one blanket and a small window offering little light on his iron bunk, he decided that if he didn't mentally adjust to this horrific situation he'd soon go mad.

A black man came by with beans and stale bread on a tin plate, which he handed through a slot to Jack, along with a spoon and a cup of what the man called coffee.

"You's be alright today, sir?" the man asked.

Jack nodded.

"Sure be hot in dis place, huh?"

"Yes. Very hot."

"I's be back for them plate and spoon after a while. They done run out of most everything else when they told me to feed you," the black man with gray whiskers said under his breath. "You must be a special prisoner."

"Why's that?"

"Well, 'cept for the crazy ones, rest goes to mess to eat."

Jack shook his head. "I have no damn idea."

The man nodded, then shuffled off down the hallway. Jack took his plate and went over to the bunk to sit and eat. In his mind he'd expected prison to be physically bad, but he had underestimated its effect on his mental state. He needed something to take his mind off his surroundings or he might end up with the crazy ones.

Sleep never came for long. Wails, screams and bangs on the bars woke him in a cold sweat numerous times. But when he did manage to sleep, he dreamed of the war. Men dying under cannon fire. Their bodies exploding into flying parts by incoming rounds. He finally sat up and swung his legs over the side of the bed with his eyes shut to try and block out the bad nightmares he'd relived over and over again.

Everett came to see him on the second day. Only an hour before some old man with a shotgun-bearing guard had emptied his overflowing night jar. Jack was grateful, although the odor lingered and a few flies buzzed as he talked to his attorney.

"I have spoken to the judge about your case." Everett began. "A man called Hefner. He seems like a judge

with actual experience. That sad truth is, most of these
appointees aren't. One I recently dealt with was a former postmaster. No bench or law experience at all.

"I managed to set your bond hearing for next Thursday." Everett rose and began to pace the cell with his
hands clasped behind his back. "I'm going to have to
raise some money."

"For my bond?" Jack asked.

The man looked around furtively to be certain they
were alone. Then in a stage whisper he said, "No, to
pay him off."

Jack was startled. "How much will that be?"

"Two thousand, I suspect. He hasn't said, but that's
the going price for murder cases."

"Why, I have no idea where we could find that much
money except by robbing a bank." No way I can raise it
sitting in this stinking prison, he thought.

Everett shook his head. "No, we can raise money without holding up banks." He smiled back at Jack. "I can get
it. But that might lengthen your stay in here, of course."

"Of course. You think it will happen on Thursday?"

"Yes, I do," Everett said confidently. "I sent word to
the Frank brothers that I need an affidavit from them
swearing you were in Kansas that July."

"But they're up there now taking cattle to market."

"Yes, they are. Albert Frank's wife, Hailey, said she'd
come down and tell the judge that you were up there
with their cattle that July."

"Will that help?" Jack recalled the woman. She looked
proper enough to him to impress a judge. At least he
hoped so anyway.

"I think so. I asked her to be at the bond hearing. I also arranged for a clean suit, tie, starched shirt and a bath and shave the night before."

Jack gave Everett a warm look of appreciation. "Thanks, sir. I'll be in your debt."

"No, you won't. The entire state of Texas owes you, and men like you, more than you'll ever get from them."

The nights were easier on Jack. He finally had something to look forward to. The night before the hearing, a man who called himself a barber came by and shaved him; then a black man and a guard hauled in two pails of water, a bar of lye soap and a towel—well, a flour sack, but it was good enough.

"I'm coming back in an hour for all of this. You be done bathing by then," the guard said, relocking the cell door.

On Thursday morning Jack wondered if they would ever come for him. But at last they arrived and put him in shackles, and with several other prisoners he was loaded into a prison wagon and hauled across town to the federal courthouse.

"What'cha in for?" a big, unshaven guy in filthy stripes, seated on the wagon bench beside him, asked.

"Murder," Jack said curtly.

"Hmm." He turned up his nose. "They sure got you fancied up. What chance have I got in these dirty stripes with an appointed law clerk? Bet you've got a real lawyer."

"I do. But I didn't kill the man."

The man scoffed. "Rich sumbitch like you won't ever do time. Prison's plumb full of dumb, poor bastards like me."

"What are you in here for?" Jack asked curiously.

"You don't want to know."

Jack shrugged. Whatever the man had done he wasn't proud of it. He decided to pay him no mind and enjoy his first breath of fresh air in five days. A cool breeze swept away most of the stink from the other prisoners' bodies.

The men in the caged wagon whistled at hussies strolling on the sidewalks and shouted about how badly they needed them.

One of the women yelled back in a French-sounding accent, "You come by Mrs. Carrie's House when you get out."

"Oh, we will! Oh, we will, darling," the men whooped and hollered.

At the building on the second floor an officer took him to a holding cell adjoining the courtroom and undid the chains. "We can shoot your ass down here as well as we can going over the fence," he muttered and showed him through the door to the courtroom, pointing out Everett at a front table.

"Good morning. You look much better," Everett said.

"I feel much better." He looked over the crowd and when he saw Hailey Franks sitting in the first row behind the fence, he nodded to her. Thank God she was there.

Jack eased himself down in the spring-loaded wheel-back chair. Damn, it felt wonderful after five days of iron bunk.

"All rise," the bailiff announced. "His honor, Judge G. P. Alcott."

Jack stood up beside Everett and then they were seated.

"What do you think?" Jack asked.

Everett nodded in approval. It stirred a little hope in Jack's heart. Just maybe he would get out of there.

The particulars were read and the judge invited the prosecution, a man called Trimble, and Everett to the bench. Jack heard him allude to Mrs. Franks' appearance to the judge. Trimble made a fuss about her testifying, but the judge waved him aside and invited her to come forth and speak to him off the record.

"This man Starr worked for your husband, ma'am?"

"Yes, in July 1866, your honor, Jack Starr was in Kansas with a herd of our trail cattle. My husband, Albert, would be here to testify, but he is up there now."

"When will he be back, ma'am?"

"September, if he don't get lost."

The judge smiled. "I thank you so much for taking your time to come here today, Mrs. Franks."

"Your honor—"

"Yes?"

"Jack Starr is a good man," Hailey Franks said. "You know, at Shedville he recovered two white women from the Comanches before he came here and turned himself in. No one paid him to save those women either."

"Thank you, ma'am. I have that under consideration as well."

There was more talking among the parties at the bench. At last Judge Alcott spoke to Jack.

"Please rise."

He stood.

"It is the ruling of this court that you are to be released on five thousand dollars bond. Are you prepared to provide that?"

"Yes, we are, your honor," Everett said.

"You must understand that you are not to leave the state of Texas or the region that you are currently residing in without express permission of this court."

"Yes, sir," Jack said.

"Your trial has been postponed until a later date."

Everett nodded and thanked the judge. When Everett came back to the table the judge dismissed them.

"Thanks," Jack said to his lawyer as he grasped his hand in a firm shake. He turned and thanked Mrs. Franks. She nodded formally, leaned toward him and said under her breath, "You need work, come see me. I could find lots for you to do."

"Thank you."

"It wasn't any problem," she said, and he could swear she winked at him before she left the courtroom.

He could hardly wait to be outside and draw a deep breath. Going down the stairs he asked Everett how much it would cost his organization.

"The judge got two. But that damn prosecutor got a thousand as well."

"Justice ain't cheap, that's for sure."

"I doubt they'll ever try you, but we need to heed the bond."

"I will," Jack said. "But I'm going to need an outfit and a stage ticket to get out of here."

"That's where we're going right after lunch. I figured you'd be ready for some real food first."

"Amen to that." He pulled his tie loose, looking out the front doors at the traffic in the street. "Lead the way, my friend. I feel a hundred percent better already."

Their lunch in the Armstrong Hotel Restaurant included slices of tender roast beef, potatoes, gravy, green beans, rolls and butter. With a china coffee cup nestled in his hands, he studied the great red drapes on the windows and put out of his memory the taste of the hot-water crap they'd served in the Austin jail. He felt fortunate to be out of there and never wanted to go back.

"How do I repay these sons of Texas for all of this?"

"Your debt is settled." Everett wiped his mouth on the linen napkin.

"I was a rather expensive case to handle."

"We've had higher-priced ones."

"I'd hate to have been any pricier."

"Jack, Texas will have to be restored to full statehood— someday. Then we can drive these corrupt officials out of town."

He agreed. It couldn't take place fast enough. Every judge and prosecutor on the take sounded scary. There were more poor folks in Texas that would never see justice done for them because they couldn't afford the cost.

After lunch Everett took him to a mercantile and he was fitted with new canvas pants, suspenders, a collarless cotton shirt, wool vest, silk rag and a wide-brimmed straw hat. A new pair of stub-toed boots that actually fit him, a holster and an oily smelling .44 caliber army-model Colt with a pouch for bullets and caps completed the look.

Jack tried to protest, but Everett insisted that a free man needed to look the part.

A man came over as they were paying up and introduced himself as Sam Sterling. "I own this store, and, Mister, I say you can have anything I have in stock. James, get him out one of those good steel hunting knives and a sheath. He may need that too."

Jack looked at the tin ceiling for help. His bill would be well over forty dollars. Everett laughed aloud at his discomfort.

It was midafternoon when he rode his gray Kentucky horse out of Austin. The horse was worth a fortune and it came from a Mrs. Grady, a war widow whose husband had been killed in Mississippi in the last battle. She said she wanted a real son of Texas to have her husband's favorite horse and had hugged him hard at the transfer. Under the wide-brimmed straw hat, he short-loped along on the open road, passing freight wagons and farm rigs. It'd take him two days to get back to Lost Dog Creek, but he had plans when he got there. Big plans.

He went to Austin flat broke, sat in jail five days and came out smelling like bluebonnets in spring. No way he could beat that. I'm coming home, Lucy, he thought.

Chapter 12

In the predawn chill, he sat on his haunches beside the fire. The pungent smell of the burning mesquite and oak filled his nose as he coaxed the flames back up to boil water for coffee, Lucy, wrapped in a blanket, joined him.

"You sleep any?" she asked.

"When?"

She elbowed him hard. "Last night, silly."

"Well, you didn't let me sleep for long," he said with a laugh. "I got some water from the spring to make coffee."

"I can do those things," she protested.

"Let me help," he countered. As she tried to take over, he twisted around to lean over and kiss her.

She flushed with embarrassment. "I don't think I've ever been kissed this much in my entire life."

"You want me to stop?"

"No. I was just saying—"

"You never had a big fool before to pick on you."

"I never said you were a fool."

"Good, because I never felt the impulse to kiss any other woman as much in my entire life either."

She looked sideways at him and then shook her head as if dismayed. "I've been feeling this way since that first night you walked in that schoolhouse."

He smiled at her, but his face dimmed soon after. "I wish this trial was over." He looked out at the hills covered in cedar and live oak that surrounded their camp.

"They may not even have one—that lawyer, Everett, told you."

"I know, but I don't want you married to a man in prison."

"I've been a widow for three years and I'm getting along fine. I think I could handle just about anything."

"Yes, but the stigma of it—"

"You can marry me or simply live with me. I don't care as long as we're together whenever possible." She wrapped herself tighter in the blanket.

"Will the kids mind?"

She frowned at him and shook her head as if amused. "They'd probably rather live with you than me."

"You want a fancy wedding or a plain one?"

"I want Sister and her family there. I want the kids there and that's all."

"Good, cause I'm broke."

Lucy wrinkled her brow in concern. "Do you need money?"

He shook his head warily. "I'll need to find some work soon. I haven't done any in years."

"I know you aren't real keen on it, but why don't you take on the cattle drive? They can pay you a small subscription fee to help cover your expenses until the drive."

Jack scratched at his beard in contemplation. "You want me to do that? Why, I'd be gone six months." He wasn't prepared to tell her his real reasons for not wanting the job.

"I understand that, but there really isn't much ditch digging needed around here." She rose to fetch her coffee grinder out of the pannier. "I better get some coffee ready."

"I bet there's lots of mustangs around here that I could gather," he said. "They're bringing good prices in Fort Worth even when they're half broke."

"There's some bands back west. You thinking of doing that?"

"Ain't no one knocking down the door to hire me, is there?"

She shook her head. "We'll make it somehow."

He liked the idea of the mustang business. They'd swing through the country and look for some bands. It would keep him occupied and provide some excitement besides the damn hard work of building traps, which he'd been doing ever since he came to town.

On his feet, he stretched his arms over his head. She glanced up. "I'm glad we're camping by ourselves for a few days."

"You don't know how glad I am to be out of that stinking jailhouse. Whew. They've got crazy people in there that wail all night or beat their tin cups on the bars. I've heard 'Shut up back there' a thousand times.

That meadowlark sounds like fiddle music to me after those five days in hell."

She hugged him from behind, wrapping her slim arms around his waist. "I'll make us some pancakes if you have the time."

"Lucy, I have all day for you, and tomorrow and the next day." He turned around and pecked her on the forehead.

"Heavens to Betsy, I won't be that slow," she joked.

In midafternoon he used his field glasses to scope the open country they were fixing to cross. So far that day he'd counted four bands led by stallions. But he was more interested in the cull males. You could sell a farmer a mare, but a cattleman wanted a horse to ride. At the perimeter of the herds were bands of outcast males and yearlings, which were kept away from the mares by the lead stallion. Those were the prizes he needed.

As they wandered around the open country they discovered some older, abandoned horse traps that looked almost functional.

"I'll drop back here in a few days and leave some salt in these traps," Jack announced.

"That's a smart idea," Lucy said encouragingly.

"I bet I could ride down toward Mexico and find me some hands that need work."

"What about your rangers?" she asked.

"Hadn't thought of them. They might even do it on shares."

"I bet they would. They've got the time on their hands too. I'd bet it'd beat hoeing corn any day."

Jack chuckled at her words. "You bet it would."

After three days of camping they headed back to her place in the late afternoon.

"Well, it's settled, then." He reached over and clasped her hand on top of the saddle horn.

"If you're sure, then I sure am."

"Next Saturday night we'll get married at the school-house."

"Yes and you be sure to invite your ranger pals."

"Oh, I will. I'm certain there'll be a crowd show up. I don't think we can get away with that small wedding you wanted."

She laughed. "Yes, no doubt. I better talk to Sister about making more accommodations."

They descended the hill toward the house. The dogs started barking in anticipation as Tally stood out front with her hands on her hips and an about-time-you-two-got-back look on her face. Luke joined her on his crutches.

"They look glad to see us." She laughed.

Jack smiled at the kids, who would soon be part of his family. "Looks that way to me."

Gathering his rangers wasn't hard. He happened upon Jangles in the road the next day and told him about the wedding.

"Cap'n, we'll be there with our bib and tucker on."

Jack chuckled appreciatively. "So I was thinking I'd

do some mustanging after the wedding. Horses are bringing a good price in Fort Worth."

"Hell, count me, Cotton and Arnold in on the deal if
you need help. There's more boys that'd like to come
along too, I'm sure."

Jack was relieved to hear the news. "It'd be a part-
nership. We'd share the profits after expenses. I can't
afford any wages. But I think if we start out just the four
of us, we'll make out okay."

Jangles nodded. "We trust you, Cap'n. By the way,
Captain McIntyre has forty dollars for you from them
Mexican horses and saddles he sold."

Jack frowned at him. "You boys all get your split?"

"Sure did."

He scowled at him. "You're lying to me."

"Damn it, we want it that way."

Jack gave him a hard stare, but could see the boy was
set in his ways. "Alright. Wedding's at seven at Lost
Creek on Saturday night. Supper follows."

"We'll have bells on our toes and ribbons in our
noses." Jangles laughed aloud.

They parted with Jangles singing "Olde Dan Tucker."
Jack rode on to Shedville to talk to Mr. Volkner, who
owned the general store. Lucy said the man would ex-
tend him credit for the supplies he'd need to go mustanging.

At the store he hitched his new horse, Gray, at the
rack and started to go inside. Business looked slow in
the small village. He stopped on the porch and listened
to the sound of the blacksmith pounding on an anvil.

Besides the store and smithy, there was a rusty tin-roofed saloon across the street—he'd have to go over and have a glass of beer when his deal was over with Volkner. He went inside and was immediately surrounded by the smell of garlic and new leather. At the sound of the bell over the door, a tall, thin man in a white apron came from the back of the store.

"Good day, sir," the man said.

"Good day, my name is—"

"You must be Captain Starr. I've heard all about you." They shook hands and the man, who had a distinctive German accent, invited him to come and sit on some ladder-back chairs.

After Jack explained his business and mustanging needs, Volkner told him he would set him up in style. "It is the least I can do for you."

Jack beamed. "Business aside, I'd be pleased if you came to the wedding."

"I *vill* be there," the man promised.

Jack left the store, ready for a beer as soon as he stepped in the midday shade of the store's porch and spotted the rusty-looking saloon. It seemed pretty shabby to him, but he was building up a mighty thirst so he crossed the street and stepped through the open door-way.

A bushy-faced man looked up at him with a mean glint in his eye from behind the bar. "What'cha need?"

"One draft beer," he motioned with a raised finger. He settled down at the bar, but noticed two hombres stand up at a side table, casting mean stares in his direction. Jack felt cold chills run up his spine. It was dark in the saloon and looked like it was stacked two deep in badgers.

As the men approached Jack started to shift in his seat. He had a bad feeling about them, but wanted to wait to see what they would do.

The shorter of the two, with a slick, black mustache, walked right up to him, his face even with Jack's. "You're the no-good cuss who wouldn't leave when he was told." The second man rolled up his sleeves as if he were readying to throw a punch.

"Hold on, now," Jack said, trying to make the men see reason. But before he knew it he heard a crash and felt a blow to his head. The lights went out and the last thing he remembered was an oily black mustache above a nasty smile.

As he came to his senses the first thing he heard was the sound of dragging poles. He could feel the bumps in the road as he went over them, jarring him in his seat. Jangles was singing "Sweet Betsy from Pike" and riding in front of him. He discovered, with a pounding headache, that he was riding in a crude travois with Jangles pulling the makeshift contraption.

"Oh, Cap'n, I was afraid ole Gray might not like them poles so I'm pulling you with my horse, Sam Brown. I left Gray in town, but we can fetch him tomorrow. We'll be at Mrs. Thornton's in an hour."

"What— what happened?"

"You went in that wildcat saloon without backup,"

Jangles said, letting out a low whistle. "Don't know as I'd do the same."

"How did you find me?"

"Mr. Volkner sent word when he heard from some kids that you were unconscious and lying on the ground out back."

"Who were those men that attacked me?"

"They collect for Hiram and I suppose they were mad at you for telling him to go to hell."

"No, I want their names," Jack said, sitting up with some difficulty and feeling a surge of anger course through him.

"Yes, sir, they're Dyke and Freeman, and the bartender is Gurley. None of us rangers ever go in there alone."

"When I go in there again I'll damn sure be ready for them."

"And we'll be there to back you."

His head hurt and the back of his hair was matted with dried blood. He felt lucky to be alive. If he made any more dumb moves like that one he'd not be around to enjoy his new bride.

He was grateful, but his temples sure pounded.

Chapter 13

"They tried to kill you," Lucy said bitterly, using rubbing alcohol to clean the cut on the back of his head. The cure felt worse than the injury as the alcohol burned the raw flesh.

He winked and made faces at Tally, Luke and Jangles, who watched him anxiously as Lucy doctored him.

"Who did this to you anyway?" Lucy asked.

"Jangles named a Dyke and a Freeman as the most likely to have been my attackers."

"Hiram Sawyer's men must frequent that tin can."

"All I wanted was a draft beer," Jack grumbled. "I wasn't lookin' for trouble."

She leaned over and looked him in the eye. "Next time you'll know better."

"Next time," Jangles said, "his ranger company is coming along."

"That old claptrap building might fall in on all of you," Lucy said. "It's not sound and neither are the people in it."

"I won't forget the warning," Jack said with a quick

kiss on her cheek. "But there's good news too. I got a line of credit established for the wild-horse business, so that's settled."

"Well," Lucy said, "we have a large canvas tarp and posts you can use to protect yourselves from the rain. Where will you set up camp?"

"I think Double Springs is the best place," Jack answered. They'd seen it on their grand tour. Sweet flowing water near the horse traps they'd found, with lots of graze for their ponies at night.

"When does it start?" Lucy asked.

"Soon as Jangles gets me a crew."

"I'll have them here tomorrow night. We can leave the next day."

Jack winked at Lucy. "I think I have a wedding in there somewhere I better attend."

"By gum, I forgot that too." Jangles took off his floppy-brimmed hat and scratched the top of his head. "Can we go next week?"

"Sure. I'm thinking she'll let me go by then."

"My, my, Jack Starr," Lucy said. "You can go when you get ready."

They all laughed.

What started out as a small wedding grew as fast as wildfire. Seven neighbor women came over early that Tuesday morning and ran off every male in the place. Led by Sister, they brought white lace material and silk to make a wedding dress for Lucy; they wanted nothing simple for the occasion. Wanting nothing more than to stay out of the way, Jack loaded Luke in the wagon and they went to find Captain McIntyre.

When they arrived at his place they found him busy shoeing horses under a great, wide, live oak. Swiping sweat off his forehead with the side of his finger, he gave them a grin. "You two got here just in time."

In the air was the smell of coal burning in the forge for the horseshoes. He dug out the horse money and paid Jack. "Them boys told me you didn't owe them a thing."

"I wanted them to have something. Texas won't ever pay them for their work."

"Look at it like this, Jack. We've all got to pull our share and rangering's our part. We accept it as part of our lives."

Jack nodded, and McIntyre changed the subject. "So, I hear there's going to be a wedding."

"A wedding is in the works, alright. Saturday night. The whole town's invited."

"Wouldn't miss it," McIntyre said with another broad smile.

"By the by, Luke wants some pointers on shoeing. What horses are left?" Jack looked over the line of ponies tied on a lariat hitching rope.

"The sorrel, but watch him: he's snippy."

"Luke, let's find something for you to sit on and we'll help Captain McIntyre out."

"A nail keg inside that shed door should do the part." McIntyre pointed out its whereabouts. "Your leg healing, Luke?"

"I think so, Captain, but not as fast as I'd like."

"Well, now you'll have yourself some real help with the men's work." He motioned toward Jack with a tip of his head.

"Yeah, sis and I sure like the idea of having him in the family."

"He won't get much help out of me for a while," Jack said. "I'm going to the west country to round up some horses. There's good cash up at Fort Worth for the usable ones."

"Hard work, that mustanging, but I wish you luck." McIntyre didn't sound or look enthused about the prospect.

"Ain't much easy in life." Jack laughed.

He went over and untied the lead to move the horse, Red, over in the shade. The sorrel reared up, but Jack talked softly to the gelding, slowly working on the rope. Lots of white showed around Red's eyes, and when he finally laid his palm on the pony's neck, he trembled all over.

"Easy. Easy," Jack kept saying, trying to prove he wasn't a threat. After some time he won a very shaky truce, hitched the horse and started with a rasp on the gelding's front hooves.

"Most important part." He demonstrated to his student, who leaned over on the keg to watch him. "Get the hoof down to size; it'll need to be flat when he strikes the ground."

As the lesson went on and his confidence rose, Luke asked more and more questions. After some struggling on the hind ones, Jack had all four hooves shaped and began shoe fitting.

"I think I can do it better when I get off these sticks."

"There ain't no rush. We'll do a few more together before you tackle one by yourself."

"Thanks, Jack. You know, Dad used to take me everywhere with him, but I was younger then and sure never learned much."

"Don't regret that. They must've been fun days." He was clipping the last nails on the final hoof.

"They were, but there was so much I had to learn on my own after Dad passed on; Maw didn't know much about men's work either, so it was tough on me. I guess we expected him to be there forever."

Before Jack could answer, McIntyre came back with a bucket of cool water and a gourd dipper for them. "Time for a break." He watched Jack carefully as he dipped the gourd in the clear water. "So they tell me you got beat up a few days ago at the saloon in Shedville?" he finally said.

"I guess I didn't belong there."

"We ought to hitch up some mules and pull that damn saloon down. The bunch that hangs there needs to move on to San Antonio."

Jack agreed. There was a lot he needed to know about local politics. For instance, how did Hiram Sawyer get to be such a banker? There was no law except in San Antonio, seventy miles east, not counting the ranger outfits, which were mostly for defense against the Comanches. Since no county had been carved out of the vast region except Mason, the rest of the land came under Bexar County jurisdiction until the legislature met again. But when that finally happened they'd need a county seat and a population to support it. That would be a while off, he realized, as he drove back with Luke to the ranch.

Before he left, McIntyre hadn't missed the chance to ask him about making the cattle drive the following spring. Jack had given him the same answer he'd given the rest. He'd think on it, but he didn't want them to pass up the chance to hire a good man.

"Reckon they've got that dress made?" Luke asked as they headed downhill in the wagon toward the house, which was darkly outlined against the setting sun.

"I bet they'll have it done in time for the wedding."

He knew Lucy would see to it. There was nothing more important to them than becoming husband and wife.

Chapter 14

Lucy made a striking bride. Her hair was pinned up. The white silk dress would have done well at a Washington D.C. gala. Jack couldn't recall seeing as many red faces at once as there were in that hot schoolhouse, all looking at Jack and Lucy in anticipation. The place bulged at the seams with people. One of the townsmen played a small accordion while Luke, on crutches, brought his mom down the aisle from the back of the room to give her away. In his starched white shirt and tie, the young man looked awfully grown up to Jack as he watched him swing across the floor on his sticks.

Jangles, his best man, stood to the side with Jack and held a small surprise the two of them had concealed. When Preacher Teck came to the part of the ceremony about the exchange of rings, Lucy raised her eyebrows a quarter of an inch, not expecting the matter to be brought up since they hadn't purchased any.

"Here, sir," Jangles said, stepping in to hand the preacher a folded linen handkerchief that nested a gold ring.

A smile grew at the corners of her mouth at the sight of it. "My grandmother's," Jack whispered, and slipped it on her finger.

She nodded, speechless. Jack was afraid she was going to cry.

"I now pronounce you man and wife," Preacher Teck said with a smile. "You may kiss the bride."

And he did.

He knew one thing: his grandma Starr would've been proud of Lucy Starr, same as she'd been of every other child in her grannyhood. He could feel the little old lady's blue eyes looking down from heaven at him. "It's about time you got married, Jacky boy," she'd say.

For their honeymoon lodging, the newlyweds used a tent that Lucy had borrowed from Sister. After the wedding they drove up to Willow Springs with a light buckboard and team that Jangles had borrowed from his uncle for the event. The day before the rangers had gone up and set up the tent for them. There was a large supply of chopped wood and a grub box full enough to last them a month.

Sometime past midnight Jack awoke to the sounds of the horses acting restless, as if there was a disturbance in the meadow.

"What is it?" Lucy asked, turning over and clutching his shoulder.

"I'm not sure," he whispered. "Something is upsetting the horses. Could be a bear. You stay here."

"You be careful. It could be Comanches."

He slipped on his pants and socks. Straining to detect any recognizable noises, he finished pulling on his foot gear and scrambled to his feet. He handed her the rifle, just in case, and with a nod he left her sitting in her new nightgown atop the pallet.

The night sky was pricked with stars, and a quarter moon cast a pearly light on the meadow. From his vantage point, he could see the two horses' silhouettes; they were looking south at something. When he turned to look, he couldn't make out anything but a dark curtain of trees. Still the team kept snorting as if they were upset. Even if it was just a bear, the horses' behavior was enough to convince Jack. He ducked back inside and exchanged his six-shooter with the rifle he gave Lucy.

"Did you see anything?" she whispered.

"Not what those ponies are seeing or smelling. But there's something out there."

Outdoors again, he used the shadowy edge of the trees to move in the direction of the team, who still held their vigil on the intruder—or intruders. Trust a horse to see and know a man's enemies before he even saw them. He put a lot of stock in that adage.

He dried his palm on the side of his pants leg, despite the night's coolness. He halted and knelt, hoping for a better view of whatever had interrupted his sleep. In a few moments he heard voices whispering.

"That ain't his gray out there. Them's some kind of light draft horses. Ain't worth nothing."

"Shut up!" The other man lowered his voice. ". . . he'll hear you."

"Waste of our damn time—"

"Let's get the hell out of here, then."

He didn't recognize either voice; they were too far

away and hidden in the trees. On his feet he moved closer to where he thought the voices were coming from, skirting the cedar boughs, but he could hear them already retreating up the hills as dislodged stones rolled down the hillsides. Chances were good he'd never know who they were. One thing was for certain: they wanted his gray horse. It was strange that he'd been targeted twice recently. First two hombres had beaten him up for no apparent reason in a public saloon. Then two hoots rode clear into the middle of nowhere to steal his gray horse and made enough commotion to wake him in the process.

He walked back to the tent. Lucy rushed out in her new nightgown and hugged him, her face pale with worry.

"I'm so glad you're alright." She nestled her face into his bare chest. "I was so worried."

"I'm fine," he reassured her. "They rode off."

"Who were they?"

"Damned if I know, but I heard them say they wanted to steal my gray horse. Seems like they left Jangles' uncle's team alone."

She peered off in the night just to be certain.

He kissed her to reassure her once more. "They rode off. Let's go back to bed."

She cast one last look down the starlit meadow to check for them, then swung her arm around his waist and headed back. "Yes, yes, let's."

The next morning when he looked around he found nothing but cigarette butts on the ground. They must have sat and looked over the scene for some time. What would they have done with the gray? There was no way to sell him in the area, because folks would recognize him. It didn't make sense. He followed the tracks in the brush but found no more evidence of them.

The week flew by and on Friday Jack and Lucy packed up to return to the ranch. On the spring seat with all their gear loaded on the rig, he looked over the valley as they rode on, admiring the rich, green meadows and the tall cedars.

"Nice place to get away," he remarked.

"You don't regret anything?" she asked, hugging his arm.

"Regret? I'm ecstatic to have you for a wife."

"You remind yourself of that if our marriage ever turns sour," she joked.

"And you, Mrs. Starr? Any regrets?"

She shook her head firmly. "I feel younger than I have in years. I just can't believe I found . . ." she trailed off, trying to hold back tears.

He hugged her with his right arm. "Don't cry."

She used a handkerchief to dab at her eyes. "Oh, I just never thought I'd have another chance to find this."

He smiled broadly. "I'll try to make you feel that way for the rest of our lives."

"I hope I do."

He kissed her. Maybe he hadn't wasted his whole life after all. The dreamy experience of the honeymoon had suspended him in another world and he wasn't at all eager to get back to reality.

* * *

In the late afternoon, they descended the hill, dogs barking and the kids in the yard awaiting their arrival. He chuckled. "Reckon they'll be on us for coming home late."

"Oh, I hope not," she said, a wrinkle of worry creasing her forehead.

He laughed. "Who cares. Sometimes a man needs a little time alone with his wife."

Chapter 15

The D-T ranch headquarters bustled with activity early that morning as the mustangers prepared to leave, just a few days after Jack and Lucy's honeymoon. Jangles had borrowed a team of mules and a farm wagon from a neighboring rancher to haul their things. Jack realized the two mules were only half broken, which must've been the reason why the rancher was all too eager to loan them out. Driving them required a rider on each side with a lead rope tied hard and fast to keep the mules on the road and prevent them from running away. But it was no big job for a ranger and it was easier than using team horses, which required more work to load and unload than a wagon.

"When will you be back?" Lucy asked, clinging to him.

"Two weeks," Jack said. "I hope we have a string of them by then."

"So do I. You and those boys be careful. Wild horses could hurt you."

He agreed to be careful for the hundredth time, kissed

her good-bye and left. By sundown they were at their base camp near the horse traps he'd found on his trip with Lucy.

Long past dark they finished eating and were getting ready to climb into their bedrolls. Jangles stopped and listened to the sounds of the night in the campfire light.

"You reckon a man could ever break that blue roan stallion that runs with a band of mares up here? I've seen him twice or so."

"Jangles, you want him, we'll get him," Jack said.

"I ain't a great horse breaker, Cap'n."

"Only way to learn is to do it. We'll all help you."

"Dang, so *that's* what your friends are for," Jangles said with a grin.

"Who said we was your friends?" Cotton asked from his bedroll, and pulled the light cover over his shoulder. The rest of them laughed.

The first day went smoothly. They drove a few mustangs in, led by an old branded horse. A good set of wild males followed him into the repaired pens. Standing at the closed gate, Jack looked over the catch. There were probably a half dozen in the trap they could turn into saddle horses.

He left them in the pen for the night and went to camp, where Cotton was getting supper ready. They could sort out the ones they planned to keep in the morning. With no time for dinner at midday, he figured the boys were starving. Amused, he found that Arnold and Jangles were trying to hurry along the cook.

"It takes time," Cotton said, brandishing a large wooden spoon at them. "Now get back."

"Let's make some halters so we can tie logs on those horses we intend to break," Jack said, putting his hands to work on the reel of rope he'd bought from Volkner. His scheme was to let the horses drag around a large log until they calmed down and were gentler. After making a few halters, supper was ready and the four of them dug in as Jack poured the coffee.

"Kinda hard to be the cook while y'all are running mustangs all day," Cotton complained.

"You're doing fine. Someone's got to fill our hollow bellies. It's just as important as wranglin'," Jack reassured him.

"I hate to miss the action."

"You won't. We'll let you help us do the breaking, and you can get kicked, bit and trampled like the rest of us."

Cotton laughed, already in a better mood. "You ever get to see Sergeant Craig when you were in town?"

Jack sobered. "No, but I sure wanted to." It had niggled at Jack, knowing the man was so upset about his trip back with Mrs. Lerner, but between the wedding and the honeymoon he never had enough time to visit him.

"I heard that him and Marsha broke up on account of him feeling so low after the rescue. That's why he never came to your wedding either."

Jack nodded. "After we get things settled here, I'll ride by and check on him."

"I sure wish you would. Marsha'd be a good woman

for him. He needs a wife and bless her, she needs him. She's my mom's cousin. And he'd listen to you."

"Maybe," Jack agreed. "At least I'll try."

Early the next morning after breakfast, they separated the horse catch on horseback. Branded horses were cut out first and turned loose if they looked like discards. The good ones that looked like they were broken were corralled. Their owners would pay for their return. They'd simply escaped and joined the wild ones. Obvious cripples were cut loose, along with a clubfooted one, a bay with a bad limp from some previous wreck and a horse with problems in his neck that restricted him from raising his head.

That left about thirty prospects in the final cut. Six were freshly weaned and too young for their purposes. They branded these with Lucy's D-T iron and neutered them. They would return for them when they were older.

After a long day of sorting and working the herd, they finally made it back to camp, exhausted, ate some leftover biscuits, fell into their bedrolls and went to sleep.

Jack was up before dawn to help Cotton fix breakfast. The crew would need to eat hardy to work another day. They fried a pound of sliced bacon, a huge pan of German fried potatoes and onions, plus two batches of biscuits in the Dutch oven. Cotton stirred the skillet of scrambled eggs while Jack woke Jangles and Arnold.

They crawled out of their bedrolls, bleary-eyed, looking like they'd been through hell.

"This is tougher than chasing Comanches," Jangles complained, pulling on his boots.

"Wait till you see what Cotton has cooked up." Jack jerked his thumb toward the campfire to indicate the food.

"Hurrah!" Arnold said. "I dreamed we all would starve up here."

Jack shook his head. He needed to hire a full-time cook next time. At least today they'd be full as ticks.

The two dozen horses they kept were worked, branded, gelded and fitted with a halter, rope and log to drag. Spooked by the trailing object, they usually threw a fit, but soon they would tire out and become tamer.

Midafternoon they went back to camp. Come morning they'd begin to break the horses. Jack felt proud of his hardworking crew. Things were moving along so well that he allowed everyone to take a siesta. At supper their spirits seemed to be lifted. Jack knew they were doing better.

In the morning they took their saddles and pads down to the pens. Using Mac as the snubbing horse, Jack roped the big bay, who threw a head-shaking fit. The boys rushed in, threw a jumper over his head and subdued him. Jangles worked a saddle blanket over his back, talking soothingly to the horse the whole time and dodging his flying hind heels. They untied the rope from his drag block, and using Mac they pulled him to a snubbing post. In a short while he was saddled and his left hind foot drawn up with a rope tied on the horn so if he fought he'd fall down. They left him and Jack rode in for another.

The big gruella he picked pawed with his forefeet and flashed his teeth. Despite his surgery from the previous day, he was not going to be easy.

"Go get a blanket," Jack told Arnold. "We're laying him down and showing him who's boss."

Jangles frowned as he tried to work closer with the saddle pad. "What're we going to do?"

"We'll put him down on his side and you can sit on his head and neck and talk to him awhile."

"What is he, four or five?"

"He ain't a baby." Jack watched the gruella shake his head furiously.

"No, he's been in some fights too. Got several scars from battles with stallions."

"He should make a good stout horse," Jack said.

Before the day was over, Arnold was bitten on the arm by a furious bronc. No broken skin, but it tore through his sleeve. He was jumpy for the rest of the day, leaping back whenever a horse flashed his teeth at him, which several did. The others got a kick out of it.

After they had successfully tamed a few horses, the crew rode back to camp, joking and laughing.

"What was it like up there in Abilene?" Jangles asked.

"No one ever went to sleep," Jack said. "Those cowboys never stopped their wild parties. They gambled till they lost all their money. They hugged and kissed every shady lady that would stand still for them and drank lots of bad whiskey."

"Were they pretty?" Jangles asked. "The women, I mean."

"Not particularly, unless you were starved for one."

"You don't act too excited about having been there." Jangles sounded a little disappointed.

"It was just another wild place. Folks didn't show good sense and there were some shootings that were uncalled for. Whiskey and guns don't mix well."

"Sorry I asked," Jangles said.

"No, it wasn't . . ." Jack gave a sigh. "It simply wasn't a good experience for me."

"Something bad happen to you up there?" Cotton asked in a low voice.

Jack looked off across the rolling hills, which were distorted by heat waves. Those boys needed an answer, but he felt too choked up to talk about it. He couldn't swallow.

"My youngest brother, Cory, was there with me." He chewed on his lower lip before he continued. "Cory was seventeen. I guess he got involved with a lady of the night in a saloon. A drunk came in claiming she was his girl. When she protested he slapped her down to the floor.

"Cory caught his arm to make him stop. The man whirled, answered him with a .45 and shot him five times."

"Five times?"

Jack nodded.

"Did the law get him?" Jangles asked.

"No. He got away."

"What was his name?"

"Julius Knotts."

Cotton looked up from the floury board where he was cutting biscuits. "You know where he's at?"

"I hear every once in a while that he's been in such and such a place. In fact I was looking for him the night I learned about the Lost Dog Creek dance and rode up there to see if he was around someplace."

"I never heard the name before," Arnold said, busy peeling potatoes between his knees.

"He goes by Jewel sometimes," Jack said.

"That the reason you been saying no to the trail-boss job?" Jangles asked.

Jack looked off at the low setting sun. It would be dark in a half hour. "The job ain't all it's cut out to be. I buried three young men along the trail to Abilene. Their mothers won't ever be able to decorate their sons' graves. They're buried at river crossings and places we had stampedes. By now the crude crosses we planted over them have been trampled down by other herds passing through, so there aren't even any markers."

He shook his head and asked them to excuse him. Everyone felt subdued.

Standing on the highest point he watched the bleeding sun dissolve away the last of the day. Abilene was over, but it still felt like a spear in his chest when he talked or even thought about Cory's death at the hands of that cruel man. One shot would have been enough, but to empty his six-gun in Cory's body seemed like cold-blooded murder.

Jangles broke his thinking. "Sorry, Captain, I never meant to stir up bad memories. I brought you some food. Better eat. You're sure going to need your strength."

He took the plate and sat down cross-legged on the ground. "Thanks. I'll be fine. Just need a little space."

"You got it." Jangles left him.

He was grateful for Jangles' thoughtfulness. Maybe sleep would put the matter to rest. Sometimes it did; sometimes it didn't.

Chapter 16

Whooping and shouting the next day, Jangles fanned the bay's ear with his hat. The best that the horse could do was crow-hop stiff legged. After some time Jangles got the horse to respond to the reins and rode him around the large round pen.

"Open the gate. I'm going to ride the hair off him."

"Don't forget we've got more," Jack reminded him.

They'd left the gruella for the boss man. Tying the horse's head to his left leg, he mounted and turned him loose, and the ride was on. Things became rowdy. Gus, as they called him, made some high-flying lunges through the air and Jack thought for a short while he'd overpower him. But in a short time Gus became confused and Jack took the upper hand, punishing him when he tried to break out. Soon Jack rode him out the gate, short-loping and teaching him to rein. The big horse learned quickly.

They all intended to rest on Sunday. Midmorning a wagon showed up bearing Lucy and Tally. Everyone busied themselves hand-brushing their hair and tucking in their shirttails.

Jack smiled, grateful to see the two of them. He hugged both of them, kissed his wife and led her over to the fire. "This is Cotton's kitchen."

Arnold offered to show Tally the horses they had caught. Lucy shooed her off with him.

"We butchered some chickens early this morning. Thought you boys might want something hearty after all this camp fare," Lucy said, presenting the chickens.

The others cheered and she winked at Jack. "I knew they wouldn't turn down a meal from me."

"No way," Jack said, and shared a private wink with Cotton. "Would we?"

"No, sirree."

"If I keep these horses up here much longer I'll need a wagonload of hay. They've eaten most of the grass in those pens," Jack told her.

"One of the Yarboroughs would bring a load up here for ten dollars, I'm certain," Lucy said, on her knees as she started the fire under a large skillet.

"Order me one," Jack said. "In two weeks we'll come out with the horses, drop by for a visit, and go on to Fort Worth."

"Will you be there for the dance?" Lucy asked, referring to an upcoming town event.

"That'd be good. We'll be there."

She smiled wide. "I'd appreciate that."

"How's Luke?"

"Antsy. He had to watch the place instead of coming

up here. He wants to join your rangers when his leg is healed."

"I'll see how we're doing when his leg is fully healed."

She shrugged, spooning lard into the pan. "I just wanted to warn you. He's gonna ask you one of these day."

"I guess he's as old as these boys."

"And he's got a steady head on his shoulders to boot."

"I'll think on it. Anyway, I sure appreciate you coming out here. It's nice to a have a woman who'll save me out here with her fried chicken," he teased.

Lucy laughed, poking him in the side with a spoon. "Don't underestimate the power of my chicken. You boys need to keep up your energy, and beans and biscuits ain't gonna do it."

Tally and the rangers returned looking refreshed; Tally's cheeks were especially rosy, and Jack figured it had something to do with all the male attention. She helped her mother fry chicken, mash potatoes and stir the huge pan of bubbling white chicken gravy. The three boys sat around the fire, hugging their knees and rocking back and forth, trying not to drool over the savory aromas.

After dinner Lucy and Tally packed everything up to leave. Lucy and Jack took a walk over a hill to have a private moment before she headed back home.

"It gets lonely," she said, holding his hand between them, "when you're gone."

"It gets lonely up here too. But if we can break two dozen horses and sell them in Fort Worth, it'll be a nice sum. I'll be able to afford some of that good barbed wire down at the blacksmith's so we can finally mend that break in the fence around the cornfield."

"I know, I know. I just miss you."

They kissed in a long embrace, then he herded her back to the waiting wagon. They could spend all day in each other's arms, but they needed to be back at the ranch before dark.

When Lucy and Tally were gone the crew lounged around, praising Jack's choice of a wife.

"She's sure a great cook," Cotton said.

"She's always a well-dressed lady," Jangles said.

"You were plumb lucky to find her," Arnold said.

Jack just smiled in amusement. He couldn't say enough about his good fortune. "Two weeks and we'll be back for the schoolhouse dance."

"We all going on to Fort Worth after that?" Jangles asked.

"If Captain McIntyre can handle things with the rangers he has, yes, indeed."

Arnold, lying on his back atop his bedroll, leapt up and let out a whoop. "Wahoo, I've never been there!"

"Neither have the rest of us," Jangles said. "You been there, Captain?"

"A few dozen times. Next two weeks we'll ride the heck out of the new horses. The better they're broken, the better they'll sell. The less trained ones we'll need to ride the most."

The boys looked forward to the coming weeks and Jack fell asleep to the sound of them chattering about everything they were going to do in Fort Worth.

Steve Yarborough delivered a load of hay midweek to feed the horses. The rangers forked the load from the hay rack into the storage bin, hoping that the horses would be easier to break if they were well fed. They had already depleted the grass in the pens and were getting antsy.

The next few days were still hard as the rangers were constantly thrown from their horses. Horses had to be re-caught and the riders resaddled them time and again. But after a time the horses began to lose some of their wildness, and Jack started to see the effects of their hard work.

Even the gruella began to act more like a ranch horse when Jack rode him. Soon enough all two dozen were close to being broken. When Saturday came they tied the horses halter to halter to lead and hitched them to Jangles' uncle's wagon to haul their gear on their way to the schoolhouse dance. Cotton took the lead at the front of the line while they snaked out of the large pen. Though a few acted up, they all soon fell in line, confined by the short lead to the next horse and the one behind. Jack and Arnold rode the line, making certain they settled in and kept up.

Jack's plan was to stop halfway to Shedville, then water and rest them at the D-T, where the corrals were big enough. He worried about leading them all in a line, but he wanted them to look well-broken when they finally got to Fort Worth, to draw more buyers.

By late afternoon the long line of wide-eyed horses pricked up their ears as the stock dogs barked their arrival. Lucy and Tally ran to open the pen gates while Jack drove the train through and untied them.

"You sure have them gentled," Lucy said, looking amazed at the horses.

"They're still wild horses," he said as he rode by, "but they'll be ranch horses in no time."

The rangers stomped in their high boots across her porch to wash up. Lucy had some of Jack's clean clothes laid out, and after he'd made himself presentable, he talked with Luke about his leg; his cast was to come off in ten days. He volunteered to watch the horses at home while the rest of them enjoyed themselves at the dance. Jack gladly accepted.

When everyone was set, Jack, Lucy, Tally, Cotton and Arnold headed for the dance. Jangles planned to meet them at the schoolhouse with their bedrolls and gear, which were packed into his rig.

At the schoolhouse Jack unhitched the team while Lucy, Tally and the rangers brought heaping dishes of food, specially prepared by Lucy, into the schoolhouse. When they were finished Tally and the rangers headed back outside to the wagon to make their own fun while the adults waltzed the night away.

Dark thunderheads were gathering high overhead

and Jack hoped they would bring much-needed rain. As everyone trickled in Jack exchanged hellos and warm handshakes with the townsfolk. By the time everyone had arrived and the preacher said grace over the food, thunder began rolling across the roof and a cool, fresh wind relieved the hot interior of the school building.

As they stood in line for food and the thunder broke loose overhead, everyone was giddy. The men ran to close the windows as the rain began to pound on the tin roof and the hard cracks of thunder sounded closer and louder. A few latecomers, wet as ducks, came bursting indoors.

With their plates piled high Jack and Lucy found a place to eat along the wall while the thunderous storm roared outside.

"Bad as the one we ran into out on the Llano," he said, recalling the day they were caught in the tough storm on their way to save Mandy and Mrs. Lerner.

"I hope there aren't any tornadoes." She looked concerned. "Luke's all alone out there."

"He'll be fine." He had to talk loud over the downpour and hail outside.

He looked up as two men in slickers burst through the door. Because the room was so crowded, at first Jack couldn't make them out. But soon he got a clear view of them and recognized them as the pair from the saloon. He realized his sidearm was in the wagon and he prayed the men wouldn't make any trouble.

Close to his ear Lucy asked, "What's wrong?"

"Those two that just came in are Dyke and Freeman— the pair who left me on the floor in that saloon."

Lucy tried to stand up and see them, but soon dropped back down. "You think they're here for a reason?"

"Let's hope they're only hungry."

Lucy was suddenly worried. "Have you seen Tally?"

"She's probably with the rangers."

"Where are they?"

"Trust me—they'll see she's protected."

"Oh, Jack, I'm afraid." She put the dish in her lap. "I need to go look for her."

"This storm will wind down. Give it more time."

"I'm afraid that . . ."

He put an arm over her shoulder and hugged her, whispering reassurances in her ear. More hail and wind tore at the eves of the building. When he looked up he saw one of Sawyer's henchmen push an older man aside.

Lucy grasped his wrist. "They're armed," she whispered, pointing with her free hand to the flash of a pistol at his hip.

"I don't give a damn. I owe them both a good lickin'."

"Oh, please don't make a scene, Jack. People might get hurt."

Jack saw the wisdom in Lucy's words. "Alright, I'll go look for Tally. The weather's let up some."

"Oh, Jack, if anything happens to you or Tally I won't know what to do."

"Stop worrying so, Mrs. Starr. It'll be fine." He rose and made his way around the room, trying to be as inconspicuous as possible as he headed for the door. His gruff responses to those who wanted to chat prevented any major delays.

When he reached the door he kicked up his heels and broke for the wagon. Water soaked through his boot seams, but he reached the wagon and saw three faces peeping beneath the tarp at him, wide-eyed.

He could see a layer of hail on the tarp and laughed aloud. "Y'all alright under there?"

"I thought we might die," Tally shouted.

"Your ma thinks you might be dead. Better go ease her mind. You can come back when you're done."

She clambered over the side of the wagon, allowing Jack to help her down.

Arnold shook his head. "It was worse than that day we got caught on the caprock."

Cotton caught the sober look on Jack's face. "You alright, Cap'n? You look upset. Somethin' happen in there?"

"Sawyer's thugs just arrived, armed. Dyke and Freeman. They're pushin' folks around. I don't wanna make a scene, but someone might need to put them in their place."

"What are we going to do?" Cotton asked, looking around. "Jangles ain't made it here yet and I'm starting to get worried about him."

"He'll make it alright. But let's focus on the thugs inside. I think the best way to take care of them is lure them out here. I'll call them out and you two can attack them from behind. We got anything heavy and loose we could use?"

Both rangers cast around in the wagon, securing two loose poles tucked under the seat. They climbed out of the wagon as the sun began to shine under the dark

edges of the storm clouds. A few folks had headed outside to check on the weather.

He caught a man who was headed back inside. "Tell
Dyke and Freeman that I want to see them in the yard."

The man cast his eyes around nervously. "I'm not com-
fortable approachin' them. They've got wild tempers on
them. Everyone knows it."

"They don't want you—they want me. I'd appreciate the favor."

The man finally agreed and Jack, with his six-gun
strapped on his hip, walked to the side of the schoolhouse and peaked around the corner. If he had to shoot
them, he didn't want the folks inside in his line of fire.

The front doors were open and light spilled out on
the front stoop and stairs. Jack's gaze was trained on the
entrance. Cotton and Arnold stood against the wall, one
on each side of the doorway, ready to attack.

The first of Sawyer's henchmen came out and peered
around in the night with his hand on his gun butt. Cotton moved quickly and hit him in the back of the head.
He went down like a poleaxed steer.

"Freeman!" His partner rushed out and stumbled over
his prostrate body. Arnold swung and missed his head
but struck him on the shoulder with plenty of force.
Dyke fell to his knees, screaming in pain. Cotton put
his boot to the middle of Dyke's back and shoved him
facedown while Arnold kicked away his pistol and a
large knife.

Jack quickly disarmed Freeman, who was holding
his head and moaning.

"Folks! Folks!" Jack shouted at those who had come

outside to see what the scuffle was all about. "Go back inside and enjoy yourselves. These two won't hurt anyone here tonight."

An elderly woman in a puffy-sleeved poplin dress nodded her approval. "Those men have been terrorizing people all night. Thank you for getting rid of them." She sniffed and walked back inside.

Cotton and Arnold laughed and jostled each other. "You're welcome, ma'am. Anytime!" they called out as they dragged the men toward the base of a tree to tie them up.

"Wait till this is over," Freeman said through his teeth.

Jack caught him by the collar and slammed him against the live oak. "You lay a hand on one of my men, I'll find you and you'd better have your funeral suit on, 'cause I'm planting you. You just got part of what I owe you tonight for that incident in the saloon. You ever come back and try to muscle your way around, I'll hang you by the neck until you're dead."

"I'm not afraid of you," Freeman spat.

Jack lost control. Teeth gritted tight, his hands gripping Freeman's shirt, he slammed the man against the tree trunk hard until he slumped over, unconscious. He stood over him, adrenaline rushing through his body.

"Captain, you alright?" Cotton asked, fear creeping into his voice.

"I'll be fine." Jack drew in a deep breath and leaned against the tree to support himself. "Tie these two up. We can see about them later."

"Yes, sir," the boys answered in unison.

Jack went back inside to find Lucy. She must have seen how upset he was when he found her. She guided him to a private corner.

"What happened out there?"

"We arrested them. But that's not what bothers me. I lost my temper." He licked his lips and stared at the shiny pine flooring.

"Lost your temper?"

He shook his head. "I've had it reined in for a long time. Freeman pushed me over the edge and I about murdered him."

"Maybe he needed it." She patted his back as he leaned forward.

"Of course he needed it. But I didn't need to lose my temper over it. Bad example for the boys."

"I'm certain they know the difference."

Red Larson came toward them and smiled. "Howdy, Lucille. One of these days we'll need a sheriff. Reckon your husband should run for office."

Jack shook his head and smiled weakly. "Not interested."

Red laughed. "You're a hard man to hire."

"Just stubborn is all."

"Those two sure needed a good lesson in manners." Red chuckled and wandered away.

"These men around here sure are persistent enough about hiring you," Lucy said, hoping to cheer him up.

"They're playin' a waltz. Let's dance," he said, ignoring her comment.

They walked to the dance floor and took their positions. "Your daughter says she survived the hailstorm thanks to the rangers."

"My daughter?" Jack asked, confused.

"When she came inside, she said, 'Dad said it was okay to stay out with them.'"

His face lit up. "She called me Dad?"

"Well, only a dad would look after a young girl."

He hugged her close as they swept across the floor. Somehow the notion that Tally had called him Dad cast all negative thoughts out of his mind. Forget Freeman and Dyke. He was a father now.

Chapter 17

When the dance broke up in the dead of the night, close on morning, the two prisoners were untied and sent packing under the threat of death. They wasted no time riding off and everyone clapped their hands, glad to be rid of them. Jack was not satisfied that the matter of the two bullies was resolved, only postponed, but he'd cross that bridge when he came to it.

Tally fashioned herself a pallet in the back of the wagon bed and went to sleep. It was near dawn when they returned to the ranch. Jack lifted his girls down as Luke came out on the porch on his crutches.

"About time you got home. How was it?"

Hugging her bedding, Tally shook her head at him and went inside the house. "It would take all night to tell you. I'm going to bed."

"Hmm," Luke said. "Maybe staying home was the right choice."

"We'll tell you all about it when we can think," Jack said, unhitching the team. "Right now we're pretty well done in."

Luke hobbled along with him to put up the team. "Wish I was going to Fort Worth with you and the guys."

"Oh, there will be other trips." Jack turned the team into the smaller pen. "Right now I just want to sleep a few hours."

"Naw," Luke said. "I smell bacon grease. Mom's about to make us breakfast."

Jack laughed. "Oh well, I'll sleep later, then." On their way back to the house he told Luke all about Freeman and Dyke.

"They'll learn they can't mess with the rangers," Luke said.

"I doubt their kind ever learns anything."

"Kinda like a chicken-eating dog. Can't ever break 'em, huh?"

"Exactly."

That evening his mustangers showed up with Jangles on the wagon and the other two on horseback. After supper they sat on the porch and talked about the drive to Fort Worth. They decided that two twelve-horse lines would be easier to lead, so they set them up for the morning.

That night, Jack and Lucy were in bed, with the sound of crickets chirping in the background.

"How long will you be gone?" Lucy asked.

"A month or so, I figure. It'll take time to get up there and more time to sell them and get back."

"I'll miss you," she whispered.

He rolled over to face her. "I'll miss you too."

"You know folks have asked me to help them convince you to take their cattle to Kansas?"

"What did you tell them?"

"I don't know what to tell them."

"My last trip up there was so bleak. I'll tell you about it sometime. For now, let's sleep. I have a big day ahead tomorrow."

She squeezed his hand. "I'll be here for you."

In the predawn, Jack and his crew washed up on the porch while Tally handed them towels and hot water.

The smell of fried bacon filled the great room when Jack stepped inside. His time with Lucy was always too short. She scurried around putting food on the table— platters of scrambled eggs, bacon, fried potatoes, biscuits and gravy and steaming hot coffee.

How she could look up and smile at him when he could give her only a few days at a time, he'd never know. But she did and she looked happy.

He said grace and they ate. As the sun began to peek into the windows, they left for Fort Worth. With Jangles and the wagon leading the way, they were off to sell the ponies.

North of Austin, a few days from home, a rancher named Ira Tobin and his foreman, Martin Brown, stopped them on the road. Jack swung off his horse and shook the man's hand.

"I reckon you have them for sale," Tobin said as his

man went from horse to horse, looking them over. "My remuda was recently stolen. We think it was Comanches."

Watching the man's close inspection, Jack said, "Shame, but there ain't none of yours in this bunch."

"Oh no, Martin's only checking their age and condition."

"I'd hoped so. We just ran them in off the range, tamed them and rode most of the fire out of them."

Tobin, in a brown suit, white shirt and fine hat, squatted on his heels with Jack. "What do you want for them?"

"Forty bucks a head," Jack said without hesitation.

Tobin made a face like he'd been punched in the gut. "Kinda high, ain't it?"

"There aren't any sleepers in the bunch."

"What about that gruella? He looks like he's been running as a stud."

"He ain't one anymore."

"I can see that. You have a ranch down where you got these?"

"Yes, I do."

"Nine hundred and sixty dollars. That's a lot of money for some untried horses."

Jack shifted his weight to his other leg. "You could probably buy horses cheaper, but I've got two dozen head, sound and all in one place. That would save a lot of time riding all over the country to complete a team, and you'd still not save much over my price."

"Let me talk to my man," Tobin said.

Jack agreed.

Jangles joined him, jerking his head in Tobin's direction. "Is fancy-pants going to buy 'em?"

Jack smiled. "He's considering it. If he does buy them we save a long trip. Comanches got his whole remuda, he thinks."

"Shucks. I was planning on having me a real fandango up there."

"He may be saving you a big headache." They both laughed.

Arnold and Cotton joined them.

"They sure are checking them ponies thoroughly," Arnold said with a wary headshake.

At last Tobin walked over to the shade where Jack and the rangers were lounging.

"I'll give you seven hundred for them," Tobin said, standing with arms folded across his chest.

"No." Jack shook his head. "We can take 'em to Fort Worth and sell 'em for more." The rancher was barking up the wrong tree if he thought he was going to swindle Jack out of more than two hundred dollars.

"What's your bottom dollar?"

Jack rose to face the man. "Nine hundred and sixty dollars. My next offer is a thousand. You want it?"

Tobin shuffled, his face turning bright red. "Can you deliver them to my ranch?"

"How far is it?"

"Eighty miles west of here, near Burnett."

"We'll deliver them."

Tobin stuck out his hand. "I'll have the money there to pay you."

Jack shook his hand. "I'll expect it."

After leaving them a map Tobin and his man rode off. Jack wondered about the man and his finances, but he soon dismissed it. Still, it was strange that they'd both left a ranch alone in Comanche country. Who had Tobin left in charge of his outfit? He'd have to trust that they were legitimate buyers.

"We sell them?" Jangles asked, hitching up his chaps and pants.

"Sold 'em. Got to deliver them, but we sold them and got our price."

"Where's his ranch?"

"Near Burnett."

"West, huh?"

"Right. Why do you ask?"

Jangles shook his head. "Oh, nothing. Just closer to Injun country, ain't it?"

"Yep. Tobin says they stole all his horses."

"That works for us, but I still wanted to see them bright lights."

Jack clapped him on the shoulder. "You're young enough—you'll see lots of bright lights in time."

More than anything, Jack felt relieved that he wasn't going to Fort Worth and would be home with Lucy in a week. They made camp and plans were laid to head west in the morning.

Later, when they were seated around the campfire, Jangles asked, "Cap'n, you ever decide to take another herd north, can the three of us go along?"

Jack looked at their faces in the orange light. "Can you three swim?"

"How far?' Jangles asked, and the other two leaned in to listen.

"Oh, a quarter mile in a raging current."

Jangles looked at the other two. "Well, we can learn, can't we?"

"Sure thing," Cotton said.

"Why's being able to swim so important?" Arnold asked.

"There're two dozen rivers to cross north of here. Some are creeks, others are simply quicksand, and some get up higher than hell in the rainy season."

"You must hate rivers," Cotton said, awed by the information.

"Trust me, there's more than rivers to face. There're rattlesnakes, rabid skunks, rustlers and men ready to loot you at every turn. Throw in stampedes, pneumonia, horse wrecks and bad storms and you've got yourself a cattle drive."

"Have you dealt with all of those things?" Arnold asked.

"Everyone leaving South Texas for Kansas with a large herd experiences all of them." He tossed some small sticks in the red coals and they flared up. "It damn sure ain't no Sunday picnic. Anyway, we better turn in; we've got two long days ahead of us before we get to Tobin's ranch."

"Sold 'em. Wahoo!" Cotton shouted. "You cut a fat hog in the ass. You knew from the start he was going to pay the price you asked for, didn't you?"

Jack nodded. "Figured so. It's hard to find two dozen solid horses in one place."

"Shoot, we'll be rich if we keep this up."

"I looked over the entire country when we were rustlin' them horses," Jack said, "and there wasn't anything left that we didn't already round up. We'll need to find some new sources until the mare market improves."

"When we were cutting them out I wondered about that too," Jangles said with a grim nod. "And we wouldn't be lucky enough to find traps already set up again, I bet."

Jack rose. "Well, I'm ready for bed. Do I have the morning watch?"

"Yep," Cotton said. "I'm first."

"When I pay you boys for the work, maybe y'all could buy yourselves some new pants. Rangers with their asses hanging out don't look too spiffy."

Jangles slapped the deer-hide patch on his butt. "I got most of the hair wore off it."

Jack let out a full-bellied laugh and went off to set up his bedroll. Those boys were dandy, but a little dressing up wouldn't hurt their looks.

In the predawn Jack took his place as guard on a high spot above the camp and horses. Crickets chirped in a chorus and a large barn owl hooted in a deep voice for his mate farther down the valley.

Suddenly, Jack caught sight of something—or someone—creeping toward the camp. One of the horses must have seen it too because it raised its head and pitched its ears up at the disturbance. Soon all the horses were on the alert; Jack could tell from their silhouettes. Something was wrong. On his feet he slipped downhill, staying in the shadows, and eased the hammer back on his Winchester.

Was there more than one person?

When the stranger started to reach for the rope of the first picket, Jack calmly raised his rifle and pointed it at the man's temple. "Hold it right there."

The man stood dead still in his tracks.

"Why'd you come to steal my horses?"

"I just need one," the man said with a slight whimper.

"Stealing one is just as bad as stealing the whole damn bunch."

"I need a horse real bad."

"Who the hell is he and why ain't he dressed?" Jangles demanded, joining Jack with his pistol cocked at the stranger.

"I was just about to ask the same thing."

The man remained silent.

"Who the hell are you?" Jack shouted.

"Wil-Wilburn Shanes."

"What are you doing out here in a nightshirt?"

Shanes swallowed hard. "It was all I had to wear."

"Better than being bare-assed," Jangles said, as Cotton and Arnold joined them.

"Where do you live?" Jack asked.

"Hoover Crick."

"How come you ain't got any clothes on?" Jangles asked, his face betraying his disgust.

"There's no money. And we ain't got any credit. Too dry around here. The cotton ain't gonna make this year."

Jangles uncocked his pistol and put it away. "You must be too damn poor to think."

"We're sure poor as hell."

"What were you going to do with the horse you stole?" Jangles asked.

"Go find something to eat."

"When did you eat last?" Jack asked.

"We had some bullheads to eat day before yesterday. But there ain't no more of them. We used green walnut hulls in a sack to make them float up. But there sure ain't another fish left in that creek. Tried every pool. Got a few minnows is all."

"How many of you are there?"

"Six. My three older brothers rode off. They said I couldn't come with them 'cause I had no clothes."

"Do you know they hang horse thieves in Texas?" Jack asked him.

"I guess hanging ain't no worse than starving to death. You'd get over it a lot quicker."

"Where's the closest store?" Jack asked.

"Mandy's Crossing. It's four miles or so west of here."

"What're we going to do with him, Captain?" Cotton asked.

"I guess find him some clothes and send two sacks of frijoles back to his people."

Shanes blinked, dumbfounded. "I ain't got no money."

"You can work that out," Jack said. "First we need breakfast. Shanes, you help Cotton here get it ready."

"You mean you'd give me a job even though I was about to steal your horse?"

"Don't make me mad. Now get to work." Jack shooed him away.

"What do you think?" Jangles asked after Shanes and Cotton had left.

"I think he's telling us the desperate truth. And I have to say I feel bad for the man. He's got it a lot rougher than some folk. Plus, it sure does beat all, stumbling on a nearly naked horse thief."

"He sure is worse off than we are," Jangles and Arnold said between fits of laughter.

At the store, Jack bought two sacks of frijoles. The boys loaded them over a saddle horse and sent Cotton to deliver them by horseback to Shanes' family.

"Tell them he's found some work and he bought this for them," Jack said. Then he went back inside and bought the boy a pair of waist overalls, two sizes too big. They nearly drowned Shanes' small, thin frame, but after a few rains or washings—and a few meals—they'd fit fine. Jack added a one-piece red underwear suit to the pile along with suspenders, a large whipcord shirt, socks, a pair of brogans and a felt hat. He told Jangles to put leather strings on the hat so he wouldn't lose it. A man not used to wearing a hat would be hatless after a short ride; experience would teach the wearer how to tilt his head just enough to keep the wind from sweeping it up and away.

"Shanes, take that outfit, go out back and get dressed. Arnold you go along and help him."

The ranger made a face over his assignment, but he grabbed some of the things and motioned for Shanes to carry the rest. The storekeeper had been quiet up until then, but he shook his head when the two left.

"Lazy loafers," he said under his breath. "The reason they're broke is they're too damn lazy to work."

"We may change his outlook," Jack said. "In my outfit, every man pulls his own weight or he's gone."

"He won't last long with you, then." The man made a face. "If he ever gets his belly full, he'll fall right back into the mold he came from."

Jack was annoyed with the man and decided he should settle up and leave before he spoke his mind. "How much do I owe you?" he asked.

"Beans and all, I'd take ten dollars."

"Why so much? Show me your list."

The man turned bright red. "Uh, maybe I made a mistake in my arithmetic." The man looked upset as he went back and refigured the total on a piece of brown wrapping paper.

"Them beans were worth two bucks a sack, that's four dollars," Jack pointed out. "Overalls fifty cents, shirt the same, underwear seventy-five, suspenders two bits, shoes a dollar and the same for the hat. That comes to eight bucks. You can throw the socks in and it still won't come to ten bucks."

"That's fine, that's fine," the man said hastily.

Jack counted out the money, adding a few cents for some hard candy for his crew, and went out on the porch to wait for Cotton's return from the Shanes' home. Thankfully he could do simple arithmetic, he thought, or else he'd have been swindled by the bastard.

He wasn't long in coming back and soon they all mounted up. The newly dressed Shanes climbed in the wagon with Jangles and they headed west. There was still plenty of daylight left.

"What did Maw say when you gave her the beans?" Shanes asked when Cotton rode up to the rig.

"'Oh, God bless that boy of mine.' She was mighty happy to receive the present."

Shanes nodded from his seat on the wagon. "I'd've figured she'd cry."

Arnold and Jack each had a line of twelve horses to lead, but by that time they were so well broken, they followed like babies. They traveled the well-used road through the rolling country with little difficulty. German farmers carrying produce in farm wagons let them go by with a solemn nod. None of them cracked a smile and Jack wondered if they ever did.

That evening they secured a place to camp beside a tank with water for two bits from a woman in her forties. Jack could barely understand her broken English, but she understood money well enough.

Jangles dug his mouth harp out of his sack after supper, beat the dust out of it, and played a few tunes to entertain the crew. After singing and laughing for some time, everyone turned in. Jack found Shanes a blanket and the boy thanked him again.

"Just pull your weight around here and we'll be square," Jack said.

Before daylight they mounted up and left. It was midmorning and Jack was scouting the road ahead to make sure there wasn't anything or anyone to impede their progress. Good horses were a commodity that caught the conniving eye of many a white man as well as the Comanches.

A rocky outcropping hung over the road, which looked to Jack like a good place to jump someone. He rode back up a canyon and gained the top. Tall grass, pear cactus beds, and yucca ran wild across the flats there. Satisfied that nothing looked out of place, he dropped back to the road. In another mile he found a freestone-bottom creek and they watered the animals in the midday heat.

Cotton handed out leftover biscuits to everyone and they all squatted in the shade to wash them down with tin cups of fresh water.

"We getting close?" Jangles asked.

"Tomorrow we should find his place," Jack said.

"Jangles said you-all are rangers?" Shanes asked.

"We do ranger work," Jack said.

"I thought rangers worked all the time," Shanes said with a frown, and narrowed his eyes in suspicion.

"In Texas," Cotton said. "You do what you've got to do so folks can live here."

"I guess so," he said, unconvinced.

"You'll learn more if you stick with us," Jack said, motioning that it was time to ride on.

"Captain Starr, kin I become a ranger someday?"

"We'll see. You'll have to prove yourself first. Let's move out, boys. Our daylight's a-burning."

They reached Tobin's ranch the next evening. The layout was what Jack expected, with corrals and buildings made out of lumber rather than adobe. He was impressed with a small irrigation system, which provided water for corn, vegetables and, farther down, green alfalfa. An engineer had laid out the watercourse, which snaked all over to follow a grade.

A woman in her thirties came out on the veranda as they rode up to the house. She wore an elegant divided riding skirt and matching blouse. She stood like a willow tree in a gentle breeze, delicate and poised, casting an eye over the horses before walking to the gate.

"May I help you?"

"You must be Mrs. Tobin." Jack removed his hat and wiped his sweaty forehead on his sleeve before offering his hand to her. "I'm Captain Jack Starr."

"My name is Nilla Tobin. These horses are for sale?"

"In a manner of speaking. Your husband has already agreed to buy them. We came here for delivery and payment."

She shook her head. "He's my brother. I expect him to return any day, but he's not here as yet. Manuel will show you where to put the horses. I'll tell the kitchen servants that we have guests; we'll eat in an hour in the main hall."

Jack nodded to his rangers and they followed her through the yard, entranced by the sway of her hips. There was something special about the woman, a certain quality about her. He never expected to find someone like her in the far reaches of Texas.

"You have a husband?" he asked.

She turned and smiled at him. "At the moment, no. Why do you ask?"

"I simply wondered."

"Are you married?" She showed him to the doorway.

"Yes, with two stepchildren and a ranch in Shedville."

"My, my, I was thinking you might be the soldier of fortune I've been looking for."

Jack blushed, something he rarely did. "Sorry to disappoint you, ma'am."

"No need to apologize. So, Captain Starr, what do you do for a living? You obviously spend at least some of your time trading horses."

"Cash is short in the ranching business these days, so I try to take whatever comes my way." He noted the gleam of her tile floors, which looked too clean to walk on. He hung his hat, gun belt and vest on a wall hook beside the door.

She was standing uncomfortably close to him when he turned to face her.

At a loss for what to say, he blurted out, "Was your husband killed?"

"Oh, dear, must we talk about him?" she cooed.

"I think it's a safe topic."

She laughed, turned on her boot heels and with a flick of her fingers she beckoned him to follow her.

In the large and spacious dining room, she spoke with a Mexican girl who was setting the table, giving directions and gesturing toward the table, then moved to a cabinet and took out a bottle of whiskey. She poured double shots in two glasses and handed one of the glasses to him. "Here's to Texas dust."

He smiled weakly, wondering where the boys were, and quickly downed his whiskey.

Nilla took a large swallow, recorked the bottle with the heel of her hand and lifted her half-full glass again. "And here's to a new Texas."

She studied him intently as they clinked their glasses. He felt like he was being examined by her dark eyes like a horse for sale.

"Why have we never met before?" she asked, leaning forward and running her finger around the rim of her glass. "You hardly look like a sedentary rancher to me."

"I have no idea," Jack said, clearly uncomfortable.

"I've been to Austin for the social season several times." She sipped her whiskey daintily, all the while never taking her eyes off of him.

"I'm sorry to say I've never been."

She raised her eyebrows in surprise. "But you were a captain in the war?"

"Yes. I was a ranger before that."

"And your wife waited for your long-delayed return, I suppose?"

"No, I came home and found my family had been murdered by the Comanches. I met my wife recently at a dance."

Nilla looked amused. "She's lucky, Captain Starr. Very lucky."

"Yes."

"I can see you aren't interested," she said abruptly. "What a waste." She drank the rest of the whiskey in one swallow, stood and smoothed her skirts. "I'm always a day late."

At that moment, the rangers clambered in for supper, followed by three of Nilla's ranch hands. The men looked like typical cowboys to Jack—simple, hardworking, good-natured boys. They wore freshly pressed shirts and Jack wondered whether it was expected of them by the lady of the house.

Nilla proved to be the perfect hostess at the meal and with her looks and charm she held his rangers' attentions. The food was generously portioned and the men ate with gusto. Shanes was agog at his surroundings, as if he couldn't believe such luxury existed in the world. The other rangers, while visibly impressed, were too busy flirting with Nilla between bites of tender beef, frijoles and fresh green beans.

After they finished the meal and thanked the hostess, Jack and his crew retired to the bunkhouse. Monk, who was the *segundo,* offered them hammocks to sleep in instead, since the bunkhouse was often oppressive during the long, hot nights. They accepted and strung them up in the twilight.

Jack hoped Tobin would return shortly; his encounter with Nilla made him want to be at home with Lucy. But as soon as his head hit the netting, he fell asleep and all feelings of homesickness were temporarily put to rest.

Before sunrise he was up and dressed. The light in the kitchen led him to the same Mexican servant from the day before, who was working hard with several other women to prepare breakfast. She quickly served him coffee and he took a stool, observing their tortilla-making process.

In addition to the tortillas, the women tossed scrambled eggs, fresh tomatoes and spices in a large skillet on the range top.

"Go ring the bell for the men," the head cook said to the youngest girl, who rushed out to do her bidding.

In a short while, through the window Jack saw the crew out back, washing their hands and faces. They marched into the kitchen, exchanging pleasantries with the three women. Nilla did not join them for the meal and Jack wondered where she might be.

"While we're waiting for Tobin, why don't you boys team up with the ranch hands and help them out for the day? That alright, Monk?" Jack asked.

"Sure. Can we use some of the new horses? Most of the ones left aren't worth much. The Comanches got all the good ones."

"Use them—they'll be yours soon anyway," Jack said.

The ranch hands and rangers left, and he went into the library to examine a few books and pass the time. He found the selection interesting and was scanning an adventure novel in a corner chair where the light came through the window when Nilla walked in.

"Ah, you can read," she said. She was in a flattering blue duster, standing much too close to his boots.

"I'm looking for pictures," he said with a smile.

"You're a deep person, Captain Starr. I've watched you and I think there's an interesting story behind your one eye," she said, referring to his black eye patch.

"I told you I was in the war and rode with the rangers. An eye is a small casualty compared to what others lost."

She took a seat on the stuffed leather, hardwood-armed chair beside him. Her legs crossed under her duster, she assumed the look and position of one settling in for a long conversation.

"Yes, I remember. So, is Kansas the answer to a rancher's money problems?" she asked.

"It's about the only market we have."

"I heard that many had to pass the winter with their herds up there. They couldn't sell them last fall."

"I didn't go this year."

"Do you raise horses?"

"No, ma'am. I was looking for a project to earn enough money to keep the bills paid."

She shook her head and tossed her long, light brown hair. "I find myself attracted to you. But obviously you don't share that attraction."

Jack was surprised by her brazenness. "Perhaps another time and place," he said uncomfortably. "So, Ms. Tobin, when do you expect your brother to come back?"

She shrugged. "You are, no doubt, ready to ride home?"

"No doubt."

"I can send a man to look for him."

"He said that he'd be here waiting for me. If he's not back here in three days, I'll have to take my horses and leave."

She nodded slowly. "You know he needs them."

"I can sell them in Fort Worth. If he's stalling me,

thinking that I'll take less or let him have them on the credit, he's barking up the wrong tree."

"Plain enough," she said. "Pardon me, but I have something to attend to in the kitchen." She gave him a flirtatious smile and left.

Obviously she wasn't going to offer to pay for them. It became clear to Jack that Tobin didn't have the money for the horses and was off somewhere trying to raise it. But Jack had already made up his mind. He would leave in three days' time, with or without the money. With the faint scent of her perfume in his nostrils, he turned back to the book. He'd have to warn the rangers. This deal wasn't over.

Chapter 18

Tobin and Martin arrived at the ranch the next evening. Jack stood on the porch in the twilight and watched the Mexican handyman lead their spent horses to the barn.

The rancher glanced up at Jack when he started through the yard gate. Tired, he strode up the path to the house, kissed his sister on the cheek and shook Jack's hand. "My apologies, sir. Money is very short in Texas' banks. However, I have the sum you requested. I'm sorry it took so long."

"I'm glad to hear it," Jack said.

"Both of you can come inside and talk," Nilla said. "You too, Martin. I'm certain Ira would like a drink. You as well, Captain Starr?"

He nodded and the men followed her inside. Tobin looked exhausted as he collapsed in a leather-cushioned chair. Nilla moved around, pouring and serving drinks to the men.

Tobin handed him an envelope. "Here's the money."

Jack accepted it and opened the flap. He counted the

money on the table in front of Tobin, and when he was finished he nodded. "Thank you. I appreciate your sister's hospitality and in the morning we'll head for home. Your men have been riding the horses and are satisfied with them."

"His men have been riding each day and helping our men with the daily ranching work," Nilla said.

"Thanks," Tobin said, too tired to muster up much appreciation for the favor. His eyes looked nearly blank as he held his glass.

"Your supper is ready, Mr. Tobin," a young Mexican girl announced.

"Very good, Consuela," Nilla said.

Jack quickly pardoned himself, eager to inform his rangers that they'd be on their way back home come dawn.

When he met them at the back door he smiled. "The horses are sold. We go home tomorrow."

"That's great news!" Jangles said with enthusiasm. "If we hurry we can make the Saturday-night dance." The others nodded their heads eagerly.

After a restless night in which he looked forward to reuniting with Lucy, Jack and his crew woke in the pre-dawn, thanked Nilla and Tobin and readied their horses for the journey home.

"Captain," Nilla called out in a husky voice. "I'll be here or in Austin should you ever . . ." Her voice trailed off as her brother stared at her curiously.

Jack nodded, still a little embarrassed by the woman's openness. Once in the saddle he joined the wagon boys and the other rangers. With a wave they left the ranch. Jack watched Nilla grow smaller in the distance, and though she made a lovely picture in his mind he wanted no part of her. The only woman who would ever mean anything to him, and to whom he would always remain faithful, was Lucy.

After two days of hard pushing they trotted up the dark, dusty, rutted road toward the schoolhouse. Weary and exhausted, Jack's thoughts were on the platters of food and icy-cold lemonade awaiting them. It made Jack think about the first time he met his wife, and he smiled.

The lights of the schoolhouse soon appeared and the rangers let out a whoop. Even Mac seemed more spirited as they turned in the lane and saw the parked wagons, rigs and people socializing on their way inside. He leapt down from the saddle and was immediately greeted by the now-familiar townsfolk. He spoke to a pregnant woman with a crying baby in her arms, offering to take the hot platter of food she had brought inside.

Jangles took Mac's reins and Jack handed his gun and holster to him to slip into his saddlebag. With a tip of his hat to the mother, he headed for the open double doors. He stopped on the threshold to let his eye adjust to the lights.

"It's Captain Starr!" someone shouted, and all heads swiveled toward the door. Gathering her dress in her hand, Lucy quickly rounded the food table and rushed to him.

"How wonderful to see you!" she said, peppering

him with kisses. "You're back much earlier than expected. Did everything go smoothly?"

He told her about their good fortune in finding a horse buyer long before they had reached Fort Worth, and she beamed with pleasure.

"I'm so glad to hear it," she said, giving his hand a good squeeze. Then she motioned with her head toward something behind her. "Look who's finally walking." Jack peered over her shoulder and saw Luke making his way toward them without his crutches.

Jack shook his hand and smiled broadly. "Well, don't you look great? Nice to see you workin' both your legs now." Jack filled Luke in on the events of their trip, but it wasn't long before Tally rushed in to hug him.

"You made fast work of those horses. Are all the rangers here too?" she asked.

"They're puttin' up the horses. We added another to our crew while we were away. His name's Shanes—you'll meet him soon enough."

Lucy tried to maneuver him toward the food table, but he insisted on waiting for his men. Jangles soon appeared and waved to them.

"Slight misunderstanding. But we settled it."

Jack was curious, but he figured he'd ask once Lucy was out of earshot. As the others trooped in, Jack didn't notice anything amiss, but as they went to the end of the food line he nudged Cotton.

"What happened out there?"

Cotton made a sour face. "Some guy made a remark about the rangers."

"Oh yeah? What'd he say?"

"Not worth repeatin', but he'll think a long time before he says anything again."

"Who was it?" Lucy asked quietly, coming up behind them.

Jack picked up a piece of golden fried chicken and spooned some squash and sweet peppers on to his plate. "Don't worry; they settled it."

Lucy took the hint and they chatted about Shanes and how Jack had discovered him trying to steal one of the horses. She shook her head in horror when he told her about his family and she vowed to send another bag of frijoles to them as soon as possible.

She led him to a corner bench and he sat down beside Sister, whom he hadn't seen since their wedding.

"How have you been?" he asked.

"Well, I can see you didn't bring a man back for me, but I guess I'll live." She laughed aloud.

"I had one picked out," he said, taking a bite of chicken, "but he wasn't good enough for you so I had to cut him." Sister and Lucy laughed heartily, and Jack winked at them as he took a bit of sweet peppers.

"Sister will need some help this fall catching calves that got by the spring roundup," Lucy said.

"Luke, Shanes and I would be happy to help. I ain't set on going after more wild horses for a long while. Figure we've caught all the easy ones."

"Will you talk to the ranchers about doing a cattle drive next year, then?" Lucy asked.

Sister paused and looked at him with serious brown eyes. "We need a real trail boss—badly."

Jack thought long and hard for a moment. "Well, I guess I can't say no to my favorite lady and her best friend. I guess it wouldn't hurt to talk to my men about it, but just remember that I can't work any miracles around here."

"Can we call for a meeting at our place tomorrow afternoon?" Lucy asked.

"I'll come over early and help you fix the food," Sister said. "I'll bring Margaret Israel and Red's new wife to help."

Lucy frowned in disapproval.

"Go ahead and say what you're thinking," Jack said under his breath, between bites of food.

"I think she came from a house of ill repute," she said with a little huff.

"Give her the benefit of the doubt. She may have had a tougher life than you two," Jack said.

Lucy gave another little huff, but softened after Jack winked at her.

News traveled fast in the crowd, and as the evening wore on Jack could see there would be several who wanted to join in the drive. He danced with Lucy; having her close stirred his heart as they gently swayed across the floor. The fiddle music soothed him, but the next square dance energized him and he was clapping and swinging in no time.

"We should start home early this evening. There's so much to do to prepare for tomorrow's meeting," Lucy fretted once the square dance was over. Jack knew that Lucy took pleasure in playing the hostess, so he rounded up the rangers and they headed out for the night.

They arrived at the D-T gate a little past midnight, filling the night with their laughter.

"I bet you didn't get much sleep on your way home," Lucy said.

"Ah, we slept some here and there. We all just wanted to get back." He reached over and squeezed her knee. "Especially me."

Leaning her head against his shoulder, she whispered, "I wanted you home too."

Chapter 19

The next day the meeting went smoothly. Tally wrote each person's name down when he arrived and how many cattle he'd pledge to the drive. Jack spoke to the group about the technical aspects of cattle driving while Lucy doled out the food.

"I can't guarantee I can do any better getting your stock to Kansas than any other driver. But I'll try. Between now and the fall, I'll figure out a fair tariff and line up my drivers. I'll be looking for some good hands. Luke and I'll build a chuck-wagon box and start gathering a remuda. If you have a good, solid horse, I'll pay you a fair price for him when the drive is over. But I want only geldings. No cows; just big steers between two and three years old. Those people up there won't buy yearlings. You send me a foot-sore steer and he won't make it. You'd be better off eating him at home."

Everyone laughed.

"Any questions?"

"When you leaving with them?" an older man asked.

"March. Spring marches north fifteen miles a day they say. I'll head them toward the Salt Fork."

"Where's that?" someone piped in.

"Wichita, Kansas," Jack answered. "Anyway, I'll give you-all some time to think things over."

There were murmurs of interest as everyone considered Jack's words and dug into Lucy's delicious barbecue and potato salad.

Jack was surprised he had agreed to another cattle drive. But they needed him. Everyone needed him. Across the room he could see his wife directing young girls with coffeepots toward those with empty cups. Most of all he knew he was doing it for Lucy. Had he lost his ever-loving mind?

Sister hung on his arm. "You don't know how much we appreciate you, Jack. We'd all been so scared we'd done the wrong thing not sending cattle north this year. It really hurt a lot of families. We all need the money."

"The drive's going to work, and we'll turn a nice profit for everyone. It'll be fine." He patted her arm reassuringly.

She smiled and led him to the food table. "I'm making sure he eats enough," she said, passing Lucy with him in tow.

Later, when everyone had gone and the two of them lay in bed together, Lucy said, "You sure eased lots of folks' minds tonight."

He shook his head, rose on his elbow and kissed her. "Everyone's but mine."

She held him and they fell asleep in each other's arms.

*   *   *

Summer passed into fall. The Comanches never showed up, but McIntyre held a confab with Jack and the rangers about doing more patrolling. With the buffalo-hunting season over, they often turned their attention to raids on the settlements, ranches and farms along the frontier. No more soldiers were assigned to the forts than were already there, and there were too few troops to scout such a large area.

The young rangers began a search for signs that Comanches were in the area. Mustangs left poop in a pile, but a moving barefoot horse—which was the manner in which the Comanches liked to ride their horses—scattered it. The rangers came by the ranch on a regular basis and Luke began to patrol with them, despite his mother's unspoken concern for his safety.

Meanwhile Jack and Shanes were busy redoing the wire-stake fencing around the cropland. A couple of Mexicans delivered Jack several oxen *caritas* piled high with cedar stakes and posts that he'd ordered. The fence job proved time consuming, and each month Shanes took a few days off to go back and deliver more food to his family. He reported that they were doing much better.

When he was gone Jack was grateful for the rest, and he would reshoe his horses and use the big gray to do light work. He was sitting on the porch swing one warm late afternoon in early fall, thinking about the coming winter and his firewood supply. Shanes had gone home and the girls were busy canning apples with a new-fangled glass Mason jar system. There were sliced apples drying on racks and cinnamon lingered in the air, drawing saliva from his mouth.

Lucy brought him a hot dish of the fruit and a spoon. She stood by the porch post looking off at the fall-painted hillside as he ate.

"Have you noticed what's been going on?"

Jack scratched his beard. "Probably not."

"Well, there's Tally and the hired man's budding romance, for one."

"Shanes?" Jack said in surprise.

"Yes. I think they're getting serious and I can't say that I like it."

Jack was silent, still dumbfounded by the news.

"I saw him kiss her behind the corral before he left for home."

Jack sighed. "Well, what can I do?"

"Speak to her," Lucy said firmly. "Fifteen is entirely too young to get married."

He blew on the hot apple chunk on his spoon. "How old were you when you got married?"

"That was different," she said, folding her arms across her chest.

"Just tell me, Mrs. Starr."

"Fourteen," she answered, tight-lipped.

"Well, how can I talk to her when you've already set your own example?"

"Well, the least you could do is send him to live with one of the rangers."

He shook his head. "Shanes is learning how to work and he's taking care of his family. He never slacks, never hides on me, never plays sick on me. He's a good worker."

"But he has nothing to offer a bride."

Jack stiffened. "Neither did I."

The words made Lucy soften. "Jack, what should I do?"

"When he returns we'll have a meeting with both of them and learn their intentions."

With a wary shake of her head, she bent over and kissed him. "You seem to have answers for everything."

He sighed. "Well, I don't know how to handle everything. I'm going up to see Craig again and try to get through to him this time."

"Your last trip sure didn't convince him that he should marry Marsha."

Jack shook his head. "He needs Marsha and she needs him. His excuse that the incident with Mrs. Lerner broke his spirit is wearing thin. He's just afraid."

"Of what?"

"Of himself and how he'll handle a wife and married life."

"What will you do to change his mind?"

"That's the thing. I'm still working on it," he said.

Three days later he had a cool ride to Craig's ranch. A north wind was blowing in and he huddled into his unlined jumper, short-loping the gray. He found his man making gate hinges from flat pieces of iron.

"Hi," Craig said, pulling off his leather gloves and shaking Jack's hand. "Been a long time. What can I do you for?"

"I came to get you," Jack announced.

"What for? You got Comanche problems?"

"No, but I've got Preacher Teck at my house and your bride will be waiting for you there. Now go clean up and get ready to ride back, 'cause I ain't taking no for an answer."

Craig peered hard at him. "You're serious."

"I'm as serious as if that girl was my own daughter."

Jack waited to gauge Craig's response, afraid he'd fight him on it. But Craig just dropped his head and laughed. "Well, then, I better get cleaned up—she ain't mad at me for not doing this sooner?"

"No, she's going to be there. Waiting for you."

"Guess you like married life alright if you're pushin' it on an old bachelor."

Jack laughed. "Go clean yourself up. I'll finish these hinges."

Strains of fiddle music wafted in the night air when Jack and his sergeant descended the hill to his ranch. Chinese lanterns were hung along the eaves and from the branches of the trees, and several rigs were parked outside the house. The rangers met them, taking their horses and congratulating Craig.

"When things calm down later tonight, you two can use our bunkhouse. I moved Shanes out for the night," Jack told him.

Craig stuck out his hand and stopped him. "I ain't never done that before."

Jack was stumped. "Well, just let nature take its course and don't be in a hurry." Lord, was that what worried him so much? That's the easy part of marriage, Jack thought.

"You think I'll be alright, then."

"You'll be fine. Don't worry."

Craig grinned and they headed inside.

* * *

The wedding went off without a hitch and the new couple soon slipped away to the fresh sheets in the bunkhouse while the rest of the group danced and partied on the D-T Ranch.

Jack felt smug about his matchmaking abilities until he rounded the corner of the house and caught an entirely different couple kissing.

"I'm sorry, Dad," Tally said, quickly disengaging herself from Shanes and staring intently at her shoes.

Everyone turned bright red. Finally Shanes blurted out, "We can't help it, Captain."

Jack shook his head. "Reckon we better have a meeting in the morning with your mom. I don't think we can put this off any longer."

"You won't send him away, will you?" Tally asked, fear growing in her eyes.

"Captain, I wasn't trying to ruin her reputation," Shanes said, desperation creeping into his voice.

Jack didn't say a word, hoping that his silence would keep them away and off each other until the meeting the next day.

He left Tally and Shanes to return to the party, where Red Larson cornered him next to the lemonade tub, his face filled with anxiety. "I think you ought to know that Hiram Sawyer says he's going to take a herd north in the spring. Anyone owes him any money is going to have to use his herd to ship their cattle."

The news was a sucker punch to the gut.

That son of a bitch, Jack thought.

Chapter 20

"He did what?!" Lucy propped herself up in their bed in the dim light.

"Last night Red told me that Sawyer has been telling folks if they owe him any money they'll have to ship their cattle with his herd."

She chewed her lip. "What will we do?"

"Why, I bet half of the folks that were here last night owe him money. They've had no income so they've all been living on loans."

"Can he stop them?"

"I don't know Texas law that well, but there's probably something in it about removing mortgaged cattle from the state."

"What about your bond?"

"I've been thinking about it. I really expected that issue to be dismissed by now, but Everett will know if I leave the state, which might complicate things for us if I have to go to trial." He stood up and stretched. "Do you think that damn Sawyer was behind my arrest?

I've been thinkin' it all along, but there's no evidence against him."

"I've never said it, but I wondered it too," she confirmed.

"If he was the one, then he's liable to pull the rug out from under me when we get ready to leave, isn't he?"

She lit a candle for them to dress by and blew out the match. "I would say yes."

"I better go see Everett in Austin."

"I'm so sorry, Jack. I shouldn't have asked you to go to Kansas, knowing about your situation."

"Well, let's put it out of our mind for now," he suggested. "Today we need to talk to Tally and Shanes."

She looked at the ceiling for help. "Oh, heavens. What should I say?"

"Ain't no need in getting all upset. Let's see what they want to do. After all, it's their lives, not ours."

"I know. I know. It's just hard when you're expecting your third child, knowing that your second one wants to run off and get married at such a young age."

"Third child?" Jack was blown away by the news.

Lucy beamed. "I'm not entirely sure just yet, but I think we can expect a baby come next April."

"Well, I'll be a horn-swaggled toad!" He picked her up and spun her around, overwhelmed with joy. He saw the tears glistening on her lashes. "Damn, that's exciting news."

With Luke out patrolling with the rangers, the four of them were alone that morning at the ranch. After breakfast Jack called everyone together.

"First of all, it looks bad to have two people living on the same ranch in a relationship out of wedlock."

"We a-ain't doing anything but, um, kissing," Tally stammered.

"I didn't say you were. I said it looked bad in the eyes of other folks. Your mother and I feel that young people who are serious about each other have to realize there are limits."

"Well, I have a resolution," Shanes nervously piped in. "If we got married, we could make everything right in the eyes of God and everyone else."

Tally quickly agreed.

"Marriage is forever," Jack said sternly. "It's a serious commitment. You would need a ranch or a better job to support a wife."

Shanes threw open his palms. "I can work. I'm learning lots of things. I know I can't sit on my backside and expect manna to fall from heaven. Tally and I could live in the bunkhouse until we find a place. I'd never let her starve, or even come close to it."

Lucy had remained silent until then. "I hope to God you know there's more to marriage than kissing. You'll have babies and bills and obligations." She began to scrub at the tabletop furiously with a washcloth before collapsing into her chair in tears. "I'm not ready for my baby to be a wife and a mother. But if it's what you really want, Tally, I'll get ready. We'll help you any way we can."

Tally walked around the table and embraced her mother. "We plan to be married on Christmas Eve." She squeezed her mother's hands. "Don't cry, please."

"Well, we give you our blessings," Jack said. "And while we're discussing big life changes we might as well tell them our news," Jack said to Lucy.

Lucy nodded. "Next spring," she said, blowing her nose in the handkerchief he handed her, "we're having a baby."

The kids leapt up from their chairs and let out a whoop. It was a helluva morning for the Starr family. He wasn't married a year yet and he'd soon be a father and probably a grandfather. He thought about his grandmother in heaven and smiled. I hope you're proud, Grandma. I'm really a family man now.

The town of Austin was already up and energized when Jack walked from the livery stables to the café early in the morning. It was crowded with folks gobbling down their breakfast before rushing off to work. His greatest concern was that Everett would be out of town and he wouldn't be able to learn the status of his case and what he needed to do to leave Texas legally on the cattle drive. He ordered food and sipped the bitter coffee the waitress poured for him. No wonder folks used cream; a cup like that needed quite a lot to mask the taste.

He waited in the hallway of Everett's office building. A young clerk opened the door on his way in to work and caught sight of him. "May I help you?" he asked.

"Is Mr. Everett going to be in today? My name is Jack Starr. Everett represented me in a murder case that's still pending."

"Oh, I've heard about you. I'm Steven. He should be here around nine or ten. Come in."

Jack busied himself reading the morning newspaper that Steven had provided. Not that he gave a damn about anything in the pages, but he needed something to pass the time and keep his mind occupied.

When Everett strode in, he smiled. "Jack Starr, what a pleasant surprise. How are you?"

He rose and shook the man's hand. "I've come for some counsel, sir. I need to take a cattle herd to Kansas next spring and wanted to know my status with the courts."

Everett let out a low whistle. "I'm afraid I can't answer that question for you, but let's go see the state prosecutor and get this sorted out. Steven, we're going to the attorney general's building," he said as they left the office.

"Penskey, the state prosecutor, has your case now," he informed Jack once they stepped outside. "He's a good man. Not prone to corruption like some others."

After a taxi ride to the attorney general's building, they were ushered into the private office of the prosecutor.

A round-shouldered man whom Jack supposed was Penskey peered up at them from behind thick glasses and asked his law assistant to find the case papers. He sat behind his polished desk, steepled his fingers and cleared his throat. "Does Mr. Starr know we have had several requests for rearrest?"

"On what charges?" Everett asked in surprise.

"Some are worried that you might be a threat to the community."

"Can I ask the name of the man who's made these

requests?" Jack asked, trying to keep a tight lid on his temper.

Penskey shook his head. "I'm afraid I can't confirm or deny anything."

"Was his name Hiram Sawyer?"

Penskey remained silent, but Jack could tell he'd hit the nail on the head.

"If you don't have a recorded mortgage on livestock, can they be moved out of state for sale?" Jack asked, switching tracks.

"Certainly. Why do you ask?"

"I'm putting together a cattle drive to Kansas and Hiram Sawyer is forcing people to ship their cattle with him rather than me, claiming he has a mortgage on them and they can't be moved without his permission."

"Is it recorded?"

"I doubt it. But Hiram acts like he's law around these parts."

The office assistant returned with Jack's file and Penskey dismissed him.

Jack leaned forward and tapped the file. "Tell me about the correspondence on this case. I need to know who's behind this. Someone pointed a finger at me that started all this business."

Penskey read through several documents and nodded. "Well, it seems that a Mr. Sawyer of Bexar County brought you to the attention of the state police regarding the matter of this murder." Penskey looked up, puzzled. "Bexar County?"

"Bexar has jurisdiction over lots of land in south-central Texas since there's no organized government in those places," Everett explained.

"Who is this Sawyer?"

"A back-pocket banker who lends money at high rates and rips off honest, hardworking people," Jack said, trying not to sound too embittered.

"Why is he after you?" Penskey asked, leaning back in his chair and steepling his fingers.

"I married a woman he had intentions on and whose ranch he's been coveting since she was widowed. But she'd never marry the likes of him and I can't say that I blame her."

Penskey processed the information. "There was a creditable enough witness at your bond hearing who claimed you were in Kansas at the time of the shooting. I see no reason why the charges can't be dropped. I'll initiate the paperwork and make sure the bond gets refunded to you."

Everett slapped him on the back. "How does that feel?" he asked.

Jack stood and shook Penskey and Everett's hands. "It's a big load off my shoulders. Thanks very much, gentlemen."

"Let's go find some lunch, Jack. Penskey, I'll expect those release papers on my desk in a few days," Everett said.

Out in the sunshine, the relief of his dismissal made him weak-legged as he headed for a nearby restaurant with Everett. He had never been quite aware of how serious the effects could've been if he hadn't found a good attorney and a reasonable state prosecutor to drop the charges. Hiram Sawyer could've ruined his life—or worse, got him shot or hung.

"What happens next, Jack?"

"I get ready for Kansas; or better yet, Kansas better get ready for me."

Both men laughed.

After he left Austin he rode south to San Antonio and went to the county records office with a list of names of people he knew or suspected had loans with Sawyer. None were listed as having liens on the books. Just as he suspected, Sawyer was too cheap to come down and file the liens. All that Sawyer had were pieces of paper with no legal value. Jack rejoiced, but he had to keep that knowledge quiet until the herd was in Indian Territory in the Nations. Sawyer'd really have no say once he was there.

His weeklong odyssey ended when he was back at the D-T ranch gate. He led Gray through and rechained him. From the top of the hill he could hear the dogs barking. Shanes ran out to wave at him, along with Lucy and Tally. Jack felt as good as he ever had in his life.

"I'm a free man," he said as he embraced Lucy and shook Shanes' hand. "They've dropped all the charges." He hugged her close again, lifting her feet off the ground.

"Better news yet. If we don't force Sawyer's hand till the end, he can't stop us."

"How's that?" Lucy asked, leaning back in his arms to search his face.

"I'll explain it all later." Recalling her delicate condition, he set her down gently.

She swept the hair back from her face and shook her head. "You must be exhausted."

He handed the reins to Shanes. "I'm not, but Gray is. We've been to Austin and San Antonio. Grain him good, Shanes."

"I will," he said. He and Tally headed for the corrals and saddle shed with the horse.

Lucy linked his left arm in hers. "Tell me all about it."

He recounted the details all the way to the kitchen table. The stiff Texas north wind outdoors made him glad to be inside the cozy house.

The next day he rode over to talk to McIntyre about the situation.

"So Sawyer turned you over to the state police?" he asked.

"One way to get rid of me. Almost."

"I don't like night riders but this is a case when people need to take things into their own hands. He needs to be run out of the country, and that saloon needs to be pulled down to the ground."

Jack shook his head. "I shouldn't be the point man on this one. It'll just give him more fuel to start the fire against me."

"I can handle it," McIntyre reassured him. If you want to be the little bird in the tree and watch, I'll send word when it'll happen."

"I don't want you to endanger yourself or your neighbors on my behalf."

McIntyre clapped his hand on Jack's shoulder. "We all owe you for what you've done. You haven't been here long, but you sure've made a difference in all our lives."

Jack shook his head to dismiss the compliment. "That's water under the bridge."

As he rode home, he thought about his conversation with McIntyre. Were night riders the answer? He didn't think so, but some folks would be up in arms when they learned the truth about Sawyer's cheating ways. Perhaps he better stay out of it.

Three days later, back to fence-building with Shanes, Jack was tamping in a new post when Jangles rode up.

"Howdy, Captain." He leapt off his horse with a clink of his spurs.

"You boys been riding hard?"

"Yep, tracing out every clue or tip we get on them Injuns. They've been careful. Not riding in the open. Hard to keep track of them." Jangles waved to Shanes, who was working down the line. Then he lowered his voice. "Captain, tonight's the night. They're closing the saloon and delivering Sawyer the word to get out or be burned out."

Jack nodded and Jangles made a swift swinging leap into the saddle and nodded back. "Ten o'clock."

He spurred his horse down to Shanes. The two spoke for a few minutes, then Jangles rode out with a wave. When the ranger was gone Shanes came over to Jack.

"Jangles ain't himself," Shanes said grimly.

"How's that? I didn't notice anything."

"Well, for one, he ain't singing."

"Good observation. He must have some things on his mind."

"Must be real serious." Shanes took a drink from the water jug.

"I wouldn't jump to that conclusion. Anyway, let's call it a day."

Wiping his mouth on his sleeve, Shanes looked back down the repaired section of fence line. "Lucy ought to be proud; we about have it fixed."

"Hog-tight, goat-proof and horse-high."

After supper that evening Jack excused himself and rode into Shedville. He kept to himself, letting other riders pass him, and trying to stay within the shade of the trees. When he reached Shedville, he sat back and watched the action from a distance. He saw a dozen riders ride up in flour-sack masks and go into the saloon. He didn't recognize any of them, but some of their horses looked familiar. There was a short scuffle inside and soon five men came outside with their hands in the air and rifles pointed at their backs.

Ropes were tied to the building and ponies were hitched at the other ends. Even from far away he could see their muscles straining as they moved forward in unison, bringing the rickety saloon down with a thunderous crash. Flames from the fallen lanterns, which had been hanging on the eaves, ignited the wreck, and a giant fire began to spread. The blaze grew higher in seconds, consuming the rotten wood of the former saloon. Jack heard the riders shout, "Leave town at once or you'll be lynched." The arrested men looked terrified and Jack could see that one of them had wet himself.

The masked crew left the scene and rode like a funeral procession to Sawyer's place. Jack followed, still maintaining his distance. When they arrived they surrounded his house in a semicircle and demanded that Sawyer come out.

He appeared at the doorway wearing a nightcap and robe, a look of confusion on his face.

"What is the meaning of this?" he demanded.

The leader of the group, whom Jack could only speculate was McIntyre, spoke up. "You have four weeks to move on. If you don't, we'll burn you out lock, stock and barrel."

Sawyer's face was purple with rage. "You can't do this!"

"The saloon is gone now." The masked leader pointed to the smoke rising over the hilltops. "See that blaze, Hiram? Your friends have even less time than you do to move on. If I were you I'd be close on their heels."

"I'll foreclose on every one of you sumbitches," Sawyer screamed, charging off his porch.

"I'd heed our warning," the leader said. "The first foreclosure will be your last. We'll lynch you on the spot."

Waving his fists, Sawyer shouted, "I'll have the law down here on all of you!"

"Find a suit and coffin on your way." The leader turned his horse to leave and the rifle-bearing masked riders began to file out.

"I know who you are! I ain't moving! This is my land."

Under the cold stars, hunched in his wool coat, Jack rode home. They'd run off Sawyer's men—there was no doubt in his mind that they'd heed the masked men's warning. But what worried him more was the next bunch that Sawyer would hire. They'd be tougher than the last bunch. Hiram wasn't the type to cut and run. But only time would tell.

He told Lucy about the saloon when he crawled into bed with her later that night.

He lay on his side and curled himself around her back, wrapping his arms around her waist. After all the nights he'd slept alone, there was nothing better than this. But it was best not to get too used to having her next to him. His bedroll would be mighty lonely for months on the drive north.

Chapter 21

Jack, Shanes and Luke broke thirty acres of land that winter for spring corn planting. The ground was ready to be harrowed and sown. There was a lot of work ahead, but a good corn crop that size would save them from buying feed the following winter. The nearby thirty acres of short oats needed rain, but it was doing well and should furnish enough hay for the milk cows and horses. It was an ambitious plan, but they had bought a good used Oliver mowing machine, so Shanes would be able to handle the farming and cut some hay if the rains came while Jack was away.

Luke was going north with the herd, but only after a long talk with his mother. He'd be joining Jack's usual crew: Jangles, Cotton and Arnold. That made four, but he needed eight more drivers and a cook before he could leave. McIntyre said he could handle the scouting without them, but he needed the younger rangers to stay on patrol. Jack spent two days a week looking for more riders to hire.

Some came by the ranch and asked for work. He

culled the ones who were too young, couldn't swim, couldn't ride a horse or just had bad attitudes.

He was offering forty a month plus a bonus if they got there in one piece. Word began to spread and three men rode in from Fort Worth to apply for jobs. Experienced riders, they'd heard about the generous pay and wanted to see for themselves whether it was true. Clayton, a lanky veteran of the war, Earl, a shorter version of Clayton, and Shanks, a tall, bowlegged drink of water, looked like good recruits to Jack. Clayton said he knew a good cook who'd be happy to join the crew. Two Mexican boys, Raul and Peso, rode in the next week. They were good hands with horses and both swore they could swim. Jack hired them, impressed with their demonstrated roping skills.

Once the beginnings of a crew were assembled they spent their time taking the hump out of the horses that Jack had collected. Some were branded range horses that the rangers had rerounded and brought down. Most of their owners either sold them to him or let him use them. He planned on taking a hundred of them. That gave each puncher a horse a day for a week. Not graining them would let the individual ponies have time to recover from a long workday and left plenty of mounts if things got tough. They'd lose some on the way, but that was unavoidable.

A Mexican youth named Estefan arrived and asked for the wrangler job. In the corral he showed Jack his roping skills. He was one of the best Jack had ever seen and he was hired on the spot.

Claude arrived strumming a small bug and singing

some song about Texas. He was no kid, and his face was the color of saddle leather and the brim of his hat was pinned up. He looked the part of a cowboy, but Jack was uncertain.

"Where all have you been?" he asked.

"Well, Mr. Jack, I was in Sedalia, Missouri, Abilene and Newton. I brung plenty of them steers out of old Mexico."

Jack was impressed and hired him, his crew nearly complete.

The last two to round out the group of drivers were teenage boys from a nearby town: Hank and Either. The latter had received his name from his pa, who'd been inebriated and ran off shortly after he was born. The name stuck.

The horses were costing him a rack of hay a week. By February the team divided into two and was going from ranch to ranch, trail branding the shipping stock with a bar burned high on the right side. It was a basic logistical necessity, but it also allowed Jack to see the quality of the livestock. He cut some of the older ones by looking at their long horns, wanting only the highest-quality steers on the drive. Jangles did the cattle appraisal for the second group.

At Collier Place there were several steers in the back pens he could see were too young to go on the drive.

"Aw," Clifton Collier complained. "Them's near two years old."

"They ain't old enough." With his saddle horn cap in his hand, Jack stood in his stirrups, looking the pen over. "I need only twos and threes."

"If you knew how badly I need the money—"

"I know how badly you need the money," Jack interrupted. "But they ain't old enough. You got some older stock, we'll take 'em."

"You're a hard man," Collier said, and watched as the hands cut out several head.

But he had to be a hard man. Unsellable cattle were just deadweight. He hoped that Jangles was being just as tough with his branding crew. There was only one market up there: big-framed steers they could hang some meat on.

It was past sundown when he and his crew came in, dog-tired and dusty. The women set to feeding them as soon as they walked through the door.

"Jangles and his bunch aren't back yet," Lucy whispered.

Jack sighed. "I better ride their way and see about them."

"Want me to go along?" Luke offered.

"No, eat your supper and get some rest. We still have lots of branding to do tomorrow."

He looked disappointed, but agreed.

Shanes walked Jack to the pens. "I went into town for supplies today. I heard that Sawyer is fixing to bring some law up here from San Antonio to stop you."

"I don't doubt it. Living clear down in Fredericksburg ain't helping him keep tabs on us. Must be driving him nuts. But my lawyer says he can't stop cattle already consigned to a cattle shipment. We get them branded, they ain't his and I have all the consignment papers dated so he can't file a lien after the fact. He's out on a limb."

Shanes laughed. "You sure know your law. Anyway, when you get back from Kansas you may be a grand-daddy, or close to being one."

Jack's eyes brightened. "I certainly wouldn't mind that. Our babies can grow up together."

Shanes looked equally excited. "I just hope I can get the corn planted to suit you."

"Don't worry about the small stuff. You're going to make a helluva farmer."

"I hope so. I want to pass these skills on to my future son."

Jack walked back to the house, his mind turning to other things. He'd liked to have Craig go along to Kansas, but when Jangles had branded his cattle earlier that week, Craig hadn't said a word about joining the crew. But Jangles was stepping up as a solid second in command, and Jack was grateful for that.

Under the stars he rode west on the dim road through the shadowy cedars in search of his missing crew. In the distance he heard a cow bawl for her calf, and around a turn three deer leapt in front of him across the path and spooked Mac sideways. Jack turned his coat collar up and the crisp night air cooled his face while he pushed on.

The lights were on at the Sorensons' place, so he reined up and Lex came out on the porch.

"You're getting around late."

"I'm looking for my crew. They didn't come in to-night."

Lex scratched his thin scalp in the light streaming from the house. "They're over at Trainer's, ain't they?"

"Supposed to be."

"I ain't seen 'em come back, Jack."

"I'll head over there. Thanks." He set Mac on a long lope.

When he dropped off the ridge and started down the grade to Wilborn Creek, there were no lights on that he could see at the Trainers' place. Jack started to worry. Jangles had planned to come back to the D-T by supper and the Trainers' ranch was supposed to be his last stop for the evening.

He shifted the holster on his hip out of a nervous habit. Things were not right. Anxious about the situation, he drew his Colt and reined Mac off the road. He paused and listened, but nothing. When he drew near the house he hooted and waited.

"Come on in, we won't shoot you," Jangles shouted from the doorway.

"What's going on?" Jack asked, dismounting at the house.

"About a half dozen Comanches rode up the hillside today while we were branding. We figured there'd be more so we stayed here just in case. Turned out the lights so as not to attract attention. You see anything?"

"No, it's darker than a cave out here. No moon. It surprises me they're even down here."

"Hell, we all seen them. Thought they might be part of a bigger party."

"It's best you stayed here. No telling what might've happened. Come dawn we'll go check their tracks."

"Good idea. You know Mrs. Trainer?" Jangles asked, gesturing to a woman with a short cob pipe between her teeth.

"Good evening, ma'am," Jack said pleasantly.

"Call me Zelda. I'm sure grateful these boys stayed. Robert and I are alone out here."

Jack saw Robert through the doorway, coming across the yard. "See anything out there?"

"No, guess they rode on. Thanks to these boys," Robert said, warmly shaking Jack's hand. "Nice to see you, Captain Starr."

Jack turned to Jangles. "Did you complete the branding?"

"Yes, sir, Captain. We have them all branded."

"You might as well stay too," Zelda chimed in. "Ain't no sense in losing your head out there. I'll find you a few blankets. You can sleep on the floor in front of the fireplace with the rest of them."

He agreed, hoping that Lucy wouldn't get too worried about him.

In the morning, Zelda fed them a big breakfast and Jack and Jangles went to check on the Comanche tracks while the others loaded the squeeze chute in the wagon. He could only hope his other crew had ridden out that morning without him to the Carlsons' ranch to continue the branding.

The war party, by all signs, was headed back north

on what looked like trotting ponies. They hadn't lingered long, but Jack told Jangles that they'd done the right thing by waiting till morning.

On the way back to the ranch, they met Red and two of his vaqueros.

"What's happening, Captain?"

"Boys had some visitors yesterday over at Trainer's. A small war party showed up on the hillside and the boys stayed overnight to be certain they were gone. Guess the bucks kept on riding, from what Jangles and I saw this morning."

"They've acted half spooked all winter. I was sure they'd have tried something by now. Their old ponies must be getting thin with no hay."

"You're right as rain."

Red and his vaqueros moved aside as the wagon and crew caught up. Jack saluted Red and they moved on.

Midday they arrived back at the ranch. Lucy, her face looking pale but relieved, ran to him. She was getting big, and he could see she was having some difficulty moving quickly.

Jack filled her in on the adventures of the previous night, but not without Lucy's face turning two shades paler before returning to normal.

"Claude took the crew this morning and went on to Carlson's. They took bedrolls in case they didn't get through."

Jack nodded, pleased. He was only weeks from heading out with the herd and everything needed to be done before they left. The women had dinner ready, so they marched to the house, washed up and ate. After the meal Jack told his crew to get their saddles and tack in top shape.

Estefan waited by the door until they all filed out. "Señor, I have some horses you need to look at."

A look of concern crossed Jack's face. "What's the matter with them?"

"Two have bad backs," Estefan attested.

They went into the corral. Each questionable horse was haltered and tied neatly in a row. Jack could see the fistulas on the first two horses, both from a neighboring rancher. After only a few days of riding, the swollen sores behind their withers were seeping fluid and blood. Damn, so that's why the rancher had turned them out, Jack thought. The problem looked chronic.

Estefan raised the hind foot on a third horse. The hoof was badly cracked and the animal would soon be crippled. Jack realized they were all range horses and he began to worry. The fourth and fifth horses had severe cases of ringbone, an affliction to the pastern bones on the front legs of horses that lamed them when they were used too hard.

The next two had bad coughs and were wind broke.

"I need seven more horses?" Jack asked the youth.

"*Sí.* These *caballos* are no good, señor."

"I guess we should put them out of their misery. I'll inform the owners later."

He complimented Estefan's work before he went about the rest of his checkups. He felt lucky to have the boy. He decided to check on Ralph, his new cook, down by the shop. The man was so organized he'd spent his days making cabinets and arranging all the food supplies on the chuck wagon.

"How's it going?" Jack asked.

Ralph was busy making a new singletree on a sawhorse bench with a clamp. "You know how many of these I broke going to Abilene?"

"How many?"

"Sixteen. Mostly it was the rotten wood they were made out of, but the mules I had were rowdy too. Jim Hamilton was the trail boss and he got to cussing me about breaking them on purpose. I got so mad I wanted to split his head open with one, but I figured that would break it and I'd be out of spares."

Jack let out a belly laugh. "He was sure lucky you held back."

"He damn sure was."

Ralph was a typical cowboy-turned-camp-cook, which he had become on account of his gimpy leg. But he could cook a mean meal, and he understood that eating was the only luxury for a cow outfit on the road. Jack noted that he'd also make an excellent nursemaid for the boys and a pretty good horse doctor to boot. But his real skill lay in his ability to whip up a gourmet feast out of the simplest ingredients. Even Lucy said his pecan pie was as good as any woman's.

Jack saw Estefan ride on horseback, driving the culls out to an open field, where he would put them out of their misery. Jack was pained to lose seven horses, but he'd rather not ride them into the ground.

He felt lucky to have a strong crew to take on the road. Estefan would have the horses culled to a decent stand. Jangles was looking for a good bell steer to lead them. Ralph was making sure the wagon was sound and ready. But his hay expenses kept growing. All of the nearby range was cropped off after a dry winter. Keeping any number of animals in one place required forage, which was why he was branding them on their home ranches instead of bringing them to his own ranch. A hundred horses and four mules could eat enough store-bought hay to put a man in debt.

The days trickled by and some showers passed through. The weather warmed, but they awoke to hoarfrost on the ground a time or two. Jack had word that the range north of them had plenty of grass for grazing. He hoped there was enough forage between Lost Dog Creek and the Red River to hang some meat on the steers' hips.

In bed with his wife, he rubbed her swollen belly and they discussed baby names. Jack suggested Cory in honor of his brother, but he was afraid he'd bring bad luck to the child.

"What about Dallas?" he asked, after staring at the ceiling for some time.

Lucy sat up on her elbow. "That's beautiful, and it would work for a boy and a girl."

Jack beamed, pleased he had suggested a name they could both agree on. He rolled over and kissed her good night.

"We won't have many more nights together," Lucy said, nestling into him. "Let's make these last ones count."

Chapter 22

The next week, Jack learned that Sawyer was back in town. He'd been stopping at ranches that owed him money, letting them know that his trail-driving crew would be by to pick up their cattle in three weeks for Kansas. Jack had expected this and had told the ranchers not to argue. He could only hope that Sawyer was dumb enough to believe they'd all agree to his terms, though the saloon incident had made it perfectly clear how everyone felt about the man.

McIntyre told him there were three hard cases riding with Sawyer, all of whom wore low-slung six-guns, leather cuffs on their wrists, and acted as tough as a pack of Louisiana fighting curs. Jack was sure these men cost Sawyer more than his last crew, and they wouldn't be as easy to subdue as Dyke and Freeman.

McIntyre scowled at Jack as he described them. "I want to tie a tin can on their tails and send them back to San Antonio."

"This is the best way," Jack gently reminded him. "If he thinks he's pulling one over on them he won't think to bring down an injunction, and by the time he realizes that no one will comply he won't have enough time to get one."

McIntyre grudgingly agreed, but Jack could see the boiling hatred in his eyes for Sawyer.

Later that day Jack began to collect the cattle and prepare for the long drive. He had enough hay scattered on the ground of the corrals to fill the bellies of the first round of cattle, but the subsequent groups would be driven ten miles north, where Ralph and Estefan would set up camp on the grassy plains and ensure that the cattle had plenty of room to graze. In three days' time, the entire herd of two thousand would be collected on what they called the Frenchman's Flats, ready to head north to the Salt Fork.

At the end of the three days he kissed Lucy good-bye. By the time he got back he'd be a father. Her pregnancy was going smoothly and she begged him not to worry. He was reluctant to let go of her, but in the end he placed his hat atop his head, mounted Mac and headed north with his crew.

Clayton and Shanks were his point riders and Jangles was his second in command. As for the rest of his drivers, each day a different one would scout ahead for the next campsite and help Ralph set up before riding back to report.

River crossing proved easier than usual. The lack of rain was a blessing for them, although he knew the ranchers were paying for it in other ways. In ten days they were on the Trinity River, which put them close to Fort Worth. They soon closed the gap and swung west of the fenced country.

Ralph and Jack purchased some food and first-aid items in town while the crew caught their breath and regreased the wagon axles. Down in the stockyard district, he ate lunch in a café and listened to the other drivers discuss when they'd be leaving for Kansas. Jack worried that he'd left too early, but he knew he had to be in Indian Territory and out of Sawyer's reach as soon as possible.

By evening he was back with the herd. The weather held and the cattle were docile now that they had established a ranking system among themselves. The worst-behaved one of the bunch had disrupted the rhythm of the drive so much that Jack had ordered he be butchered and served for dinner. Ralph kept the carcass under a wet canvas to keep it from spoiling, breaking up some of the monotony of eating beans everyday. They roasted some cuts, fried some and pounded others into steaks; the rest was made into stew. The boys respected his decision-making abilities. They'd lose money on the head, but it was a small loss compared to the damage he could've caused if Jack had let him live.

At their first campsite north of Fort Worth, Jack could smell a skunk from the chuck wagon. His nose wrinkled, he dismounted and tied his bay horse to the front wheel.

"What in the hell happened here?"

"Rabid skunk came up over there. Had to shoot him

with my .22," Ralph said. "I already had the wagon set up, so I didn't want to move. You'll get used to the smell in a while. I sure have."

Jack wasn't certain he'd ever get used to it. "You sure he was rabid?"

"Anytime you see a drunk-acting skunk in the daylight, he's rabid."

"I've heard of cowboys getting bit at night and dying a sad, pain-filled death," Jack said.

"I had a friend who died from a bite," Ralph began. "Went delirious. He asked us to put him out of his misery when it got really bad. We drew for the high card, and I was the one who had to pull the trigger. Worst day of my life."

Jack closed his eyes. A man never forgot something like that. He knew that Ralph had done the right thing, but the job of compassionate executioner was never an easy one. He went and found one of the whiskey bottles and poured three fingers' worth of the amber liquid into two tin cups for himself and Ralph.

"We need a little pick-me-up," Jack said. He raised his cup. "To your friend. May he rest in peace." Ralph clinked his cup against Jack's as they settled into canvas chairs.

They sat in silence for some time until Jack spoke up. "You ever know a guy named Julius Knotts?"

"Name sounds familiar," Ralph said, taking a sip from the cup.

"He shot my brother in Abilene years ago."

"I'm sorry to hear that," Ralph said. "I take it you've been looking for him ever since?"

"Ever since."

"It's hard, Captain, to live with things like that. Damn hard."

"Don't I know it. My life took a good turn when I met and married Lucy. But I've never forgotten my brother. The war. All those bad drives."

"She's a good woman. She may not be able to erase those memories, but she'll support you the rest of the way and that's all that matters."

Jack nodded appreciatively and they sat in silence once again.

Finally he said, "When the boys come let's move this camp. Even this damn whiskey tastes like skunk."

Ralph laughed and agreed.

A week later Jack and Jangles scouted the snag-choked Red River. On the far shore was Indian Territory. This was the last chance that Sawyer had to stop his crew. Ralph and the chuck wagon could go over by ferry in the morning, but the rest of them would cross the river in a serpentine formation with the steers. Jack knew that some of them would break, and some might even drown, but it was the best way to go.

"It won't be easy," Jangles said, "but I guess a million head have crossed here."

"They have. But it's one of the tougher ones," Jack admitted.

"I'll ask Claude to say a prayer. He reads the Bible all the time."

Jack agreed. "Some intervention from God could only help with this one."

At daybreak they had the herd lined up. Jack told them to undress at the river; Jangles would see that all their clothes got across in the chuck wagon. They could swim easier naked.

Claude gave a long prayer once they reached the shore, asking God to protect them on their journey across the river. When the prayer was finished they lined up to cross the river. They had a new lead steer—a big dapple red—that would take them across, but Jack was worried that he'd turn out to be like the previous two lead steers they'd tried, both of which failed them. But a good bell steer was worth a fortune for a reason: they didn't come easy.

The naked riders looked like white ghosts in the pale morning sunshine, which was just beginning to filter over the horizon. Jack figured the temperature was less than fifty degrees, and he could only imagine what the water would be like. A shudder went through his body. He prayed they didn't have to spend too long in the river.

Red took to the water and started swimming for the north shore like he'd done it a million times. Some steers leapt way out on their bellies while others calmly waded in and began to swim. The naked cowboys led their horses across the water as best they could. A few of the less intelligent steers swam downstream despite the drivers shouts and curses, but the first of the herd to cross were soon shaking the water from their bodies and collecting on the north bank. Shanks, one of his point riders, was trying hard to get them started uphill. He and Claude, joined by one of the dripping Mexican hands, finally got them going up the road. Things started to go more smoothly after that, but there were still more than two dozen head either stuck on snags and bawling or floundering where the bank was too steep and the water too deep to wade in.

Jack caught sight of Luke trying to drive some of them upstream, but the cattle kept circling back. He waved his jumper and shouted to Shanks, figuring he'd know what to do. Shanks shouted and waved to a spot where the bank gently sloped upward from the river.

Luke went around the river bend and out of sight downstream. Jack couldn't help but worry. If anything happened to the boy it would be his fault, and Lucy would have his hide.

"You see Luke?" Jangles asked.

"Shanks told him to go farther down."

"I ain't seen him since he went around the corner. It must be deep over there."

"I wouldn't worry about Luke. We still have three head caught on snags."

"What do we do about them?" Jangles asked, loading the clothing in the chuck wagon as they prepared to go across on the ferry.

"Our best swimmer needs to go out there and tie ropes around them; we'll fish them out with the horses."

"Bet you won't get many volunteers for that job."

"We'll see."

Jack and Jangles loaded the wagon and mules aboard the ferry and boarded on their horses. When they reached the other side, Jack rode Mac off the barge and short-loped him through the post oaks until he saw Shanks and Luke driving the remaining wet steers through the brush. He was proud of Luke—he'd saved over a dozen head that day.

Wrapped in blankets, the shivering hands crowded around the fire Ralph had built on the shore. Jack dismounted.

"All the hands here, Jangles?"

"Yes, sir."

"Good. Now, who's going to swim and help us fish out those three snagged steers?"

"It's only two now, Captain. One got loose and swam up here," Jangles said.

"I can swim out there when I warm up a little, Captain," Arnold said.

Jack clapped him on the shoulder in appreciation.

Barefoot and naked, Luke joined them, shivering down to his bones. Ralph threw a blanket over him.

"How did we do?" Luke asked, his teeth chattering.

"Pretty good. Just need to get those snagged steers and we can head on out," Jack said.

"So I didn't freeze my ass off for nothing," Luke said, and they all laughed. "It's hard to herd cattle, hold on to your horse's tail and swim at the same time. Doesn't help that those steers are dumb as rocks too."

As the crew warmed up, Arnold, rope in hand, swam out to the first steer. The angry bovine wanted to fight him, but the ranger finally got the loop around his horns.

Arnold waved for them to go ahead and swam back to the shore. Shanks and two of the Mexican hands created a lariat at the end of the rope that could be tied to multiple horses. Urging them on, the horses slowly pulled the floundering steer out of the snag. The men and the horses kept slipping on the shore, which had been muddied by thousands of cattle hooves, but they finally pulled the steer from the snag. He came swimming to shore, lowing angrily.

Raul heeled him and stretched him out while Jangles removed the loop of rope.

Arnold, who had been warming by the fire, took the rope and started out toward the second steer. "Let's get this over with."

He waded out and as he drew closer the steer started to throw a fit, and Arnold was forced to swim out and come in from the back. He climbed on the steer, riding him like a horse, and fashioned the loop around his huge horns. The spectators shouted and applauded. When he was finished he stood up on the steer's back and dove back into the muddy water.

Arnold swam to shore as the men pulled the steer through the water. Suddenly the longhorn flipped over and all they could see were his four legs thrashing above the water. Jack felt sure they'd have to eat him, but the steer righted himself and sprayed water like a geyser. Raul rode in and took off the lariat and the steer joined his brothers on the shore. The men cheered. They were finally in Indian Territory, and out of the reach of Hiram Sawyer.

Chapter 23

"They can't bother us up here," Jangles said. "Right?"

"Right," Jack said, cradling a cup of hot coffee in the light of the burning post oak logs.

"There's no authority on this side of the Red River," Jangles said, a little awed.

"Yep, no Texas lawman can come up here and serve papers to us. Only a U.S. marshal can do that."

"Hell, I'd like to have shown my ass to that damn Sawyer back at the river," Jangles said with a laugh.

"You wouldn't need to," Cotton said. "We were all bare-assed for you."

The whole crew laughed.

"How far are we from Kansas?" Cotton asked.

"A month," Jangles said. "But it won't take us a month to get back here."

"No, it won't, since our load will be considerably lighter. But remember, it may take time to sell these steers," Jack warned.

"I'd like to be home by the Fourth of July," Cotton said. "I think we can make it."

"We ain't across Indian Territory yet," Jack said with a laugh. "We still have a long way to go."

They turned in for the night, relieved that the day was finally over.

"Nice to be warm at last," Arnold said from his bedroll.

"Damn nice. I never was so cold in all my life," Cotton answered.

"Hell, Cotton, you didn't offer to swim back and get those steers."

"Naw, I figured ten more minutes in that cold water and I'd be a steer myself."

Somewhere out in the night a buffalo wolf gave a long, mournful howl while the boys talked from their bedrolls. Jack rolled over and closed his eyes and sleep came swiftly.

A few warmer days followed the river crossing. Plum thickets were in bloom and Indian paintbrush flowers added a look of brightly burning flames to the prairie. Firewood grew scarce as they moved along, and the drivers had to drag every dead branch they could find on the way to their next campsite. Ralph had a leather sack made from old cowhides under the wagon to hold the wood. When they ran out they gathered dry cow pies and buffalo chips. Jack hadn't seen any of the shaggy beasts since his first drive to Kansas, when there were still small herds roaming the prairies.

As they were plodding along one day, Jack was overwhelmed by a bad feeling. He watched the clear azure

sky all day while the temperature rose. The winds grew
still and sweat ran down his face.

Earlier he'd mentioned it to Ralph over breakfast. "I've
got a gut feeling you'll need to pick high ground for
our camp tonight. There wasn't any dew on the ground
this morning, and my grandfather always said you're
liable to get a gully washer when that happens." Ralph
had agreed and set out early along with Luke to scout
for the next camp.

Jack noticed how the good grass they'd found in the
Indian Territory was beginning to show on his herd.
He watched several steers rise at the bell call and lick
the hair on their sides in swirls. They looked healthy,
but the realization didn't ease his bad feeling about the
weather.

By afternoon they reached their new campground. The
steers were scattered, grazing with cowbirds. Most of
the cowboys lounged or slept in their bedrolls. Rest
was short and far between in a driver's life. Each had to
pull two-hour shifts to guard the herd each night, which
gave them even less rest than they wanted. Some of the
cowboys would spend the early evening mending their
pants or reading the Bible; others would study tattered
copies of the *Police Gazette*. But most simply slept.

Too tired to argue and too busy to do much more
than punch cattle, Jack noticed that even Jangles hadn't
been singing much since they'd crossed the Red River.
But he knew he needed to trust his men to take care of
themselves.

He pushed a white-legged horse called Socks to a high

point west of the camp to scope out the surroundings. There was a small glimpse of a cloud bank that he could barely make out in the northwest. He wasn't sure if they were out of reach of the coming storm, but he prayed they hadn't used up all their good luck.

Riding back to camp, he knew the best thing to do was to head out before the storm struck. Otherwise, he risked a stampede. He didn't want to lose a single head—not if he could help it.

He dismounted at the chuck wagon and Ralph met him with a cup of coffee. "You see anything?"

"There's a cloud wall up there. Doesn't look good for us. Are there any rivers nearby?"

"Naw. It's pretty much all rolling country. I don't think we'll have to worry about flooding. But I'll rope and stake the wagon, just in case."

Jack nodded. "I'll tell the boys to keep their horses saddled."

He put Socks on the picket line and walked to where the men were playing cards. "Everyone, keep your ponies saddled. We may have a big storm coming in."

Cotton shook his head. "We've been lucky so far."

Jangles agreed and discarded two cards.

"It might miss us, but if it's coming we'll have to head the cattle up and go."

The boys nodded gravely and Jack returned to the chuck wagon. "When's your young 'un due?" Ralph asked, lugging his Dutch oven full of browned biscuits to the fly.

"Late April, early May."

"Your first child?" Ralph asked.

"Yeah, I left the bachelor game a little later than some."

"I'd say you're lucky. Mrs. Starr is a real nice lady."

"I'm satisfied," he said as he squatted down and cut in half the steaming hot biscuit Ralph had given him. "Satisfied" was an understatement. Lucy fit him like a good glove and he missed her terribly. The hardest part of the job was their separation. But if they stayed on track he'd be home long before fall.

The storm rolled in after sundown. A wall of roaring thunder, steel blue lightning and torrential rain bore down on them.

The crew quickly pulled on their rubber slickers and swung into their saddles. The smell of nitrogen and sulfur filled the hot air.

"Everyone needs to be careful and keep track of each other—this is going to be a real test for us," Jack shouted between loud cracks of thunder.

"You nailed it down?" he shouted at Ralph as the wind shook the hooped canvas top of the wagon.

"Best as I could," the cook yelled back.

They rode off as Estefan led the remuda through stinging sheets of rain. He was glad he could count on the boy to keep the horses together, and he knew there was little chance of Estefan losing a single one.

Jack's main concern was the steers. In the flashes of lightning, he could see the hard drops of rain pelting their hides, followed by nickel-sized hailstones. He began herding the stragglers with Jangles, beating a reata on his chaps to move the slowest steers along. Even in a thunderstorm, some steers needed to be driven hard.

Wind threatened to force him out of the saddle and Socks spooked easily at the lightning, swinging hard to the right whenever a particularly large bolt would touch down. Jack spurred him on, chasing after the longhorns who hadn't joined the line yet.

Soon the four riders had all the cattle lined up and moving. The rain was so oppressive that it was hard to see between the lightning flashes. Jack and Jangles shared a quick nod in passing, then were separated by the curtain of rain. Everyone moved in unison with the herd.

Filled with a deep sense of urgency Jack tried his best to keep everyone moving. But it was worse than the storm on the caprock, especially now that they had two thousand steers to contain and manage. He wondered how many of his boys would be hurt, but just as he started to make a loop around the herd, he felt Socks stumble and go down underneath him.

He kicked free of the stirrups, hoping he was clear enough of the cattle not to get trampled if he needed to leap for it. But when Socks' head hit the dirt, he was propelled out of the saddle before he could make the jump. He landed hard and rolled just shy of the herd.

Raul rode up and offered his arm to swing Jack up behind him. Knowing that Socks was lost, he had no choice but to accept Raul's arm. The driver rode east away from the herd and Jack dropped off. Raul rode on to tend to the herd.

There wasn't much he could do until daybreak but worry about his crew and wait for them to catch up. What felt like a lifetime later, the rain let up and moved northeast. He could see enough by the stars to backtrack the cattle and find the wagon. If Ralph was alright, he'd want to catch up with the crew and make breakfast.

The boys would be beaten half to death. They'd had no sleep and they'd chased cattle all night in the pounding rain. He could sleep for a month himself.

When he reached the wagon in the pink predawn, Ralph was straightening the hoops and tarp of the wagon cover.

"You alright, Captain?"

"Yep, just lost my horse. He went down in the storm and Raul hauled me out of there."

"Glad you made it okay. I'm about ready to hook up, so we can go see where they ended up."

With the mules hitched to the wagon and both men on the spring seat, they headed north. The wagon rocked from side to side over the rough spots and the mules brayed woefully, tired from the storm. But Ralph reined them in and they trotted complacently into the night.

Jack saw Jangles coming up hard, sliding to a halt when he finally reached them.

"Oh, thank gawd." He shook his head in disbelief. "You alright, Captain?"

Jack stood up in the wagon. "I'm fine. How's the crew?"

"We're looking for one of the boys. Either's missing." Jangles said.

"They figure he's alright?'

"He had a bad runaway horse that got spooked by the storm."

Jack was worried, but he didn't want to jump the gun

until they had more information. "Did you see Socks on the trail?"

"Yep, I left your saddle beside the trail. Had to shoot him. His leg was broken when I found him."

Jack thanked him and Jangles nodded. "I'm going to look for Either."

"Good young man," Ralph said as Jangles galloped away. "I figured he was just a kid when I first met him, but he's a solid second in command. He's the real deal." He slapped the lazy right-hand mule's back with the lines and continued on.

Jack felt trapped on the wagon seat without a horse. He wondered what else they'd lost and he wished he could join Jangles in the search for Either. There was no telling what could've happened to him.

When they spotted Either's sack beside the trail, Ralph pulled over. Jack loaded the saddle, pad, and bridle on the chuck wagon, then they drove on. There was no sign of the horse. An hour later they found the crew dressing two fallen steers under a lone cottonwood.

"How is everyone?" Jack asked.

"Fine," Shanks said, using his large knife to skin the second one.

"Did Either show up? Jangles was looking for him."

"I'm here, Captain. My horse ran away and I got lost in the dark, but even on this great prairie a man can't help but run into a crowd of two thousand steers."

"I'm glad you could take care of yourself," Jack said, clapping him on the back. "Now, one of you boys ride back and find Jangles. He's worried and looking all over for Either."

Raul volunteered and the rest continued carving up the meat.

"Boss man," Shanks said, waving the knife at one of the hanging steers. "Ain't no way we can eat both of them before they rot. We been talking; there were two Injun women here this morning and we gave them all the guts. They said they had nothing left to eat."

"You want them to have one of the steers?"

"Thought it would be the right thing to do; there ain't no market for them out here."

"You know where they live?"

"It can't be far."

"You get 'em skinned, load one on a horse, take a couple of the boys and go play Santa Claus."

Everyone laughed, feeling good about the charitable act.

"I'll have some breakfast shortly," Ralph promised.

"We couldn't find but them two crippled steers this morning," Luke said. "Pretty damn scary business, running out there in the dark. I wondered what I'd tell Maw if you didn't show up."

"I had the same problem when you went out of sight around that bend in the Red River."

Luke smiled sheepishly. "Hell, I was alright."

He hugged the boy's shoulder. "Well, now we don't have to tell her a thing."

Luke laughed. "Amen. Amen."

Chapter 24

After the crew was reassembled, they rested for two days. The Indian camp, which consisted mostly of women and small children, had a big feast and the women brought Jack a brightly colored embroidered shirt as a thank-you gift.

"Thank you," he said politely, not sure if he'd ever have an occasion to wear such a garment. "Where are your men?" he asked.

"Building railroad far away." The oldest of the women waved her arm toward the north.

"You reckon they're working or off raiding?" Jangles muttered under his breath after they'd left.

"Exactly my thoughts. Tomorrow I'll ride up north and look things over. Can you get this outfit on the road if I leave early?" Jack asked him.

"Do you think anything's wrong?"

"Probably nothing to do with Injuns. But it reminded me that the last time I was up here there were some gangs that raided cattle drives and folks moving through on the Kansas–Indian Territory borders. They were peddling moonshine liquor and causing trouble. They'd avoid U.S. marshals by going into Kansas when things got too heated."

"You need any backing?"

"Naw, just keep the cattle moving. I'll be back before you have to cross the Canadian."

After he left camp he short-loped Mac toward Kansas. When he crossed the Canadian on the ferry, which was run by a grizzly faced black man, he asked him, "Is there still a gang or two up here causing trouble?"

Pulling on the towrope hand over hand, the man nodded. "They be several of dem up here."

"Ever hear of a man called Julius Knotts?" he asked.

"I's don't know them names. They's come through here sometimes and I minds my own business."

"I understand."

"Yessuh, de best way to get youself killed is to ask questions of the likes of them."

"You hear any names of their gangs?"

"No, suh."

Jack found a store at the next road crossing. JENNINGS' STORE, the hand-painted sign read. He dismounted and went inside. The store had a crisp smell, and the woman behind the counter wore a clean dress and a starched apron.

"May I help you?"

"I was looking to buy some lunch."

"We have meat or cheese sandwiches for ten cents, sir."

"You have ham?"

"Yes, wonderful smoked ham on freshly baked bread."

"Sounds good—I'll take two of 'em." He waited until she had prepared the sandwiches before asking his next questions.

"I'm looking for a man called Knotts. Julius Knotts. You ever heard of him?"

She tilted her head. "Why do you ask? You don't look like the law. Are you a bounty man?"

"I might be; I might not be. You know where he is?"

She smirked, placing a hand on her hip. "For a price, perhaps."

"How much?"

"Ten dollars. I don't think that's an unfair price. Everyone's got to get by."

Jack wasn't sure he agreed, but he counted out ten silver dollars on the smooth wood counter between them and leaned over until his face was level with hers. "Where can I find him?"

"He's staying at Barney Snows' place," she said as she quickly tucked the money into her apron.

"You're sure?"

"He's been there for a few months."

"Who's this Barney Snows?"

"A bootlegger and outlaw. Word has it he was the mastermind behind the robbery of the Seminole Annuity two years ago."

"They never caught him?"

"They caught a few others and hung them for it at Fort Smith, but no one could lay their hands on Snows. They never did get any of the gold back either."

"There's another two dollars in it for you if you can

draw me a map," he said, smiling broadly and flashing his teeth.

"I will, sir—" She looked around to be certain they were alone. "But you've got to promise you won't tell anyone."

"On my soul, I promise."

"It could sure get me killed if that bunch knew I was giving out information about them."

"I won't let that happen," Jack said, shaking his head.

"Okay, I'll draw you the map."

She took a sheet of butcher paper and pencil and quickly sketched out a route. Jack stood over her, watching the long, clean lines she drew with such precision. At last he might've found the scoundrel. If Knotts stayed put until the cattle were sold he'd be back for him. A smile crossed his lips; he might even bring some Texas Rangers along for the party as well. For the first time since he stood in the streets of Abilene that hot summer night over his brother's dead body, he felt good. Lighter, as if a weight had been lifted. Come summer he knew the matter would be resolved.

He thanked and paid the woman, pocketed the map and circled south to rejoin the crew shortly after supper.

"Have a good day?" Ralph asked, bringing over a cloth-covered plate of food for him.

"Good enough day, thanks." He dug into the pan-fried steak and beans. "Any troubles?" he asked Jangles, who took a place on the ground beside him.

"We lost another horse. Figure he got snake bit the night before."

"We're gettin' kinda hard up for horses," Jack said between bites.

"That, indeed. We'll try to avoid losing any more. You do any good today?"

Jack nodded and lowered his voice. "We'll do something about it later. But I found the guy who shot my brother."

Jangles' eyes lit up. "That's swell news! We can go over there in the morning."

Jack shook his head, raising his hand to stop him. "We've got cattle to move to Wichita. We can settle with him on the way back."

"But, Captain, what if he takes off before we get back?" Jangles asked anxiously.

"Well, that's a risk I'm willing to take. I promised Lucy I'd make this my first priority, and I'm not going to risk the cattle drive for a personal revenge mission."

Jangles nodded. "You're at least takin' us rangers, right?"

"Don't I always?"

Jangles smiled. "I reckon so."

"At the rate we're going, we should be there in two to three weeks. If we sell the cattle quickly, I can give Knotts what's coming to him."

"You got any notion if the market's up or down?"

"No, but I'll ride up there when we get closer and look for some buyers."

"You know this job gives me a bellyache sometimes, but I kinda like being the boss," Jangles said with a grin.

* * *

A storm approached the next afternoon, but in the end the clouds slid north, much to Jack's approval. The cooler air made the next two days and nights easier to handle.

"Can you see the North Pole from Kansas?" Cotton asked, huddled under his unlined jumper at breakfast one morning.

"I doubt it. I never saw the glare from it up in Abilene. But I did see the northern lights," Jack said.

"What're they?"

"Some strange, colored streaks in the northern sky at night."

"How far are the Rocky Mountains from here?" one of the boys asked.

"Five hundred miles, I'd guess."

"Ah hell, I ain't gonna go there, then. My butt's too sore now."

Everyone laughed.

Before they stopped for the day, Jack met a lone cowboy headed south. He was unshaven and red-eyed, like he'd been riding without sleep for days. His clothes were wrinkled and well-worn, and the horse he rode was a common bay with a bushy mane.

"You ain't got the makings have you?" he asked Jack.

"Nope, I don't smoke."

The rider twisted in the saddle and looked over the line of cattle passing them. "You're going to be the first herd up here."

"That's our intention," Jack said.

The man made a sour face. "I don't know if that's a good idea. There's a group of delinquents in these parts called the Caughman Gang. They'll probably sweep in here on you and take the whole herd."

Jack frowned. "When should I expect them?"

"First rainy night, I'd say."

"Who leads them?"

"A mean old bastard. Got flaming red hair to match his temper. He don't leave any witnesses."

"Any special place he's liable to strike?"

"After you cross a river, usually. Everyone's worn out and his bunch steps in."

Jack stuck out his hand. "Name's Captain Jack Starr. Didn't catch your name."

"Smith." He shook Jack's hand firmly.

"Well, Mr. Smith, here's a few dollars to buy the makings. It's a long way back to Texas without a smoke." He doubted the man's name was Smith, but he'd given some valuable advice and Jack was grateful.

"I'm beholden to you, Captain." He spurred his horse and moved on. Jack thanked his lucky stars for meeting the mysterious stranger.

In camp that night, he called the boys together after supper and told them what Smith had told him.

"You figure he was serious?" Jangles asked. "Or just bumming money?"

"We wouldn't be the first crew shot dead by rustlers," Jack said.

"We'll sleep with our guns," Jangles said.

, "Post a camp guard."

"We can do that. And they do it in the rain, huh?" Cotton asked.

"Unless we get too close to Wichita before it rains again. I figure they use the rain for cover to take advantage of the confusion."

"I'll be gawdamned," Jangles swore. "If it ain't one thing, it's another. Captain, we'll be ready for them, rain or shine."

Jack began using his field glasses to see if anyone was sizing the herd. But nothing seemed out of the ordinary until the rain moved in a few days later. Before they halted for the night he saw three riders pass by, headed south, standing in their stirrups. They avoided looking in his direction, but he knew it was a sign.

His camp was armed through supper. They stayed under an extra fly that Ralph had attached to the wagon while they ate. Wind whipped the sheet and rain pounded from all sides. A more miserable night to ride the herd and watch for bushwhackers couldn't have been designed.

Jack heard someone say "Psst" over the wind and he knew someone was coming. Either was under the wagon armed with a rifle and Jack nodded to him in the dim light of the fire.

"Get your hands up!" a gruff voice shouted from the darkness.

That would be the last thing the outlaw ever ordered, Jack decided. Either answered the order with several loud cracks into the darkness. The crew reached for their holsters and in seconds six-guns blazed and men screamed as the drivers cut them down. Despite the fact that they couldn't see well for the misty rain, it was over before they knew it.

Outside the fly's protection Jack waited for Ralph to light his candle reflector lamp so he could survey the scene. A Colt in one fist, he raised the lantern with his other hand to see the outlaws on the ground, their limbs splayed, either dead or dying. The whole shootout took less than two minutes. Had they not been warned it easily could have been his crew on the ground.

"Any get away?" Jack asked.

"Naw, there's two I shot over here," Either said.

"Your surprise worked pretty good, Captain," Jangles said. "I was worried the shots might frighten the cattle, but they never even got up. Guess they couldn't hear it from a distance." Jangles gathered the rustlers' hardware.

"How many more are there?" Cotton asked.

"Ask him," Jack said, jerking his head toward one lying on his back with his eyes half open.

"Where's the rest of your bunch?" Jangles asked the man, but the outlaw coughed weakly, a bubble of blood forming on his lips, and died.

The Mexican hands managed to drag the dead ones from the other side of the wagon near the fly.

Jack stood back and wondered about the grizzled cowboy who'd warned him. Was he once a member of this gang and wanted revenge? No matter who he was, Jack owed him one. Jack was happy to exact some justice on this drive. It was all practice for when he'd come face-to-face with Cory's killer.

Chapter 25

They buried the outlaws in a shallow mass grave, then tailed up the lead steer at dawn and struck out north for the Salt Fork. His men were showing signs of wear and tear; they were as testy with one another as curs. Thankfully there was only a week or so left until they reached Wichita. Ralph said he knew a place where they could find decent water while the cattle and horses grazed.

The overall improved conditions of the cattle impressed Jack. They'd been putting on a lot of pounds since they reached northern Texas, and subsequent creek crossings after Red River had been a breeze, since most of them were shallow in this part of Indian Territory. They'd lost more than a dozen horses so far, but the remuda looked surprisingly well. Only his sleepy-eyed, cranky cowboys looked the worse for wear, but they'd have to hold tight. Kansas was nearby.

Midmorning, two men in suits rode up to Jack, who rested on a rise. They nodded to each other as they reined in their horses. The taller one spoke first.

"U.S deputy marshals McCory and Snyder." McCory indicated the man beside him, who was shorter and had a mustache. Snyder nodded.

"Jack Starr. What can I do for you?"

"We're looking for some whiskey peddlers bringing liquor out of Kansas."

"I guess that goes on all the time, the territory being dry and all."

"It sure is hell to enforce too. There're more miles than deputy marshals."

Jack nodded sympathetically.

"You got a real early start. Bet you're the first new herd we've seen this spring."

"Yes, and I'm eager to get home. You hear anything about the steer market?"

"Must be alright. They've been shipping out the herds that wintered over in these parts with no problem."

"Good to hear," Jack said, pleased.

"You ever hear anything about the Caughman Gang coming up here?" McCory asked.

"I heard about so many I can't keep track of them all."

"The leader is a big man with a bushy red beard. He's cagey, but we'll catch him. Him and his gang have been robbing whole herds on the way into Kansas, and drivers on their way out with their pockets stuffed full of money."

"I'll try to remember that," Jack said. He wanted to tell them that Caughman and his gang were planted under territory sod. They were out of the robbery business and roasting in hell, for his part. But he thought better of it. He didn't want to let on that he'd been tipped off by a possible ex–gang member. He owed the cowboy that much.

He saluted the deputy marshals and they moved on.

Short-loping Mac, he came over a hill half an hour later and reined up at the sight of two women in bright red and blue dresses, standing beside a light buggy with a shattered wheel. Hair piled high on top of their heads in elaborate styles, they held their wide-brimmed straw hats at their sides and considered the broken spokes, which didn't look repairable from Jack's point of view.

"Good day, ladies," he said.

The blonde in the blue dress smiled like a sly fox and used the side of her hand to shade out the sun. "Well, darling," she drawled in a thick Georgia accent. "Ain't you a sight for sore eyes."

"Looks like you two are in a fix," he said.

"We ain't never in a fix with a man around," the brunet said, and winked at her friend. She pulled up her low-cut dress, which barely covered her white bosoms. "But I must say we're not often rescued by someone as good-looking as you. What's your name, sugar?"

"Captain Jack Starr."

"I'm Strawberry Rose and she's Texas Flower." The blonde indicated her darker-haired partner. "How do we get out of here alive?"

"My boys are breaking camp just north of here. When I reach them, I'll come with four of my boys for you and your luggage. Where are you headed?"

"We're going to Wichita, same as every other traveler in these parts," Rose said.

"Well, I'd be happy to take you gals on with us."

"Yeehaw!" Flower yelled, lifting her skirt and petticoats and doing a quick jig in her high-buttoned shoes. "He ain't going to leave us out here for the Injuns to eat."

"It'll be several hours before I can get there and back," Jack warned.

"One of us can ride the buggy horse and the other can ride double with you on your pony," Rose suggested, and her partner giggled. "That way, you won't be leaving us in harm's way." She batted her eyelashes prettily.

"You girls are plumb resourceful," he said, laughing out loud. These two beauties should perk up the crew, he thought.

Flower rode behind him, hugging his waist, but he worried the whole time that his horse might buck them off. In an hour they found the chuck wagon. Ralph's eyes about bugged out of their sockets at the sight of the girls.

Jack rode up to the wagon and lowered Flower down to the ground. "Ralph, take Flower here with you to camp. Their buggy broke down, so we'll need to send some boys back for their things when we make camp." He introduced Rose, who was riding the buggy horse behind them.

After doffing his hat Ralph pulled Flower up to the spring seat. "I'll see to it, Captain."

"Whew," Flower said. "This is a heck of a lot nicer than riding behind you, Captain. But I still love you." She threw kisses to Jack.

The camp felt more alive than ever that evening. A

couple of the boys pulled out fiddles and Flower danced
for them while Ralph and Rose fixed supper. Meanwhile Jangles took a few of the boys to fetch the girls'
luggage. As everyone laughed and chatted, Jack could
tell that every one of the boys was smitten with them. It
was too bad the girls couldn't stay on with them for the
rest of the trip, but they had places to go and things to
see. The cowboy's life wasn't for them.

Before turning in for the night, Jack spoke to Estefan
about picking the gentlest horses for the girls to ride on
their way into Wichita. The buggy horse would carry
most of their luggage and the rest of their possessions
would be loaded onto the chuck wagon, which they
would deliver once they had reached town themselves.

The next morning the girls thanked and kissed everyone in the crew good-bye and rode off waving ker-
chiefs at them. Jack was thoroughly amused by the turn
of events. He hoped the boys' spirits would remain high
until they got to Wichita.

By the end of the week, he rode into the tent city on
the bank of the Arkansas River. He recognized a cattle
buyer crossing the street on foot. The man waved him
down. "Hello, Mr. Starr. It's Larry Sorrel. You brought
cattle up here before, right?"

Jack reined in Gray and nodded to the man. "Nice to
see you again, Mr. Sorrel. I've got a good herd coming
in behind me as we speak."

"I could certainly use some cattle. How many you
got?"

"Close to two thousand head."

Sorrel let out a low whistle. "What's the makeup of the herd?"

"Steers: twos and threes only."

Sorrel's eyes brightened. "I'm interested. Where are you at?"

"Six miles south."

"Great. I'll be by in the morning to ride through them."

"Bring your wallet," Jack said.

"I pay the best prices in town."

"We'll see, won't we?"

"Don't promise them to anyone until I have a chance to bid on them, okay?"

"You have my word, Mr. Sorrel. See you in the morning," Jack said, tipping his hat.

He hitched Gray outside a tent marked MIDWEST CATTLE BUYERS. HIGHEST PRICES PAID FOR YOUR CATTLE. Jack went inside and nodded to the young clerk at the desk.

"May I help you?"

"I have a herd of steers from Texas I just drove up yesterday."

The clerk gave him a look of boredom and went back to his paperwork. "There's paper and pencil there. Leave the information."

"I rode up here to talk to a cattle buyer."

"They're all busy."

Jack stood back from the wooden desk, which looked out of place in a tent pitched over thinning grass. He had to work hard to rein in his temper. After weather-

ing storms and battling river currents, he wasn't about
to let a snot-nosed clerk tell him who he could and
couldn't see.

In two steps he reached over the desk and had the
clerk by the coat collar. He lifted him out of his chair
and halfway across the desk, jerking him up to his face.
"Gawdamnit, I want to talk to a cattle buyer, not some
weaselly little clerk that don't know beans about this
business. Now, you find me someone to talk to or I'll
turn you into cattle feed, am I clear?"

The clerk was too terrified to speak and only nodded his head quickly to show that he understood.

Breathing fire out of his nostrils, Jack shoved the
man back down into his chair.

Looking white as a sheet, the clerk ran behind the
sheet partition. Jack could hear him whispering to another man behind the sheet. "Sir. Sir, there is a madman
out there who wants to talk to you, sir."

"Did you tell him I was busy?" the man asked gruffly.

"He was rather persistent, sir."

"Well, I guess I could give him a minute."

"Sir?"

"Yes, Adam?"

"He's violent, sir."

Jack couldn't help but laugh at his effect on the boy.
In a matter of seconds, a short man with a full mus-
tache appeared in front of the sheet. "My name is Charles
Manning. How can I help you, sir?"

Jack cleared his throat. "I wanted to speak to someone about my herd. I didn't drive two thousand cattle
several hundred miles to fill out a slip."

"We don't take cows or heifers—"

"I have two thousand two- and three-year-old steers. Not a cow or heifer in the bunch," Jack interrupted.

"Well, that would be a first for me."

"If you find one cow with our road brand on it, I'll pay you a hundred dollars."

"My, my. You sound quite sure of yourself."

"Driving cattle is my business. Are you interested in the herd?"

"I must say you have one of the first herds up here this year. I'll have to see how the market is doing this morning."

"Fine. But are you interested?"

"I'd be happy to take a look. Now, where is this herd located?"

"Six miles or so south and west of the trail."

"And your name again, sir?"

"Captain Jack Starr."

"Good to meet you, Captain Starr. I'll be out there tomorrow."

"Thank you, sir." He left the tent and walked out into the brilliant Kansas sunshine. One more buyer would be enough. Then word would be out about his cattle, piquing interest and encouraging others to drive out for a look-see.

"Captain, oh, Captain!" It was Rose with her arms full of purchases, standing in the middle of the street. "How are your wonderful cowboys?"

He tipped his hat to her. "Doing fine, ma'am. We'll have your other things up here in the early afternoon."

"Why, Captain Starr, any old time you want to bring

them by is fine. We're working at the Beguine House. You can't miss it. We're in a tent right now, but the lumber is being shipped here. Come by and see us any time, Captain. Things are a little slow until the other herds get in here."

He agreed and waved good-bye. A good stein of cold beer would hit the spot before he went back to the herd. He entered the Texas Saloon tent and noticed the place was nearly empty. The makeshift bar—planks on barrels—and a smiling barkeep welcomed him and he ordered a beer.

"You bring cattle up?" the red-faced man in the white apron asked.

"Yes. Reckon I'm the first herd up here."

"Good. We all moved down here and figured we'd starve if some of you-all didn't start coming."

"Oh, I suspect there's a lot of herds starting out by now."

"We sure need the business."

After draining the last drop of beer, he left the Texas Saloon and started for Gray. But he couldn't miss the pair of hard-eyed hombres loafing around his horse. Both wore bull-hide chaps, vests and six-guns. One looked no older than Luke; the other, maybe near his own age, had a bad scar from a knife cut across his left cheek.

"Can I help you?" Jack asked, wondering what the interest was in the gray horse.

"This is my horse," the older one said as the two men blocked Jack's way. "How in the hell did you get him anyway?"

"You got proof he's yours?"

"Mister, I don't need proof he's mine. I raised him from a colt."

"I'm sorry, but a widow woman gave him to me in Austin."

"That's right—some damn rebel stole him from me."

"The law says possession is nine-tenths of the law. You show me some convincing proof, we'll talk."

"I'll show you—" The man jerked his six-gun out, but Jack's smoked lead first.

He whirled on his feet to face the younger one and fired a second round as the older man folded, firing his six-gun into the dust. The gray broke loose and skidded sideways. The second man tried to raise his gun hand, but Jack shot him again. He fell facedown.

"Where's the law?" Jack shouted as faces began to appear from tent flaps and building projects.

He bent over and discovered the older one had almost fifty dollars in greenbacks and stuffed the money back into his vest pocket. The sound of boot heels hitting the boardwalk told him someone was coming. A man caught Gray and led him back across the street.

Jack thanked him and nodded to the marshal with a sawed-off shotgun, a silver star pinned on his thin wool duster.

"What happened here?"

"These two men were blocking me from my horse. The older man claimed my horse was his. He went for his gun and I shot him. Then I turned and faced the second one's Colt. I had no other choice but to shoot him too."

"Sounds like self-defense to me."

"It sure was. There's money enough to bury them in his vest."

"Who in the hell are they?" The lawman scratched behind his ear.

"I never saw them before."

"Strange he'd accost you, isn't it?"

"It sure wasn't worth dying over."

"You're right as rain about that. My name's Cord. Ervin Cord. I'm the law around here. Ride careful, stranger."

"Captain Jack Starr, sir."

"Couple of you boys tote these bodies down to the funeral home," the marshal told the onlookers. "Gawdalmighty, there's already been two men killed and I ain't been on this job twenty-four hours." Cord shook his head. "We can handle it from here, Captain."

Jack nodded and went for Gray. What else was going to happen? Who were the two dead men? Maybe they'd find some identifying papers on them. Once in the saddle he shook his head over the matter and set Gray on a lope.

Who'd put those two up to that? Only time could tell him. He still found it odd. Maybe he'd find out before he left to go back to Texas. Either way it upset him. All he wanted to do was sell the steers and get going. But even if he managed to sell the steers quickly, he still had a big matter to resolve in Indian Territory: Cory's killer.

Chapter 26

Back at camp Jack sent Shanks, Earl and Claude to town with the ladies' things. Smiling, he gave each of the three men a five-dollar advance. "Don't get head-busting drunk. We'll need you, so get on back here."

The threesome and two packhorses loaded with trunks and hatboxes rode out while the remaining fellows shouted catcalls and suggestions for what they should do once they reached town. Jack merely shook his head.

Later, while sipping coffee and sitting on a log that one of the cowboys had dragged near the chuck wagon and cooking ring, he told Ralph about the shooting incident he'd had in town.

When he finished, Ralph shot him a serious glance. "There may be more to that deal than meets the eye."

"Only they ain't alive to tell us."

"Who wants you dead?"

"I've got a list an arm long." Jack wondered if those two dead men came from his past. But there was nothing with which he could tie them to his years in uniform. He'd probably never know.

What kind of damn fools were they? It was almost like they were committing suicide. The notion stayed with him all day.

Meanwhile Jangles wanted to resettle their camp elsewhere. The cattle had mown all the grass nearby.

"Better give it two more days," Jack told him. "I want the buyers to find us."

"We can make it that long," Jangles said, and squatted down beside the log. "But not much longer."

"This is good grass country," Jack said to the ranger.

"I've been thinking the same thing. They say east of here over in the hills it's even better."

"Maybe we should take a look-see. What makes me curious is the way folks are drifting into Kansas and taking up homesteads. I sure wouldn't want to be alone on the empty prairie like that."

"I talked to a couple guys passing through. They say them hills ain't much good for a plow and no one's stopping over there. But there's head-high bluestem grass for grazing. Might be a good place to raise cattle."

"It might work."

They were quiet for a moment before Jangles asked, "How did it go in town?"

"Alright. Two guys claimed that Gray was theirs and ended up with their boot toes pointing up at the sky."

Jangles blinked at him. "Who were they?"

"Damned if I know. Fools, is all I can say."

"You better take some rangers along next time."

"Good idea," Jack said. He was tired of talking about

the incident, which more than disturbed him, so he said his good nights and turned into his bedroll early.

The following day the first buyer, Larry Sorrel, arrived in a surrey-covered buggy. Estefan gave him a gentle horse to ride, saddling the red cow pony with Sorrel's own saddle.

"By golly, Starr, you have good help."

"It's a far piece up here from the hill country. No use in hauling worthless folks along on a cattle drive."

"I believe that."

Jack clapped him on the back. "Let's go see those longhorns."

They rode together through the grazing herd. Many of the cattle were lying down, chewing their cud. Sorrel, like all cattle buyers, had an eye for detail. As he rode through the herd he obviously noticed lots of things and commented to Jack about a funny set of horns or the color pattern on a steer's hide, simply making conversation. He also avoided a snorty steer or two.

When they had seen all of them, Sorrel nodded. "Good cattle."

"We culled them at home. Made some folks mad, but no sense in bringing culls this far."

"You know the market's around eight cents a pound?"

"Last fall it was ten cents."

"That was then. Things aren't quite as good these days. What do you think?" Sorrel asked.

"I ain't selling them to the first man that comes along. Hell, as good as they are, someone may offer me twelve cents a pound for them."

"Oh, you might get more than that, but that's the best I can offer. Eight cents."

"Sorrel, thanks for coming, but I'm gonna have to pass. Ralph will have dinner ready soon; you're welcome to stay over for it."

"No, thanks, I've got business."

"Appreciate your coming out."

"No problem. But just remember, Starr—they may offer you less."

"We'll see. They're straight steers and there are few to no culls. That's gotta be worth something."

"I know, but the demand isn't here right now. Trust me."

Jack shook the man's hand and saw him off. Cattle buyers always had excuses. He'd see what he'd get from the other buyers and act accordingly.

Charles Manning showed up a few hours later. He drank some of Ralph's springwater before he and Jack made a swing through the cattle.

"You weren't lying," Manning said. "I don't believe there's a head of female stock in your herd. Good, big, uniform steers. But I have to tell you, I need to wire an outfit in Illinois, so I'm not making any bids until I do that."

"Whatever suits you," Jack said. "You're welcome to stay for supper."

"Naw, I need to get back to Wichita."

Manning went back to town and Jangles frowned at Jack. "They all this hard to deal with?"

"It's a cat-and-mouse game."

"They'll get to stirring and more buyers will be by," Jangles said confidently.

"Guess I ain't patient enough."

"You're just anxious to get back home."

"I guess I am. Lucy may have had the baby by now and I'm dying to see whether I've got me a little boy or girl."

"When Shanks gets back tomorrow morning we can leave him in charge and ride over to see those grass hills," Jangles suggested. "Might take your mind off the homesickness."

"That sounds like a good plan," Jack said.

Before sunrise, satisfied the boys could handle the herd, they ate a quick breakfast that Ralph had fixed for them, packed their bedrolls and short-loped across the prairie, waiting for the peach glow of dawn to blossom.

It was only a short while before they began to see the bluestem. The country was too rough to appeal to any farmer and his plow, but the area was well watered with creeks and springs, and fat whitetail deer were abundant. Plum thickets were in full bloom and sage hens crossed their path often in a burst of wings.

By noon they were convinced the country had been overlooked and would make powerful ranch land.

"You ever wonder how well cheap yearling cattle would do up here on this grass?" Jangles asked.

"I been thinking the same thing. We could assemble a herd of them cheap and bring them up and try it this fall."

Jangles looked a little let down. "I bet it gets cold up here."

"I don't know. It's still a ways south of the North Pole." Jack shook his head. It wasn't going to be like being on the gulf either.

"Maybe we ought to try it?" Jangles perked up.

"We can get the credit to buy the cattle," Jack said, "and get us the supplies for a year. If the cattle do good we should make some money. Two of you rangers could also stay up here and watch after the cattle and we could go three ways on any profit."

"I think Cotton would like to be in on the deal."

"I'll let you handle that. For myself, I've seen enough to make up my mind."

Jangles stood in his stirrups and surveyed the waving brown grass, which was beginning to green up at the base. "I'd sure be proud to be your partner in this deal."

They shook hands on it and headed back for camp. Clouds were piling up in the northwest and Jack grew concerned that the approaching storm might be a bad one. They pushed their ponies harder. No way they could beat the force sweeping across the rolling prairie toward their camp, but Jack hoped that Shanks, who should've returned to camp by now, had a plan to get everyone moving if they needed to.

Not stopping, they put on their slickers as they were riding. Soon large, cold raindrops began to beat on them, followed by sheets of hail. I should never have left the herd, Jack thought. It would be all his fault if anything serious happened. I was out looking at grass, dammit. Focusing on future projects when I should've been taking care of the current one.

Daylight had turned to night by the time they reached the chuck wagon. It was still an hour or more to sunset, despite the darkness. The storm threatened to tear Ralph's fly off. Lightning cracked overhead like a bullwhip and rolled off across the Kansas prairie.

Jack dismounted, handed his reins to Jangles and ducked inside. Ralph, wearing a slicker, blinked at him through the raindrops.

"Where's the herd?" Jack asked.

"Shanks moved them out before the storm. He had all the boys ready," Ralph said above the roar of the rain.

"Good. We'll tie up the horses and we can wait here. No sense wandering around in the dark, not knowing where we're going."

A flash illuminated the canvas tent. Ralph agreed and Jack went to help Jangles. Their horses hitched, they came inside. Jangles was glad to hear that the herd had moved on, but only time would tell what their losses would be.

The rain finally moved east and they went outside. Stars began to twinkle. But there wasn't a sound of lowing cattle in the night. They could be several miles away, depending on how far they got beyond the storm. Hopefully there had been no stampedes. The steers were supposed to be gentler by now.

At dawn Cotton rode in and dropped heavily out of his saddle.

"How are we?" Jangles asked.

"Alright. Everyone with the herd's accounted for. They're heading them back this way. But we can't find Estefan or the horses."

"When did he head out?" Jack asked, worry lines creasing his forehead.

"He left when we did."

"Jangles and I'll go look for him. Ralph, Cotton'll help you set up camp; we're out of grass here anyway. We'll see where Estefan ended up."

"Sure," Ralph said. "That guy's half horse anyway, so I'm sure he's fine."

After grabbing some biscuits, the two left to locate the horse herd. Jack used his field glasses to try to catch sight of the remuda. Midday they found two dead horses with a D-T brand. No doubt the victims of a lightning bolt.

Jack dreaded the notion of finding more losses. There might be others injured and dead. Damn, where was that boy?

After loping for a few more miles he saw, through the lenses, the very thing he was looking for: horses descending a hill and Estefan leading the pack.

Chapter 27

When Jack finally found his horse herder, he was babbling to himself in Spanish about the storm. He'd lost his sombrero somewhere. His facial expression looked somewhere between vacant and upset.

"How are your horses?" Jack asked, looking over the grazing cow ponies.

"I lose four of them, *patrón*."

"Lucky we didn't lose them all and you too."

With a bright-toothed smile Estefan nodded. "*Sí*, I prayed a lot, señor."

"Them boys could use some fresh horses. I believe they're south of here. You did fine, Estefan. You're a real good man."

The youth seemed to gain his bearings now that he was among men again and began to whistle as he swung his coiled reata, beating it on his chaps. Soon they were off on a long trot.

Midday they found the main herd scattered and grazing. Shanks came to meet them.

"How many do you figure we lost?" Jack stood in his stirrups to stretch his muscles.

"Not more than ten. We've looked hard for strays and drop-offs. But our horses are about done in."

"You guys did great. Better get fresh horses."

Estefan came on a trot with two fresh mounts in tow. Shanks swung down and began undoing his latigoes. Either came and claimed the second gelding. Estefan rode off hard after some more mounts.

The chuck wagon was set up and several of the cowboys pitched in to help Ralph with dinner. Things were happening fast, but Jack was glad his crew knew what it took and no one shirked his part, whether it was making biscuit dough or frying sliced bacon.

Jack relaxed a little and the stiffness in his shoulders began to evaporate. He wished he could sleep for five days. He dismounted and sat on the ground. His entire outfit had been through a helluva night and then some. But they were tough to beat.

While they were eating, Sorrel drove up in his buggy with a lathered horse.

"Why did you move so damn far?" He gave them an angry look.

"It wasn't by choice." Jack wiped his mouth on his sleeve. "The cattle chose this place."

"I've got a buyer for the cattle. Ten cents a pound. He wants a five-percent cutback."

Jack shook his head at the man. He knew there was a market for cattle, and that meant he had some say in the final outcome. Culling five percent from his herd was out-and-out robbery. Folks back home in Texas needed every dime he could deliver.

"Give me two days to think on it?"

"No longer, and you give me a chance to match anyone else's bid, since I came out here and talked to you first."

"I might trade with you, but the five percent is off. You can cull any sorry or crippled steer, but not five percent across the herd." They shook hands and Sorrel took the afternoon meal with them. Then in the late afternoon he headed back for Wichita.

Charles Manning found them the next morning. Jack felt even more confident after Manning made his offer. He proposed eleven cents a pound and a two-percent shrink. Jack told Manning he'd let him know. The cattle buyer acted put out.

"When're you going to decide?'

"In twenty-four hours."

Two more buyers showed up that day around sundown and both offered less than Sorrel and Manning. Each time, the men looked perplexed that Jack even thought there were better offers than theirs to be had in the country.

Seated cross-legged beside each other on the ground, eating supper, Jangles said to Jack, "I'm really learning this cattle-selling business. First you need an edge, like having all steers. Hell, if I'd done this myself, I'd have rounded them all up: cows, calves and big steers. I never knew it was that complicated, but I see why now. I've been watching herds go north since the war was over.

They were all mixed, and now it's no wonder to me that some do good, but the majority lose their butts."

"That's a big part of it. Men come here and get mad as hell because no one wants to give them anything for the rest of their stock." Jack held out his cup for Ralph to refill it.

"Maybe we can finally get some sleep tonight," his cook said as he poured the coffee.

Jack agreed. "I hope so too. I'm going in tomorrow to cut the best deal I can. These cattle need to be on a train."

"Amen," the crew said in unison.

"What will they weigh?" Jangles asked.

"I have no idea; but the scales will tell."

"What are you guessing?"

"Seven fifty, maybe more. They're big cattle."

Jack hardly slept. Cattle prices, weights, how to divide the money, how to pay the boys—he felt like he was on his side rolling off a tall, grassy hill, his thoughts bouncing around and getting mixed up in his head. If he could cut a profitable deal the folks of Little Dog Creek could be debt free and would never again have to work with back-pocket bankers like Sawyer.

Midmorning in Wichita, he found Sorrel in his tent. The man rose from behind his desk to greet him. Sunshine filtered through the canvas, giving off a dull yellow light.

"What did you decide?"

"Eleven cents, no shrink. You can cut back any crippled or sorry one you see—we'll help with that."

"My gawd, that's high, Starr."

"I'm going to a buyer right now who has already promised me that. You said you wanted first crack at them, but if you can't meet my price I'm gonna have to be on my way."

Sorrel tapped a pencil on the desk, concentrating hard on the open flap. "Alright, I'll take them. You're a hard man to deal with, but I respect your commitment to fairness. I have cattle cars coming day after tomorrow. I'll order more. You should be loaded out in five days."

They shook hands firmly.

"How much cash will you need here?" Sorrel asked.

"Five thousand to pay the boys and buy supplies."

"The rest?"

"Cattleman's Bank, San Antonio, Texas. Let Wells Fargo deliver it."

"That's close to where you live?"

"Close enough. I'm damn sure not packing it home. I want it deposited to Mr. and Mrs. Jack Starr, just in case. You have a bookkeeper I can hire to help me figure all this out?"

"Roth, he's my man." He indicated the man at the adjoining desk, working in a ledger. "He'll help you when we get the deal done."

"Good." Jack went over and shook the man's hand.

Back at camp excitement built and everyone scurried around to prepare for the transfer. Cattle were cut and driven to Wichita in herds of four hundred. Jack was in the scale room when the bawling steers were crowded onto the platform scales.

"They're going to average seven ninety," Roth said as he finished settling the weight markers on the balance beam of the scale and marking the total weight down on his sheet.

Jack watched them drive the cattle off. "They're going to make eight hundred pounds."

Roth nodded and another bunch was driven onto the scales. The puncher in charge shouted, "Twenty-nine head are in this bunch."

Roth waved that he heard him.

In three days the herd was on their way to some farmer's fattening pens. The deal was concluded at the bank, a wood-framed, unfinished structure with two shotgun guards in the lobby and a huge green safe chained to the wall.

All the paperwork was settled. Jack rose, shook the banker's hands and went back to look at Roth's figures. He knew there were 1,880 animals. Not a bad deal— every rancher that consigned cattle would get nearly eighty dollars a head, less his five-percent fee and expenses. His crew would get close to two hundred a man with pay and bonuses for less than four months of hard work. Jangles and Ralph had twice that amount coming to them.

Kicking back in a swivel chair, Jack studied the figures on Roth's sheet—each rancher's amount due. Lucy would earn more than twenty-seven thousand dollars for her steers. His five percent would top more than eight thousand. With a weary head shake, he smiled to himself. The Frank brothers had paid him nine hundred for his part on his last trip to Wichita, then acted like Jack was robbing them when it came time to dole out the money.

Before he left Sorrel's office, he paid Roth twenty dollars for his help. The man looked at the amount and his eyes bugged out behind the small glasses on his untanned nose. "Why—why—you don't owe me this much, Mr. Starr."

"I've got what I owe folks itemized on this here list. It's all straight. I'm damn sure happy to pay anyone who deserves it. You enjoy that money."

Before sundown, he was back in camp and paid the boys. Flush with money, several rode off to town to whoop it up. After the boys left he saw his horse wrangler, Estefan, drinking coffee.

"No big fiesta tonight?" he asked the youth.

"No, señor. I have a family to feed to Mexico. My father is dead. Shot by banditos. My mother has five children younger than me. Someone needs to take care of them."

"I admire a man with a sense of responsibility," Jack said. He looked around and noticed that his rangers had also stayed behind.

"Jangles," he called out. "You rangers ain't going into town?"

"We thought about it," Jangles said, taking his mouth harp from his lips, "but women like Rose and Flower, they sure ain't cheap, and the cheap ones are uglier than a turned-up-nose sow. We decided we'd have ourselves a better time in San Antonio once we got down there."

"Arnold, you ain't dying to go into town?" Jack asked.

Cotton gave him a little push and teased, "Tell the captain why you stayed behind."

"Well, Captain, we kinda sampled the, uh, two ladies when they were here. They were sure nice, but we decided we could wait a while longer, since we could never afford their kind in town."

Jack laughed. "Well, I better send a telegram to the ladies of San Antonio that the rangers are coming."

They all laughed, and Ralph poured a last round of coffee before they headed to bed. "Sure is nice to know we'll get a full night's sleep for once. Even nicer to know we're heading home tomorrow."

"Amen," they all said.

Jack couldn't agree more. He thought, Lucy, we're greasing the chuck-wagon axles and I'm coming home to you and the baby. Hold on for me.

Chapter 28

"Captain Starr! Captain Starr!" A woman was calling him in the night. He could hear her talking to someone, a sense of urgency in her voice.

"I know this is their camp. There's the D-T brand on the wagon." She raised her voice. "Ralph! Jangles!"

"What is it, Flower?" Jack called out to her, pulling on his pants in the moonlight.

"They've shot Shanks and pistol-whipped Claude," Flower said, almost out of breath.

"Who did?" He was pulling on his boots at record speed now.

"Some tough ones. One's named Cutter. He's the ringleader."

"Never heard of him." He turned to the man who was with her. "I'm Jack Starr." They shook hands.

"Tom Charles. I drove Flower out here," he said.

"What did they do to Shanks?" Jangles joined them, still buttoning his shirt.

"Shot him. He's at the doc's office. I don't know how bad he's hurt."

"Thanks for driving out here, you two. We'll get some horses and head in to town right away," Jack said. "Where can I find this doc?"

"Doc Leonard has a tent office on Main Street," Flower said.

"Boss, I'll get Estefan and the horses," Jangles said, and hurried off.

"Take just a minute to make some coffee," Ralph said, limping over to join the group. "Cotton, find a candle lamp."

"Yes, sir," Cotton said.

The lamp soon lit, Arnold scrambled to stoke up the fire while Ralph filled the coffeepot with water. Jack told Tom and Flower to take seats on a peeled cottonwood log. His ear tuned for the horses, he talked with Tom about the cattle sale and their plans to return to Texas.

"I guess there'll be thousands more coming soon," Tom said.

"I reckon so," Jack said. "But I'm glad to avoid the crowds. We'll be on our way just as everyone else is coming in."

Though he chatted easily, Jack's mind was on his boys. How had Shanks and Claude gotten into it with this Cutter fellow? Was Shanks still alive? He desperately wanted to get into town and see how they were doing, not to mention the other boys who'd gone with them.

"Where can we find this Cutter?" Jack asked Flower.

"The Texas Saloon, I reckon. That's where it happened."

He'd find this SOB and either plant him or make him

wish he was dead. His crew members were like family, and as their leader he'd do anything and everything to protect them. He was starting to get antsy. Hurry up, Jangles, he thought. Find Estefan.

The sound of the approaching horses had his crew on their feet. Saddles were grabbed up and more lamps lit for them to see by as they sorted out the horses with Estefan. The horses saddled, they mounted quickly.

"Ralph, you're in charge. Anything happens to us, you get these boys back home."

"We'll cross that bridge when we get to it," Ralph said. "Take care of yourselves and get those bastards."

Jack nodded as he, Jangles, Cotton and Arnold reared up and charged off for Wichita.

In the first light of dawn as they rode up Main Street, Jack saw several men passed out and snoring along the road. One man stood on the boardwalk, draining his bladder in the street as if he were in an outhouse. The boys snickered, but Jack remained focused.

He caught sight of the sign he'd been looking for since they had arrived in town: DOCTOR MICHAEL LEONARD, PHYSICIAN.

Jack dismounted and entered the tent. An orderly sat up, half awake, and blinked at him. "Doc ain't here, so I hope you ain't dying."

"I ain't, but I think my cowboy Shanks is here. Gunshot wound earlier tonight."

"Sorry, we moved him to Bigelow's," the orderly said with a yawn.

"What's that?" Jack asked, growing impatient.

"Oh, you didn't know? He died."

Jack was floored. "When did he die?"

"Not long ago. Bled out."

"Is another cowboy named Claude here?"

"No, two Mexican cowboys took him to the hotel. Said they were his friends."

"Must be Raul and Peso. Was he alright?"

"I guess somebody beat him up pretty bad, but he'll live."

Jack turned to his rangers, his jaw set. "Let's find Claude first and make sure he's alright. Then we clean house at Texas Saloon."

The rangers nodded, their faces grim. They walked a block and a half to the hotel, their boots clunking on the boardwalk. A sleepy desk clerk yawned and greeted them.

"Did you see two Mexican boys come in here with a wounded man?"

"Yes, second floor. Room three."

They marched upstairs and knocked rapidly on the door. The door opened a crack, a six-shooter pointed straight at Jack's face.

"Easy, boys," he said to his Mexican cowboys. "It's just me."

The gun was lowered and the door flew open. "We're so glad you came, boss man," Raul said.

"How is he?" Jack studied the bandaged face of the sleeping cowboy in the bed.

"He is alive," Raul said. "The doctor gave him laudanum so he could sleep."

"You boys did a good job."

"Did you hear about Shanks?" Peso asked.

Jack nodded his head mournfully. "Dead."

Peso dropped his head. "They shot him in the back. We barely got out of there."

Raul agreed. "In Mexico I would have gone back and killed them all, but we wanted to get Shanks and Claude to the doctor."

"You did the right thing," Jack reassured them.

He dug out some money and handed it to Raul. "This should cover the doctor's bill and hotel fare. I want you boys to stay here until he's well enough to travel. We're gonna take care of some business."

"What will you do about those bad hombres?" Raul asked.

"We're gonna get them; don't worry." They left the room and headed back out to the dusty street. They walked the half block back to the tent marked TEXAS SALOON.

From across the street, Jack could see people moving around inside. He huddled the boys together, their heads bent low. "We go in guns drawn. Jangles, you herd the bartender out from behind the bar. Cotton and Arnold, spread out. I doubt Cutter and his gang are still in there, but I figure they have cribs out back. He may be in one of them."

"How many are in there, you figure?" Jangles asked.

"No telling. But if anyone reaches for a gun, consider them one of Cutter's crew."

The rangers nodded and they crossed the empty street, four abreast. When they entered the saloon the bartender jerked up and blinked in disbelief.

"One word out of you and you won't see another daybreak," Jack said, his Colt drawn. "Where's Cutter?"

"I don't know—" the bartender began, until the muzzle of Jangles' .45 jammed into his side.

"Where is he?" Jangles whispered.

The barkeep swallowed hard. "Third crib on the right."

Jack nodded. "Watch him, Arnold."

"Yes, sir," Arnold said, aiming his gun straight at the bartender's head.

"Jangles, take the second room. Cotton, you cover the hall," Jack said.

When they were both at the flaps, guns ready, Jack nodded. They swept back the canvas covers.

Jack saw the man reach for his weapon on a crate beside the bed. But Jack was fast. He fired and the man screamed. He'd blown part of his hand away. In her panic to escape, the half-dressed woman in the bed fell off the far side onto the grass floor. Half crawling, she left the crib, screaming.

"Don't try nothing," Jack warned, motioning with his gun barrel. "Get out here."

"I ain't dressed." He held his bloody gun hand in the other and stood up, wearing only his underpants.

"I don't care. Get out in the hall."

Two more men stood, hands held high, in the hallway.

"These men work for you?" Jack demanded from his prisoner.

Cutter looked up at them, then shook his head. "Never saw them before."

Jack couldn't be sure whether he was lying. "Bring them along."

As they marched them out, two men wearing U.S. deputy marshal badges suddenly burst into the saloon. "Hold it there. What's going on?"

"We've made a citizen's arrest, sir," Jack said, holstering his Colt. "These men killed one of my riders and beat another half to death. Now, either you take him and his men to jail or we're going to lynch 'em."

"Where do you gawdamn Texans get your gall?" one of the marshals asked.

"Mister, in Texas we're rangers. You better get him to the doc's office or he's going to bleed all over this dance floor."

They exchanged tough looks and one of them finally nodded. "I'll take him down there."

The other one turned and looked Jack in the eye. "What are the charges against them?" he asked, motioning toward the other two men with their arms raised.

"Accessories to the crime."

"You have witnesses?"

"Sure do. Two of my men saw the whole thing happen. I'll have them here at your convenience."

"Alright, you two come with me," the marshal said, cuffing the men. "Next time get the law to do this," he said to Jack.

"Next time maybe you'll do a better job of covering the crime in this town. My man is over in the funeral home. Shot in the back. There ain't no excuse for that."

The marshal was quiet for a moment before answer-

ing. "I'm real sorry to hear that. We'll take care of everything from here."

Jack nodded. "My name's Starr. Jack Starr."

The marshal shook his hand. "My name's Earp. Wyatt
Earp."

"Nice to meet you, Marshal Earp. I just sold a herd
and I'm anxious to get back home, but we will be here
for the trial if you need me."

"I'll know in a few days what the state will do about
them."

"What now?" Jangles asked.

"Breakfast. Let's go find some," Jack said.

They found a small café opening its doors for the
day. After the meal they ran into several of their hungover hands, who were saddened to hear the news about
Shanks and Claude. Most of them had spent the night
at cards or with women. Most rode with them back
to camp. Jack knew the next few days would be long
and hard. He'd arranged for the funeral home to bring
Shanks' body to them once the official inquiries were
over.

The corpse arrived the next morning. Jack helped the
rangers dig a grave on a small rise. He figured Shanks
would rather be planted out there rather than in a yard
with a bunch of outlaws and gamblers.

He finished the services with "How Great Thou Art."

After two verses of the hymn he closed the Bible and
said, "Lord, we're delivering you a great cowboy. He
was a good friend, an honest man and a generous man.
Lord, take him home. He belongs with you. Amen."

"Amen," the sad crew echoed.

Jack walked with the crew back to the chuck wagon and they all had a drink of whiskey in Shanks' honor. Ralph had stew cooking and the smell wafted gently on the breeze toward the crew.

Claude, Raul and Peso had come back just in time for the funeral. The congenial older man, still in bandages, thanked Jack for his help and told him what had happened. Cutter had been cheating at cards all night. Shanks challenged him and tried to leave the game, fed up with losing all his money. When he started for the door, Cutter stood up and shot him in the back.

"I protested and they started beating me. Next thing I knew I was lying in the alley, half conscious. I guess Raul and Peso found me later. They said they got word through Flower."

Jack patted Claude on the back. "I'm glad you're alright. Let's put this all behind us and eat some of Ralph's delicious stew."

Chapter 29

Jack met with the Kansas prosecutor, Jerome Lonagan, who wanted to make a plea deal with Cutter and his attorney, the next morning. Manslaughter and four years—no parole.

"He won't ever shoot anyone with his right hand again. Why, I bet he can't even wipe his ass with it," Lonagan said.

"He brought it on himself," Jack said gruffly.

"This is the best deal I can make. Otherwise you and your men will have to come back and testify at a trial."

Jack sighed. He was eager to get back home to Lucy and the baby, and he trusted that Cutter would learn his lesson in four years. "I guess we'll take that then. We're anxious to shed this Kansas dust, but I need to know that justice will be served."

"Trust me," Lonagan said. "You haven't been to a Kansas prison. Justice will be served."

They left for Texas the next day. Jack had posted a letter to Lucy the day before, telling her he was leaving for home. Claude sat on the chuck wagon seat beside Ralph. The mules stepped lightly as Jangles played them out on the harmonic. They rolled southward as he sang "John, John, the gray goose is gone and the fox is on the town, oh . . ."

The second day they approached Indian Territory. Jangles asked Jack about Julius Knotts.

"Captain, you're not gonna pass up your chance to get 'em because you're eager to get home, are you?" Jangles asked.

Jack was silent for a moment. "We don't have any authority up here and I'd rather not have another run-in with the law that could prevent us from getting home."

It was Jangles' turn to fall silent. Finally he said, "Sir, with all due respect, that's nonsense. Julius Knotts deserves what's coming. Besides, you've got three rangers who'll back you up. I have a feeling this is your one and only shot."

Jack nodded. "You're right, Jangles. I need to take care of this now." They hatched a plan and Jangles went to share the plan with Cotton and Arnold. Jack knew he was doing the right thing. One by one he'd eliminate anyone who had hurt his family, friends and loved ones, leaving no stones unturned. Besides, Knotts would be good practice for when he finally confronted Hiram Sawyer. He knew Sawyer would be waiting for him, itching to get his revenge.

At dawn Jack mounted Mac and the four rangers left camp in a short lope, riding stirrup to stirrup. They scat-

tered a few prairie chickens and sent several fat ground-
hogs scrambling for their dens. A pair of sleek coyotes
spun off and tore over the hill. "What was that bluestem
country like?" Cotton asked. "I'd like to have seen it."

"Great grass country. The hills are rocky, but that
would only keep the homesteaders out and leave plenty
of space for us ranchers. Big springs and plenty of water in the creeks. God intended it to be cow country,"
Jack said.

"Are we going to try to get a herd of yearlings this
year?"

"I plan to. They say snow doesn't usually last long
up there. But it'll be colder than South Texas."

"We'll just wear more clothes," Cotton laughed. The
others agreed. "Me and Arnold sure want in."

"I figure we can get a bunch back up here by next
spring, then sell them next fall," Jack said.

"Yearlings are cheap in Texas," Jangles said. "How
many will we buy?"

"As many as a banker will let us have," Jack said.
Ten-dollar yearlings could be worth sixty to eighty dollars by the following fall if the grass that fattened the
deer so well worked on cattle.

Midday they drove up in sight of Julius Knotts' stomping grounds. Everyone checked the loads in their pistols. Loaded rifles under each stirrup, they spread out
to advance on the corrals and a low-walled sod building
with a tin roof. A rooster crowed and a hen cackled. A
milk cow bawled for her calf from her pen. A woman

stood in the doorway in a blue dress and used her hand to shield her eyes from the midday sun.

"Julius Knotts here?" Jack asked.

"I don't know who you're talking about," she said warily.

"You know him, lady. Is he here?"

She sighed. "You the law?"

"No, we're Texas rangers."

"What do you want him fur?"

"Murder."

"He's been gone for a week. I don't know where he went or when he'll be back."

Jack looked around and dropped out of the saddle. "Move aside from the door, ma'am."

"He ain't in here."

Jangles, standing in the stirrups, nodded sharply, then rode around to the back of the house to cover the other exit.

"Halt or I'll shoot!" Jangles shouted from the rear.

Shots were fired.

Jack yelled to Cotton as he ran for Jangles, "Keep a gun on her."

He raced around the building and found Jangles dismounted and standing over a man lying facedown.

"He tried to shoot me, but his gun misfired. I had no choice."

"You did the right thing," Jack said as he dropped to his knees and rolled him over.

The bullet had entered squarely in the center of Knotts' chest. Blood poured out of the black hole to stain a once-white shirt. Jack closed his eyelids and straightened his body.

The woman rushed to him, covering her mouth as she fell to her knees.

"You want us to bury him?" Jack asked soberly.

She shook her head. "Tie him up in a blanket and put him in my rig around the corner."

"Ma'am, he chose how he died. But we're civil enough to bury him and do it the right way."

"The U.S. deputy marshal at Enid will pay me a hundred dollars for him. Dead or alive."

"We'll take him to the marshal at Enid for you," Jack said.

She refused his offer.

They headed back for the chuck wagon and Arnold spoke up. "Strange lady. She never shed a tear about him. All she wanted was the hundred dollars."

Jack nodded. "I reckon she was his woman. Guess she's thinking about what she'll have to live on now that he's gone."

"I guess so. It's just strange to me."

Jack nodded. Knotts was finally gone, but it wasn't exactly what he wanted; worse, it didn't bring Cory back. He was glad Knotts couldn't kill another innocent person, but he'd rather he'd ended up behind bars to think over his sins. It would've been more of a settling of debts than shooting him dead in his yard in front of his wife. Things didn't always tally up in a man's life the way he thought they ought to. All he could do was be grateful that Julius Knotts would no longer haunt him.

Chapter 30

Jack realized they'd made good time; they had crossed Indian Territory in a little over two weeks. After stopping to rest, they grained Ralph's mules and swapped horses midday for fresh ones. When they came down to the Red River ferry the cowboys laughed and teased each other.

"You happy, Arnold?" Jangles asked. "You won't have to swim buck naked this time."

"I've never been so damn happy to see a boat."

"How are you going to drive dumb yearlings up here and not cross rivers?" Jangles teased.

"I'll make it," Arnold said. "But I damn sure won't like it." He spat to one side.

By the time they were in the Trinity River bottoms, Jack called for a three-day rest. The boys, except for Jangles, were ready to catch some extra sleep. Jack and Jangles left them at camp and rode in to Fort Worth to talk to a buyer about the yearling market.

"You know, my wife may not appreciate me being gone all summer," Jack said. He hadn't thought much about it, but here he was working on another scheme that would separate them and he'd sure missed her while he was away. He'd have to go along to get the boys settled. He just hoped Lucy would understand.

"Why, she ought to be tickled pink. Those cattle made her a fortune."

"But having her husband away is a steep price to pay," Jack reminded him.

"Ain't that something?"

"What's that?" Jack asked.

"A woman being mad 'cause her man is off making money."

"Well, I think she married me to have a husband, not a cattle trader."

Once they arrived he talked to a few commission men at the stockyards. Most said they could assemble a herd of yearlings for less than ten dollars a head. One buyer said if he had time he could find most for seven-fifty a head.

"I sure do like the idea of making money," Jangles said as they left the office, the smell of oats and leather following them out of the door.

"We better keep it quiet. No telling how this will go and we don't need hundreds of other traders doing the same thing."

"Oh, I will. I'm just excited we may have a real deal."

"You bet. Bankers come next."

"How much money do we need?"

"Twenty-five thousand bucks."

"Good Lord, who's going to loan us that much money?"

"That's why we're going to see the banker," Jack said with a laugh.

Jangles chuckled. "I'm learning, Captain. I'm learning. Old man Sawyer loans my paw money. Costs him a pretty penny too. And it ain't never much. Just enough to get by on till he makes some money."

"That's the difference between going to someone like Sawyer and going to a legitimate banker. Your paw is going to pay him high interest for a short-term loan, but it ain't worth that much to a real banker."

When they arrived at the bank, they met with a loan officer named Mr. Rosencroft. The pale-skinned, short man with large-framed glasses perched on his nose didn't look overly impressed with two trail-dusted cowboys holding their hats grimy hands until Jack showed him the receipts from Wichita. Then his eyes opened wide and his mouth fell open in disbelief.

"We're on our way home. We live sixty miles or so north of Fredericksburg in the hill country," Jack explained.

"This is a very impressive amount of money. It's the highest receipt I've ever seen from a cattle trader. What's your secret?"

"I have several of them and trust me, they all work," Jack said.

Rosencroft smiled. "Let me bring Harold Davis in here. Mr. Davis is our senior vice president. Will you excuse me?"

When he got up to leave, both Jack and Jangles rose and nodded to him.

Jangles checked to be sure they were alone. "I believe the fish has bitten the bait. He liked to have swallowed his tongue at the sight of those receipts."

Rosencroft came back into the room with an older, heavyset man in a very expensive suit. Jack extended his hand as Rosencroft introduced him as Mr. Davis.

"Have a seat," Davis said as he sat on the edge of the desk. "Allan here advises me that you two gentlemen are here to apply for a substantial loan." He paused.

"Twenty-five thousand dollars," Jack said. "Nothing more; nothing less."

"And you would need this money for how long?"

"Fourteen to fifteen months."

"You have collateral to back it?'

"Two thousand steers, a chuck wagon and eighty good horses."

"And you could sell them in that short timeframe?" he asked, looking a bit skeptical.

"I don't know what the market will be then, but anywhere around fifteen dollars a head would satisfy your loan."

"How much did this herd you just delivered earn you?"

"Almost eighty bucks a head."

"Eighty dollars a head?" Davis' eyes bugged out in disbelief.

"Yes, sir." Jack shifted his hat to his other hand.

"That's unbelievable. Why, cattle here fetch only twenty or thirty dollars a head."

"Mr. Rosencroft asked for my secrets, and while I can't tell you all of them I can tell you the most important one: deliver eighteen hundred and eighty head to the rail cars and have them all accepted."

"No cutback?"

"None."

Davis let out a low whistle. "You obviously know the cattle business, Jack. When will you need this money?"

"In the next thirty days, if I can manage it all."

"Perfect. Do you own a ranch?"

"My wife does. It's fixing to get much larger."

Davis nodded. "Allan, get all the particulars on this loan and have it on my desk in the morning. I want the loan committee to approve it immediately so Jack will know exactly what he can buy."

They shook hands. Davis left and Mr. Rosencroft began asking questions and copied down the receipt details. Their business finished, Jack and his man walked out of the Texas Ranchers and Merchants Bank into the too-bright, hot afternoon sun.

"Whew. That was easy." Jangles reset his hat on his head. "I can't wait to tell the boys."

"A lot easier than I expected," Jack said.

"Man. We walked in there like lepers, but before we knew it, it was Jangles, Jack and *Allan*."

They both chuckled and crossed the busy street. They were three blocks from Sloane's Livery, where their horses were resting.

"Let's get some lunch."

"I think we earned it," Jangles said.

Jack caught him by the sleeve to stop him, motioning to two men across the street. "Isn't that Sawyer's men?"

Jangles followed his gaze. "Yeah, that's Dyke and Freeman alright."

"I wonder what they're up to. Probably no good."

"No telling, but it's probably underhanded," Jangles agreed. "Well, they heeded our warning and left town, so maybe we'll let it slide this one time."

As they were mulling it over, a newsboy shouted, "Read all about it! Rich New York banker's ranch headquarters attacked and burned down by Kiowa-Comanches! Read all about it!"

"Here, kid, give me a copy." Jack handed him a dime.

"Is that where we were when we were coming back from the Lerner rescue?"

Jack nodded. He'd warned Hardy to watch out for them, but he wouldn't listen. *Damn.*

Chapter 31

Jack wired Lucy to spread the word that they would be at the Cattleman's Bank in San Antonio in ten days to disperse the money. Those who couldn't come he would pay at the schoolhouse at a later time. He climbed into the chuck wagon on top of the bedrolls, and while Ralph drove south he caught up on his sleep.

Waking up drenched in sweat, he made his way forward until he was standing behind the spring seat.

"Whew, it's hot in this wagon."

"Hot anywhere in Texas in June. But we're making good time," Ralph said.

"Nothing out of the ordinary?"

"Not so far."

"I saw those two who used to work for Sawyer slinking around in Fort Worth."

"Not the most solid of citizens," Ralph said. "The boys told me about them beating you up."

Jack swung around and climbed on the seat beside Ralph, his dusty boots planted on the dashboard. "The boys and I got them good at one point, but I'd like to give them another hammering. I'm sure they're earning it somehow."

Ralph chuckled.

"I've tussled with so many of their kind lately, it's starting to make me sound like some vengeful devil."

"Aw, hell, the world's a better place without 'em."

"I guess you're right." They rode along peacefully for a time while Jack looked out at the prairie.

"We'll be in San Antonio way ahead of time," Jack said.

Ralph nodded. "I know a señorita that I'd like to go see."

"Rent a rig to go see her. I'll pay for it."

"Thanks, boss. I'll take you up on it. Bet you been missing that wife, huh?"

Jack agreed, but at least he'd had fine memories of his time with her to carry him through the last few months. To know she was coming for him at the bank was enough to make his stomach churn with excitement.

They stopped near New Braunfels and camped for the night on the river before heading in to San Antonio. Everyone took baths and washed their clothing, wanting to look presentable for their women.

"You going to make another drive this summer, Captain Jack?" Either asked.

"I'm thinking on it."

"Me and my brother, Hank, would sure like to go back with you."

"That's good to hear. I'll let you know when I have more details."

His clothes drying on some bushes, he sat in the shade wearing only his underwear.

Luke walked by, chewing on a grass stem.

"How's you doing, son? How'd you like your first cattle-driving experience?" Jack asked.

"It was interesting. But I'm looking forward to sleeping in a bed."

Jack chuckled. "You glad to be getting back home?"

"Yeah, I reckon I've seen Kansas. From now on I'm staying here in Texas."

"I'm thinking about going back in a short while."

"I heard, but to tell you the truth I'd rather stay behind next time. I know you'll need a point man without Shanks, but I've seen all that I wanted to. I think I'm meant to be a rancher, not a driver."

"No shame in that. But you're absolutely sure? I know you'd make a great point man."

Luke chewed his grass stem. "I'm sure. I'll work Texas for you."

"Alright, but you made a good hand."

"I never wanted anyone to say I was just getting by as the boss's son."

"You did good at that."

"Reckon Maw will be there when we get there?"

"I hope so."

"So do I, Dad. So do I."

Chapter 32

At the north edge of San Antonio, Jack rented a pasture for the remuda and Estefan stayed with the herd. They left the mules and chuck wagon there so the boys would have a place to come back to when they were tired of running around in the city. Ralph drove off in his rented rig to see his lady while the rest of the crew headed for the saloons. Jack excused himself.

He had rented a room at the Palace Hotel, where he planned to meet Lucy the next day. He climbed the stairs wearily, sprawled out across the bed and slept till dawn. Eager for a shave and a haircut, he went downstairs and asked the desk clerk if any shops were open early. The clerk recommended a barber shop one door over.

"John will already be up and ready for business," he said.

Jack thanked him and left. Almost everything around Alamo Square was still closed. He walked up to the door of the shop marked BARBER and knocked. Soon a face appeared beneath the raised shade and the door swung open.

"Good morning, sir. Come right in," the barber said cheerily.

"The clerk at the Palace Hotel sent me."

"That's one fine lad, sir." He turned the chair around for Jack to sit. "My name's John."

"Mine's Jack. I need a haircut and a shave, although you could probably tell by just looking at me."

The barber chuckled. "I can handle it." He slung the black sheet over his chest and pinned it behind his neck. "You must have been riding a long ways."

"I've been to Kansas and back."

"That's quite a long ways."

"No kidding." Jack sat patiently while the barber lathered him up, until he noticed through the front glass window two familiar men standing outside on the sidewalk beside each other. It was Dyke and Freeman. Both men were looking around as if they were surveying the scene; then Dyke reached for the door handle. Jack lowered the barber's hand from his face, motioned to the window outside, and eased his Colt into his lap. When they burst through the door with their guns drawn, the barber drew back.

Jack flew from his seat and shot Dyke. He fell onto Freeman, who blasted a hole in the ceiling while Jack shot him in the side.

Black gunpowder smoke clouded the air, burning Jack's eyes so badly that he and John stumbled outside, coughing, to get a breath of air.

"Whew. Who were they?" John asked.

"Two hired gunnies that work for a man named Sawyer."

"What's going on here?" the night marshal ran up and asked John.

"There's two men in there on the floor. They busted into my shop with their guns drawn to rob us, I guess. Jack here shot them."

"Damn, don't you know that San Antonio's not a shooting gallery?" the perturbed marshal said to Jack.

John sounded upset when he replied, "Way I saw it, Les, he saved my life."

"They dead?"

"Damned if we know. Smoke got too thick inside for us to even breathe in there."

"Aw, hell. I'll go see." Gun in one hand, he used a handkerchief over his nose to keep the bitter smoke out of his lungs. He returned shortly, coughing too. "They're both dead or dying. Who are they?"

"One's named Dyke and one's named Freeman. They live up at Shedville, or did, and worked for a man named Hiram Sawyer."

"I guess I could contact him and see what this was all about," the marshal said, still coughing.

Opening all the windows and doors and waving a sheet to waft the gun smoke outside, John and Jack tried their best to clean out the place. When they were finished, John went back to shaving Jack's beard while the marshal and his men removed the bodies.

"Why did they want you?" John asked, still a little shaken up. Jack told him his history with Sawyer while John shook his head in disbelief.

"He hired them two to get to you?"

"Someone had to do the dirty part," Jack said. "I just

figured they'd have learned the lesson when we burned down the saloon and chased them out of town."

"Well, I don't rightly know that their kind ever does learn," John said, shaving Jack's right cheek with a straight edge. Sloshing the blade in a pan of hot water, he shaved another strip along his cheek.

"So, what are you doing in San Antonio?"

"Waiting for my wife and my new baby on my way home from cattle herding." As he said the words out loud he realized he still didn't know whether he had a son or daughter. Though he wanted to have some alone time with Lucy, he was sure glad to be meeting his new child.

They spoke pleasantly about Jack's time in Kansas, and after John finished the shave and haircut Jack stood up to pay. John smiled and said, "It's on the house," but Jack slipped the money into his barber apron, shook his hand and left.

Jack spent the rest of the morning eagerly awaiting Lucy's arrival. After a quick breakfast with some of the other hotel guests in the dining room, he settled himself in the lobby with a newspaper to wait for Lucy.

Suddenly Lucy swept into the hotel lobby, the baby wrapped in a blanket in her arms. He flew out of his seat, his stomach churning with excitement as he gave her a full, long kiss on the mouth. When he pulled away from her, she placed the baby in his arms.

"Jack Starr, meet your new son, Dallas Starr," she said.

Short of breath, he rocked the little fellow in his arms. He was a proud father.

"Is Luke here?" she asked as she looked around the lobby.

"He's off with the other hands, but he's healthy and excited to see you. And I warn you, he's grown up a lot. Knows exactly what he wants in life."

As they went upstairs to their room, Lucy said, "Jack, I've been so worried about you. Sawyer's herd was stolen by a gang, and many folks have lost everything. The ones who went with you are mighty glad they did."

Jack narrowed his eyes in suspicion. "Who said the herd was stolen?" He shifted Dallas between his arms.

"I'm not sure who found out first, but the word was Sawyer and his drivers were jumped and the entire herd was stolen."

"We'll see about that. I'll send a few telegrams."

"What do you mean?"

"I think it might be a scam."

Lucy's eyes widened. "You don't really think so, do you, Jack? But how will you find out? Who will you wire?"

"A lawman named Earp and a couple of cattle buyers I met, along with the Kansas Brand Inspectors."

"What good will it do?" she asked, taking the baby.

"We might get their money back for them if it's a hoax. We just have to hope we can get to Sawyer."

After he settled them in the room, he went to the telegraph office and sent ten dollars' worth of wires. Amazing how he could ask questions of people a thousand miles away and get an answer back in a few hours.

"Where shall I send your replies?" the operator asked.

"I'm staying at the Palace Hotel," Jack said.

"I'll send you the wires as soon as they arrive."

He gave the man two bits as a tip. "Well, thanks, Mr. Starr!" the man said, shocked at his generosity.

Back at the hotel, he tossed off his hat and settled into the bed with Lucy and the baby. "You get it all done?"

"Almost, but the rest can wait. I need to spend some time with my wife."

He took her in his arms and held her like they were slow dancing as the hot wind swept the room. It was stifling, but he didn't care. He didn't care about a damn thing except his wife and his tiny son nestled between them.

Jack sent out a second set of wires that day and the next morning U.S. Marshal Tim Harris answered.

My associates in Wichita, Kansas are investigating the matter up there. I believe we have a case of fraud, as your wire indicated. Will keep you informed. Tim Harris. United States Marshal.

Jack filled her in over breakfast. "According to the Kansas Brand Inspectors that herd was sold by Hiram Sawyer."

She beamed at him. "No one else would've been able to figure that out, Jack Starr. Thank goodness we have you around."

He kissed her. "Our bank meeting is at one o'clock today. Almost everyone will be there."

"It's a big day for most of them. As for me, I can't believe you managed to bring in so much money for our family." She reached over and squeezed his hand.

"Well, I wanted to get the most I could for our friends and neighbors. And by paying out the money at the bank, folks will know they got an honest deal."

When they arrived at the bank, the large office room where they were meeting was full of folks who were eager to shake Jack's hand. His crew was lined up against the wall, shaking hands and taking compliments from the grateful folks.

Bank President Claymore called the room to order. "I've sent for more ice and lemonade. I didn't expect so many people. You have really overwhelmed us. I'm glad you-all came so far for this event. It certainly is an important day for not only you, but the state of Texas as well. The money you spend will build our economy and help it grow strong.

"You will receive a receipt for your money and you must sign for it. When you're ready, you can take it to one of our tellers and fill out a deposit slip and we'll place it into your account. In case you want cash, we'll pay you from the signed receipt. But this bank is strong, and we would appreciate you leaving it with us. The interest you'll accrue will only make this venture more fruitful for you."

Claymore turned back to Jack. "Mr. Starr, do you wish to say anything?"

All eyes were on Jack. "I'm glad we did this. I lost one man. He was a good man. But there could have been more. I'm not a preacher, but I'd ask anyone that was so inclined to say a prayer to God and thank him for watching over us and making this a success."

Red Larson stepped out of the crowd to lead the prayer while the men removed their hats. After saying a quick word about Shanks, Red continued.

"Lord, we sure want to thank you for sending us Jack Starr. Wasn't no accident that he came by here and stayed. Thanks, Lord, for giving him the strength to go up there and make the best cattle deal we had ever heard of. Bless his new baby, Dallas, and his wife, Lucy, who, like the rest of the wives, must have talked a lot to you while the men were gone.

"Lord, love, guide and protect us in this life that we may better serve you."

"Amen," everyone echoed.

"Thanks, Red," Jack said.

Afterward, as everyone received their sale receipts, Jack watched their faces. Their eyes were wide with disbelief and their heads shook. Some even cried with joy.

"We can't thank you enough," one gray-haired lady said. "My husband and I are going to have real granite tombstones made for ourselves. For years I figured we'd never be able to afford one and it worried me. God bless you, Jack Starr."

Tears streaming down her face, the woman who'd fed him the night before they went after the bandits ran toward him and threw her arms around his shoulders. "Oh, we owe you so much. I'm going to add a new kitchen to the house and buy a decent rig for me to go to town in."

Lucy deposited all but a thousand dollars. She gave the money to Jack to hold for her. "That's for things the kids might need. I also have to pay Shanes. He's got a real corn crop coming in. Not a weed in it. He's quite the farmer."

The drive home required two days. They stayed at Lucy's cousin's house overnight, but Jack was itching to get into his own bed.

When they finally descended the hill to the ranch, Jack could see Sister pacing up and down the front yard. She looked up when the dogs started barking and smiled, her hands on her hips.

"She'll be happy with her receipt," Lucy said. "She wasn't expecting much."

Lucy waved Dallas's tiny hand at Sister.

"I just wish that Luke had come home with us," she said with a frown.

Jack smiled. "Boys have to sow their oats. But he'll be back. He loves this land."

He leaned over and kissed her and she smiled up at him. "My husband is home at last." They both laughed as he helped her and the baby down from the wagon.

Two weeks later U.S. Marshal Harris arrived at the ranch with two deputies. Jack went out to talk to them.

"Come in for dinner," Jack said.

"No, Jack, we're going to Fredericksburg to arrest Hiram Sawyer. Just thought you'd like to come along."

"You have a warrant, I take it?"

"Yes, we do. We also have his bank accounts frozen by a court order both here and in Kansas."

Jack grinned broadly. "Of course I'll come. I can't wait to see the look on his face when he hears the news."

"Good, get your horse and bedroll and come on out."

Jack told Lucy the good news and headed out on Mac.

Two days later the posse arrived at Sawyer's place. They dismounted in the yard and Sawyer came to the door without his coat.

He looked to Jack to be a lot frailer than he was that morning on Dog Creek when he told him to ride on. His unshaven face looked white as snow.

"You're under arrest, Mr. Sawyer, by the U.S. government for fraud and larceny across state and territorial lines."

"You'll never make it stick. I'll have lawyers wring your case out of court," Sawyer said with a sneer.

"Hiram," Jack said, "you'll regret not killing me up at Lost Dog Creek last summer."

He chuckled softly. "I do. I do every day."

"Well, before you die inside the federal penitentiary, I'm sure you'll have many more opportunities."

"You son of a bitch," Sawyer said under his breath.

Jack remounted Mac. "No, Sawyer. I'm afraid you're the son of a bitch."

Epilogue

Hiram Sawyer lasted eighteen months in federal prison in Ohio before he died. He was buried there.

Jack Starr and his partners, Jangles, Cotton and Arnold formed the Prairie Cattle Company and through the good years of the 1870s bought many sections of land in the bluestem hills of southeast Kansas. Their real estate holdings were extensive. As a grass-stocker operation, they paved the way for an industry that flourishes to this day. Dallas Starr took over the operation of the Kansas ranches in 1890 when Jack died from a sudden heart attack while working cattle on their Texas operation, which Luke ran for the family. Lucy lived to be ninety and was buried beside her man at the Lost Dog Creek Cemetery.

Tally and Shanes farmed a large tract of black land south of Dallas. Shanes, who had taken his education seriously after Jack taught him how to read, was elected as a state senator for two terms. The boy who Jack and his crew caught in his nightshirt became a respected Texas civic leader and an outstanding area farmer.

Dallas' two sons inherited the Kansas holdings. The depression of the 1930s cut deep into their operation. The Kansas ranches were broken up and sold. Dallas' great-great grandson, Jack Starr III, owns the old home place and the D-T brand. He is now a corporate lawyer in Austin.

On a weather-worn tombstone in the cemetery, the words are written: HERE LIES CAPTAIN JACK STARR, THE MAN WHO SAVED AN ENTIRE COMMUNITY.

"A writer in the tradition of Louis L'Amour
and Zane Grey!"

—*Huntsville Times*

National Bestselling Author

RALPH COMPTON

AUTUMN OF THE GUN
THE KILLING SEASON
THE DAWN OF FURY
BULLET CREEK
RIO LARGO
DEADWOOD GULCH
A WOLF IN THE FOLD
TRAIL TO COTTONWOOD FALLS
BLUFF CITY
THE BLOODY TRAIL
SHADOW OF THE GUN
DEATH OF A BAD MAN
RIDE THE HARD TRAIL
BLOOD ON THE GALLOWS
BULLET FOR A BAD MAN
THE CONVICT TRAIL
RAWHIDE FLAT
OUTLAW'S RECKONING
THE BORDER EMPIRE
THE MAN FROM NOWHERE
SIXGUNS AND DOUBLE EAGLES
BOUNTY HUNTER
FATAL JUSTICE
STRYKER'S REVENGE
DEATH OF A HANGMAN

**Available wherever books are sold or at
penguin.com**

No other series packs this much heat!

THE TRAILSMAN

Follow the trail of the gun-slinging heroes of
Penguin's Action Westerns at
penguin.com/actionwesterns